"... my reason for telling my story is not money.
I'm doing if for my poor dead Papa and myself
and the thousands of black men like him
in ghetto torture chambers who have been and
will be niggerized and deballed by the white power structure
and its thrill-kill police ..."

Other Titles by Iceberg Slim

Pimp

Trick Baby

The Naked Soul of Iceberg Slim

Airtight Willie & Me

Long White Con

Death Wish

Mama Black Widow

ICEBERG SLIM

CASH MONEY CONTENT

Mama Black Widow

Copyright © 2013 by Robert Beck Estate

Cash Money Content™ and all associated logos are trademarks of
Cash Money Content LLC.

First Trade Paperback Edition: May 2013

Book Layout: Peng Olaguera/ISPN

Cover Design: MJCDesign

Cover Photograph by Inge Morath
with the permission of Magnum Photos

For further information log onto www.CashMoneyContent.com

Library of Congress Control Number: 2013932033

ISBN: 978-1-936399-19-2 pbk

ISBN: 978-1-936399-20-8 ebook

10 9 8 7 6 5 4 3 2 1

Printed in the United States

Mama Black Widow

PREFACE

One early evening during the first week of February in 1969 I visited Otis Tilson. He was an incredibly comely and tragic homosexual queen with whom I had been acquainted for most of the twenty-five years that I had been a black pimp in Chicago, Illinois.

Otis lived in a third-rate hotel at Forty-seventh Street and Cottage Grove Avenue. He was colorful in fresh makeup, platinum wig and rainbow print hostess pajamas with the outrageously full legs.

His almond-shaped hazel eyes sparkled as he eagerly took the paper sack containing the gin I'd brought him and said in a throaty contralto, "Iceberg, you were an angel not to forget my medicine."

We sat on a battered sofa in his one-room kitchenette. A tall, young black stud with a natural hairdo and a hostile face got off the rumpled brass bed, glared at me and slammed the door going out.

I said, "Otis, he's got rocks in his jaws."

Otis raised a water glass and took a big belt of gin.

He giggled and said, "He's jealous and fatally in love with my old hot yellow asshole, and also he's afraid I might suck a new cock."

I said, "How is Sedalia?"

He wrinkled his tiny tip-tilted nose and said, "I haven't seen Mama since I walked out on her in '68. I guess that rotten bitch is doing as well as anybody can in a wheelchair."

A moment later as I was setting up my tape recorder, Otis's smooth yellow face became serious and he said passionately, "Iceberg, my real reason for telling my story is not money. I'm doing it for my poor dead Papa and myself and the thousands of black men like him in ghetto torture chambers who have been and will be niggerized and deballed by the white power structure and its thrill-kill police.

"This goddamn society is crooked and corrupt from top to bottom. Lots of police, judges and prosecutors put their heads together and frame homosexuals into long jail terms. The hysterical bastards are really punishing the cocksucker and the faggot-hot-to-be-fucked-in-the-ass that are inside themselves."

Otis paused and looked at me sheepishly.

He said softly, "Iceberg, was the machine turned on?"

I nodded.

He said, "I guess you'll have to erase what I said. I got carried away. I'll be careful and watch my language."

I said, "The hell you will. Any book I have any connection with has to tell it like it is. You were beautiful. The gutsy language is you, the street and life, and it's real.

"I know something of what happened to you and your family, and I guarantee all you need do is tell your story like it is to prove a thousand points about this black hell and the poisonous pus of double standard justice, racial bigotry and criminal economic freeze-out, infecting and grotesquely bloating the hideous underbelly of white America's shining facade of democracy and freedom and opportunity for all.

"Start your story with Dorcas and that first time you lived with her as a stud. I'm going to lift your whole story off the tape and put it in the book, gutsy and like it is."

In writing the book, I found it necessary in the interests of literary unity, clarity and values, to restructure and realign some scenes and events from Otis's rambling and often tearful account. And I supplied transitional bridges. Except for my minimal involvement, the unforgettable story is his.

There are no esoteric psychiatrist dialogues, dead preachments or leaden footnotes on the living pages of this book. The dialogue is in the gut idiom of the queer—the black ghetto—the Deep South—the underworld. Critical social delineations are in the stark dramas of the internal and external conflicts of Otis Tilson's heartbreaking struggle to free himself from the freakish bitch burning inside him. And also in the tragic lifestyles of Otis's older brother and two beautiful sisters adrift in a dark world of pimpdom and crime and violence where good is condemned and evil applauded.

1

MAMA, YOU MOTHER . . . !

She lay beside me in the late March night, naked and crying bit-terly into her pillow. The bellow of a giant truck barreling down State Street in Chicago's far Southside almost drowned out her voice as she sobbed, "What's wrong with me, Otis? Why is it so hard for you to make love to me? Am I too fat? Do you love someone else? Yes, I guess that's it. And that's why you haven't married me. This is 1968. We've been sleeping together for a whole year. I wasn't brought up like that. Let's get married. Please make me Mrs. Tilson. I hope you're not stalling because I married twice before."

I just lay there squeezing the limp flesh between my sweaty thighs and feeling desperate helplessness and panic.

I danced my fingertips down her spine and whispered tenderly into her ear, "Dorcas, there's no one else. I think I've loved you since we were very young. I just have to stop drinking so much. Maybe we'll get married soon. Now, let's try it again."

She turned over slowly and lay on her back in a blue patch of moonlight. Her enormous black eyes were luminous in the strong ebony face. Desperately I set my imagination free and gazed at her tits, jerking like monstrous male organs in climax.

I felt an electric spark quicken my limpness. Frantically I closed my eyes and gnawed and sucked at the heaving humps. Her outcries of joyful pain pumped rigid readiness into me.

She pinched it. She moaned and held herself open.

She screamed, "Please! Please, fuck me before it falls again."

I lunged into her and seized her thighs to hold them back. But as I touched her fat softness I felt myself collapsing inside her.

I was terrified. So I thought about Mike and the crazy excitement I had felt long ago when I pressed my face against his hard, hairy belly. Then in the magic of imagination, instead of Dorcas, it was the beautiful heartbreaker Mike that I smashed into.

Later, I lay and watched Dorcas sleeping. Except for added weight and faint stress lines etched into the satin skin, she looked the same as she had on that enchanted spring day when I first met her twenty years before.

What a chump I had been then to dream that the daughter of a big shot mortician could really be mine.

Mama had warned me then, "Sweet Pea, don't you get your heart broken. A slum fellow like you don't have a chance with a girl like that. Her father will see to it. If anyone despises poor niggers more than dirty white folks, it's so-called high-class niggers like him."

Mama had been right. He had helped to marry her off and broken my heart. The prejudiced bastard was dead now.

By sheer chance I had run into Dorcas a week after his death. She was a trained mortician, but she was lonely and needed help.

I knew right away that there was still lots of warm sweet voltage between us. Two days later I moved from Mama and the tenement flat where I had spent most of my life.

I hadn't dated a guy since I moved into the funeral home with her. I put off marrying her because I knew that freakish creature I called Sally was still alive inside me. I was afraid of Sally. I couldn't marry Dorcas until I was certain that the bitch Sally was dead.

I thought about the freshly embalmed corpse of Deacon Davis lying in the mortuary morgue downstairs. I would have to groom and dress it by midmorning for viewing in the slumber room. I tried until dawn to sleep. But it was no use. I couldn't get the corpse of Deacon Davis off my mind. I decided to prepare the deacon.

I eased out of bed and slipped on a robe and slippers. I took a ring of keys from the dresser top and went down the front stairway to the street. I went down the sidewalk through the chilly dawn to the front door of the mortuary.

I unlocked the door and stepped into the dim reception room. I walked across the deep pile gold carpet into the office. I switched on a light and sat down at the old mahogany desk. I took a fresh fifth of gin from a drawer and sipped it half empty.

The shrill blast of the desk phone startled me. I picked up and said, "Reed's Funeral Home."

Mama's high-pitched, rapid voice chattered over the wire, "Sweet Pea, it's been over a week since you visited or called me. You know I have a bad heart and I'm all alone. Don't let that woman make you neglect your mama. Think about it and let your conscience be your judge."

Before I could reply, she hung up. I started to call her back, but decided against it. I took two more belts of gin and went through the darkened chapel on my way to the morgue at the rear of the building.

The heavy odor of spoiling flowers and the harsh chemical stench of preserved death burst from the slumber room. I walked into its shadowy blueness and paused beside a cheap chalky casket with a bouquet of stale blossoms lying on the foot of it. There was a poignant message scrawled on a smudgy card:

"Happy journey, Papa, to the arms of sweet Jesus. See you soon. Lettie, your loving, lonesome wife."

I stared down at the tired dead face, creased hideous by the life-time terror and torture of its blackness. I remembered the puckered emblems of hate on the corpse's back.

I turned away from the pitiful corpse wrapped in the shabby suit. I walked unsteadily down the long murky hallway to the morgue. I opened the raspy door. There he was, a skeletal black blob on the porcelain table that gleamed whitely in the half darkness.

I walked across the room and the scraping of my feet against the concrete floor was like shrieking in the tomb quiet. I flipped on the high intensity lamp over the table. I slipped on rubber gloves and stood hypnotized, sweeping my eyes up and down the white-haired wasted corpse.

I shook with rage as scenes and sounds of the awful past shattered and filled the bright stillness. I was nine years old when the corpse everybody respectfully called Deacon Davis lived on the third floor of the Westside tenement where Mama still lives.

I remembered that first time in his apartment. His hand was hot between my legs, caressing the throbbing tip of my stiff little organ.

His voice was hoarse with excitement. "Kiss mine and lick it, you dear little boy, like I did to yours. Mine is a magic wand to make any wish come true when you make it cry tears of joy."

I put the long, crooked thing in my mouth until I spat its slimy tears. I cheated the wand and made two wishes: That poor Papa found a steady job. And that Mama wouldn't be so bossy and cruel to Papa anymore.

To my complaints of wishes unfulfilled, the deacon would grin and say, "I know what's wrong. My wand must cry deep in your bunger, my dear boy."

For more than a year, until he moved away, the deacon shoved his wand deeply into me. The deacon sure ruined me. He really did.

I leaned over the corpse and roughly jabbed my thumbs into the sunken eye sockets. I pushed back the withered eyelids and stared into the brown orbs filmy and vacant.

I whispered, "Dear Deacon Davis, you can't know how thrilled I am to see you again. I just don't want you to go to your grave unpunished. You bastard child-raping freak. I'm going to shave you and dress your nappy hair. Then I'm going to punish you for ruining me. But no one will know except you and me, dear Deacon Davis."

I groomed the corpse and got a razor-sharp scalpel. I lifted his wrinkled shaft and held it erect at its tip between a thumb and index finger. I stood there with the glittering blade in my hand.

I glanced at the deacon's face. The blank sable eyes were staring at me. I felt suddenly queasy and faint. The scalpel clattered to the tabletop. I jerked my hand away from the shaft and pressed the eyelids down. I just couldn't do a vicious thing like that even to a filthy freak like Deacon Davis.

I was putting underwear on the corpse when it groaned as trapped air escaped its chest. I went to the office in a hurry for a stiff drink of gin. I came back to the morgue and split the burial suit coat and shirt down the back and dressed the body.

I wheeled the white satin-lined casket to the side of the table. I attached pulleys over the table to the corpse and lowered it into the casket. Then I wheeled it into the slumber room for viewing by mourners who believed the deacon was holy.

Funeral services for Deacon Davis were held two days later. The anguished wails of his surviving brother and sister moved me not at all.

I drove the hearse to the cemetery. Two elegant black limousines driven by chauffeurs Dorcas hired at a ten dollar fee followed behind me. At least thirty private cars behind them crawled through the dazzling sunshine to the grave. The deacon was well thought of, all right. But then I'm sure that the mourners didn't know about his dirty passion for little boys.

A nice funeral like that was much more than the deacon deserved. But I was really glad I hadn't used that scalpel on the deacon. I've always, at least in one respect, tried to be like my idol, Martin Luther King, Jr. To not hate anybody.

To tell the truth, I've never really hated a living human soul except cops. There may be cops who are human, but I've never known any.

The day after the deacon's funeral I called Mama more than a dozen times. I didn't get an answer, and the line was never busy. I was awfully worried, so that evening around seven I killed the fifth of gin and drove my old Plymouth to the Westside.

I drove past raucous clusters of ragged kids frolicking on the sidewalks and stoops in the twilight down Homan Avenue past 1321, the six-flat slum building that my idol and his group had taken over in February 1966. The plan had been (in violation of the law) to collect the rents and spend the money to make the building fit for human occupancy.

I parked at the curb at the end of the block. A gorgeous black brute striding down the sidewalk toward me mesmerized me. The bulgy thigh muscles undulated against his tight white trousers. I forgot all my resolutions to keep Sally shackled and scrambled to the sidewalk and stood fumbling with my key ring.

His raw body odor spiced with the scent of shaving lotion floated deliriously on the warm air. I inhaled hungrily. I was flaming. I really was. He came abreast of me, and I saw the imprint of his huge dick. I was dizzy with a hot roaring in my head. I almost fainted with excitement. I really did.

I had an insane urge to stroke his thing. Instead, I caressed my eyes over his crotch, and then waltzed them to the depths of his dreamy brown eyes, searching for a flicker of sweet kinship for "the" secret message. I saw only a cold quizzical indifference as he passed me. The beautiful bastard was straight!

Almost instantly I felt like shouting with joy and relief that he was, and that the bitch, Sally, had been denied. I went down the cracked walk toward the grimy, familiar front of the six-unit building that Mama now owned.

I glanced at Mama's front window on the first floor. I saw the curtains flutter above a red and white sign, "Madame Miracle— Come In—Get the Golden Touch Blessing—Win and Hold Money and Friends—Discover How to Punish Your Enemies—Ward

Off Evil Spirits—Enslave Sweethearts—Wives—Husbands—I am
blessed with infinite wisdom and power."

I went past several cursing preteeners shooting penny craps on
the stoop. I opened the front door and stepped into the building's
musty vestibule.

A bandy legged old man in faded blue undershorts was piling his
ancient pocket watch wallet and small change on the rumpled heap
of his puke-stained trousers and shirt lying on the floor.

I paused beside him. I heard the door open leading to the first-floor
hallway. A tall, elderly woman with a fierce face was standing with
arms folded across her chest glaring down at the muttering old man.

She screamed in a shrill voice, "Nigger, this ain't our apartment.
This is the vestibule. You drunk sonuvabitch. Pick up your filthy
rags and get your black simple ass upstairs before I knock the shit
outta' you."

The old man blinked his sad eyes like a frightened puppy and
mutely worked his thick lips. I felt a sharp pulsing of sorrow and
anger looking at his eyes. They were whipped, hopeless, pitiful eyes,
so much like poor Papa's before he crawled off to die.

I went up the short stone stairway past the husky hag and opened
the splintered glassed door. I walked scabrous tile to Mama's door.
I put my key in the lock and stepped inside. It was very dark except
for cloudy rays of the street lamp that filtered through the living-
room curtains.

I said loudly, "Mama, it's Sweet Pea. Mama, are you here?"

There was no answer. I went down the hallway toward Mama's
bedroom at the rear of the apartment. I thought about Mama's heart
condition that was all in her mind. Her doctor had told me confidentially there was no organic trouble at all, just that Mama had
deep mental needs for her attacks.

Then I remembered the movement of the curtains when I came
up the front walk. I shivered. Mama had made enemies with her
witchcraft. I wondered if she was dead and the murderer was still

in the apartment. I stopped and stood uneasily at Mama's bedroom door, listening to the wild pumping of my heart.

I shouted, "Mama, are you here?"

No answer. The feeling was overpowering that something ghastly had happened to her. I almost knew somebody was behind that door. Perhaps the murderer was crimson with Mama's blood, panting, trapped, waiting for me with a butcher knife or hatchet in the dark in the other side of that door.

I decided to go back to the car. I turned and walked quickly back toward the front door. Then I glanced at the murky mirror on the wall next to the front door.

I froze. My legs wouldn't move any more. There was a kind of wavering shifting movement in the blackness behind me near Mama's bedroom. I almost tinkled on myself as I stared in the mirror and saw a mass of the blackness split off and glide toward me.

I spun around and faced the thing. I opened my mouth to scream, but nothing came out. The thing came closer and giggled. Then I saw a slash of white in a familiar black face. It was Mama in a long black robe smiling at me. I started crying in relief.

I blubbered, "Mama, darling, why did you do that to me? Why didn't you answer when I called to you? OH! Mama, I thought something bad had happened to you."

Mama held her long arms open and crooned in her racing voice, "Come here and kiss me and tell me you love me. Mama didn't want to frighten her pretty baby, but I've been mad with you for neglecting me. Come on, Sweet Pea. Come to your mama."

I felt a tremor of rage, not toward Mama really, but just for those spidery arms reaching out for me. In my anger I got the weirdest thoughts standing there. A lot like the terrible thoughts I used to get when I helped Mama with the dishes.

I'd have to lock my trembling hands together so I couldn't obey the terrifying impulse to stab a kitchen knife into her. It was awful because I love Mama and always will. But standing there in that hallway I thought how funny Mama would look without those arms. And what if I had found her not dead but with those clutching creatures chopped off cleanly with no pain, no blood, just open-mouthed surprise to see herself without them.

Then suddenly I was sorry for my mean thoughts. I rushed to her arms and buried my face in her bosom. She crushed me to her so hard I could hardly breathe. I raised my head and kissed her lips.

I sobbed, "Mama, I've missed you. I love you so much."

We stood there hugging and kissing like we hadn't seen each other in years. Mama led me into the living room and switched on a brass cherub lamp on a table at the end of the white sofa.

We sat on it close together. Mama scanned my face with bright black eyes. They were tiny, unblinking eyes that I could never look into for long. When she was upset or angry they seemed to glow balefully.

But her eyes were warm and kind when she gently placed her hand on my thigh and said softly, "Sweet Pea, I see you, and I just can't understand how we could live apart for a whole year. How do we stand it, precious?"

I didn't answer. I looked at her thinking how she'd changed; she'd been good looking and shapely down South. She'd even lost her thick Southern accent with hard study and desire.

I moved my thigh away and said, "Now Mama, please don't start. It's not like I'm living out of town. I'm never going to stop calling you and visiting you. Think back, Mama, and remember what happened to Frank, Carol and Bessie. It makes me want to bawl to think about them.

"Mama, I'm the only kid you got left. I'm forty years old, and this is my big chance to stand on my own and be a man. Try to understand. Help me, Mama. Only you know what I've gone through."

The warmness deserted her eyes. A toil-coarsened hand thoughtfully pulled at the tip of her wide, flat nose. I sat there on the edge of the sofa, waiting for her to speak, afraid that I had said the wrong

thing. I'd always tried very hard not to displease her. I suffered when
I did.

Finally, she clasped her hands beneath her chin and murmured in
an icy voice, "That stale slut is poisoning my baby's mind against me.
That's what she's doing. She's trying to make you stop loving . . ."

I took Mama's hands and pressed them against my face and cried
out, "NO! NO! Stop it, Mama. You're wrong about Dorcas. She's a
sweet person. She really is. She wouldn't try anything like that. Visit
us, Mama, or let her come to see you. You would find out that she's
a good woman."

Mama jerked her hands away and spat out, "I wouldn't go to
that deceiving bitch's funeral. Sweet Pea, you're the biggest fool
on God's green earth to forget how she and her highfalutin father
treated you like dirt and hurt your heart.

"Sweet Pea, it's bad enough that you're sleeping with that treacherous slut. But before you leave me I want you to promise me that
you'll never marry her. I'm telling you, Sweet Pea, that woman is a
snake waiting to destroy you. Now say it, baby. Say that you won't
break my heart and marry her."

I felt like I was suffocating under Mama's pressure. I could hardly
breathe. I was so ill and angry. I really was.

I stood up and said sharply, "Mama, please! Give me a break,
will you? I can't promise you that. Dorcas has always loved me.
Her father didn't break us up. I did, with stupidity. She never really
loved the two guys she married.

"Mama, I think I love her. I'm going to marry her as soon as I get
my mind together. So don't call her names. I love you, but I'm not
going to stay tied to your apron strings and play with myself until
I'm a dried up old man. I'm sick in my head, Mama. With Dorcas
I might get well. So give me a chance and stop putting pressure on
me. I can't stand it."

Mama's face was a tight black mask. I leaned over and kissed her
forehead. I turned and walked to the front door. I glanced over my

shoulder. Mama was coming toward me with her eyes almost closed and an odd smile on her face. Her silk robe rustled like a centipede snagging on autumn leaves. I flinched when she took my face between her palms and stared into my eyes.

She crooned too sweetly, "Sweet Pea, you're trembling. I know you're sorry you hurt me. I forgive you. Now come to your senses and come home soon to stay. We'll be so happy."

I twisted my face away and opened the door.

I said, "Mama, you didn't want me to make love to guys, and you don't want me to have Dorcas. I'm human. I have to have somebody."

She smiled broadly and said, "Precious, Mama will make a bargain with you. Come back home and I won't mind who your friends are, just so you respect me and your home and don't wear women's clothes. Fair enough?"

I could feel tears filling my eyes. I shook my head slowly and said, "Mama, you're really something, aren't you? You never give up. Respect? You don't give a damn about my self-respect. You wouldn't care if I went down on every guy in Chicago, just so I don't marry Dorcas. Right?"

Mama came toward me with those awful arms outstretched. I backed into the corridor and turned and walked toward the vestibule door.

I could hear Mama pleading, "Sweet Pea, don't leave like this. Come back and kiss me. I'm your mama. I'm the only one who loves you. Please come back and kiss me. You're killing me, Sweet Pea. I feel an attack coming. You better come back here. Come back, Sweet Pea."

I went through the vestibule to the sidewalk. I glanced back at Mama's window. She had her head wedged between the white curtains, and her glittery little eyes were glaring at me. The street lamp shone through the telephone wires and imprinted a spidery web against the curtains.

2

SALLY FREAKS OFF

I was fluttery and depressed when I left Mama. I drove aimlessly to Madison Street and parked in front of a straight bar near the corner at California Avenue. The visit to Mama had torn me down inside, and I felt so guilty about quarreling with her.

I felt a familiar palpitating anxiety and confusion. I knew I had to be careful that I didn't wind up in a hotel bed beneath some strange brute bulling himself into me.

During that part of it, I'd be ecstatic. And even later, alone, I'd lie there popped dry—but still feeling marvelous with spastic orgasmic waves ripping deep inside me—like a woman.

Then the horror part would start. I'd remember the contemptuous look on the coldhearted fruit hustler's face as he patted my twenty dollar bill in his pocket. I had been so hungry for love and affection. He had performed with neither. Then he'd toss some inane con over his shoulder as he hurried away to the streets to snare another freakish sucker.

Each time I'd want to die as I lay there alone with the pungent slime oozing from me. I'd cry my heart out in the lonely darkness in remorse for the abuse, humiliation and shame of it all, and guilt that I had set the bitch inside me free.

I lit a cigar and went into the crowded bar. I took a stool near the front window and ordered a tall cool Tom Collins from the elderly black bartender. Several guys who knew me from childhood stopped and made small talk.

Two cigars and five Tom Collins later I felt better. My watch read 10 P.M., so I went to the phone booth at the end of the bar and called Dorcas. I told her I was starting out for the Southside.

I went through the bar bedlam to the sidewalk. A rib joint firing up its ovens belched eye-stinging gouts of smoke into the sky.

The night people were crawling Madison Street like maggots on a corpse. Thickly painted queers and whores, white, black and high yellow jiggled corrupt behinds inside loud minidresses. They leered dirty smiles at the shabby tricks prowling for an orgy for five bucks. Black pimps with brutish faces stalked the turf in long flashy cars.

I unlocked the Plymouth and started the grumbly motor. I leaned across the seat to lower the window on the sidewalk side. I heard urgent high heels. An instant later a seamed white face framed by a red wig thrust through the open window and grinned at me. It belonged to Lucy, an old queen friend of mine, in full drag. His voluptuous face was a debauched image of the world-famous comedienne's.

"Tilly, my gawd, it's simply creamy to see you," he gurgled in a gritty contralto voice.

I said, "Hi, Lucy," and opened the door.

He gracefully slid his wide hips into the seat and adjusted the hem of the tight gold lamé microdress cut high at his droopy thighs. He slit his large blue eyes and pouted his scarlet mouth in fake anger.

He said, "Tilly, I don't know why the hell I'm so glad to see you. You dropped out of circulation eons ago without so much as a hint to your friends. I supposed that you were shacked up with some utterly divine cock that you couldn't bear to risk sharing.

"Oh, which reminds me, Mike is back in town on his bare ass, but creamy and cute as always, and Gypsy was stomped to death by that crazy, jealous Mexican of hers. I'm still slaving at Spiegel's mail-order house. And I'm shacked up with a living dream."

I sat there thinking, *Mike is back! Mike is back!*

I forgot I had told Dorcas I was on my way home. I scarcely heard Lucy as he chattered on and on bringing me up to date on the romances and happenings among the queers I had deserted.

In a mechanical daze I drove Lucy several blocks up Madison Street to an old apartment building. He begged me to come up for a moment to have a drink for old times' sake.

I followed him into a first-floor rear apartment reeking with sandalwood incense. An amber light shone from a pole lamp. The small living-room walls were aglow with Lucy's phosphorescent paintings of nude male figures.

He went across a burnt orange carpet to a yellow bar. I sat down on a yellow leather sofa. He brought a glass tray and put it on the yellow cocktail table in front of me.

He sat beside me and said, "See, Honey, I remembered your poison: gin and soda."

We sat there sipping, chatting and listening to Ray Charles records for quite a while. Then Lucy dropped a red devil, so just to be a good sport, I dropped one, and I really started to feel groovy. I really did.

Lucy took my hand and led me into a pink and blue bedroom. She switched on a bed lamp. A coal-black young guy with gleaming processed hair was lying on his back beneath a satin quilt. He was fast asleep.

Lucy cocked his head, gazing raptly down at him. He said, "The poor baby is sleeping off a binge. Isn't he gorgeous?"

I said, "He's attractive all right, but don't you think he's awfully young and innocent? He couldn't be more than seventeen. His parents could make trouble for you."

Lucy giggled and flung the covers back. He leaned over and pulled the boy's huge dick from between his sinewy thighs and hefted it lovingly in his palm. The boy smiled in his sleep and scratched his belly.

Lucy said, "The goddamn creamy thing goes nearly twelve inches hard. It's so big, I'll soon be crapping in a washtub. He's the greatest lover I've ever had.

"There's no parental danger. He's got ten brothers and sisters, and no father that he remembers. His mother is happy he's found someplace to eat. In fact, I'm something of a good fairy, no pun intended. I take food and clothing to her often."

Lucy went to the dresser and got a pink ribbon from a drawer. He tied it into a bow around the base of the boy's manhood, kissed it and pulled the covers up.

Lucy turned and said, "My gawd, we've been yakking, and I almost forgot Stel's birthday party. You remember Stel, the lesbian on Warren Boulevard?"

I looked at my watch and said, "I remember her. I can't forget her. I met Mike at her place. It's only midnight. If her parties are anything like they used to be things are getting groovy about now. Come on, I'll drop you off."

Lucy smiled slyly and said, "The hell you say. You're going to get into some pretty clothes and go to that party. They wouldn't forgive me if I didn't bring you."

She went to the closet. I stood there with my head in an euphoric whirl and watched her rummage for a dress for me.

I wanted to shout out, "Lucy, forget it. I'm not going to that faggot party."

But I couldn't make the words come out. The pill and the alcohol and that bitch, Sally, were too powerful to resist. Incredibly, I vibrated at the prospect that I might see Mike again.

Thirty minutes later I had put on a padded bra and dressed. I stood wide-eyed and thrilled before the full-length mirror on the closet door. I was dazzling in the shimmery white silk microdress and blue-black wig that hung to my shoulders in Grecian curls.

My size-six feet were elegant in white satin squared-toe pumps with rhinestone buckles.

I stepped closer to the mirror. Lucy clipped mock pearl earrings to my earlobes. I gazed at my huge hazel eyes flashing emerald sparks beneath the curly canopies of dark auburn lashes.

Despite my age, my smooth yellow skin still stretched tautly over my high cheek-boned face. My full lips were curvy and glistening beneath pale pink lipstick. Golden freckles speckled my delicate tip-tilted nose. I was enchanted with my face. I really was. I guess I loved it so much because it was Papa's face in every detail.

Lucy said, "Tilly, I've said it before, and I'm saying it now. You are the creamiest thing in drag I've ever seen. Thousands of women in Chicago would froth at the mouth with joy if they had your legs and face and could wiggle inside a size ten dress the way you do.

"That round rear end of yours is so sexy a goddamn vice cop wouldn't wake up that you're not really a glamorous twenty-five-year-old broad. Take this mink stole, bag and gloves. Let me put a spot of perfume behind your ears. Now let's drop another pill and get the hell out of here."

It was 1 A.M. when we got to the street teeming with cars and people. Under the crazy hypnosis of pills and alcohol I had the strange feeling I was in a fantastic flower garden, hearing the hum and buzz of insects. Bright neon blossoms flashed, rippled and sparkled in the bewitched night.

One of a gang of young guys in a car at the curb shouted at Lucy as we passed. "Lucy, you know you can't handle cunt. Bring that beautiful bitch back here and let me sock this nine inches to her."

I tossed my hips and giggled when I suddenly remembered that a killjoy I vaguely knew as Otis Tilson wasn't around to squelch my fun.

I felt positively beautiful. I was like an awed spectator watching myself reveling in the absolute surrender to the freak bitch, Sally.

I had to park half a block away from Stel's place because of the string of cars bumper to bumper. Lucy and I stood on the porch of the fourteen-room house pressing the doorbell again and again. Finally we heard footsteps and someone opened the peephole. The door swung open, and we stepped into a white-carpeted entrance hall.

Torchy, a young blond queen in a bloodred mini, said excitedly, "Lucy, Tilly, follow me. You're just in time for some sport. Stel's Penny was out with some stud since yesterday morning. She came home fifteen minutes ago, stoned out of her mind with a raunchy cunt. Stel is furious. Everybody's in the barroom catching the scene."

We followed Torchy down a flight of rear stairs to the barroom that had once been a basement. It was the Mecca for many of the Westside black and white queers. It was spacious and had all of the fixtures and geegaws of a commercial bar.

About forty laughing people, black and white, encircled an attraction of some kind at the rear of the room. I heard muffled screams. We went over. Lucy tiptoed and peered down at whatever it was and started laughing.

I couldn't see a thing on my tiptoes, so I half turned to spot a chair or something to add to my five feet two so I could see the action.

I felt a sudden viselike pressure around my waist, and then I was airborne. I looked down at a gorilla face crinkly in amusement. My hundred and twenty pounds were perched neatly on the ridge of the widest shoulder I'd ever seen. The black giant had his paws locked around my calves balancing me like I was a baby.

I said angrily, "What the hell are you doing? Put me down."

He flung back his shiny shaved skull against my thigh and laughed.

He said, "Baby, I ain't going to let you fall. Go on and dig the happenings."

I looked down into his brown eyes. They were so warm and nice and that face of his was so pathetically ugly I just had to be kind to him. I smiled and put my arm around his bull neck.

I looked down at struggling brown-skinned Penny, her eyes bucked in panic. Two brawny white lesbians were holding her down while Stel shoved ice cubes up Penny's guilty tang. It was almost poetic punishment for a hot delinquent pussy.

I swung my eyes away and scanned the crowd for Mike. He wasn't there. Shortly, the excitement was over and chastened Penny slunk upstairs. Gargantua lowered me to the floor and grinned down at me.

I said, "Thanks for the trip."

He said, "My name is Lovell, but everybody calls me Big Lovee. Who are you?"

"I'm Tilly, and it's a pleasure to meet you," I said and turned and walked away to Lucy sitting at the bar.

Stel went behind the long redwood bar to serve her guests. I sat at the bar sipping Tom Collins and chatting with Stel and Lucy. At least twenty people came over to say hello and how glad they were to see me again. Lovee sat at the end of the bar gazing hungrily at me.

Lesbians and their women were paired off and in small groups with queens and studs in the shadowy booths lining the long room. The scene was swept by a romantic pinwheel of colored bulbs revolving slowly in the low ceiling.

The hubbub of their chatter and wild laughter almost smothered the souling of Lou Rawls moaning from a jukebox that blazed in the corner like a pastel bonfire.

I felt cozy and intoxicated, but not only because of the pills and drinks I had taken. There was somehow a sweet and wonderful atmosphere of equality and brotherhood among queers. I guess they were so despised and discriminated against in the straight world that in mutual anguish and suffering they found emotional sanctuary among themselves.

At 3 A.M. Lucy and I helped Stel serve chitterlings with spaghetti and coleslaw. It wasn't my favorite dish. While growing up I had eaten enough hog guts to stretch from coast to coast.

I danced with Lovell and several other guys. I was having a ball, and poor Lovell had his nose wide open for me. He sat and glowered at me when I wasn't in his arms. When I was, I felt his hard thing prod my navel.

Around 4 A.M. people started to drift away to the street and to the bedrooms upstairs. I went to the john at the top of the stairs to tinkle. I pulled down the borrowed satin panties and sat down because it was easier with a dress on.

The john door opened, and there was Lovell half swacked with a ravenous look of adoration on his ape face. The musical fall of the tinkle must have been a powerful turn-on for the ugly brute, because he fell to his knees in front of me and started kissing and licking my kneecaps and thighs.

It tickled good. But there was no lock on the door and I was afraid someone might walk in. I giggled and tried to shove his head away.

He blurted out a whiney plea, "Tilly, please give me a chance. I'm black and ugly, pretty baby, but I got a boss head and a groovy dick. All my life I ain't loved nothing but sissies, and you the finest one I ever saw.

"I ain't jiving you, Tilly. I'm a poor boy, but a good boy, a long way from home, so lonesome and needing someone to love. Now scoot up, angel, and let Big Lovee send you to heaven."

It was all so sudden, inconvenient and awkward that I couldn't let myself go. I stood up quickly and pulled up my panties.

I flushed the john and said in a gentle voice while washing my hands, "Lovee, maybe later. Please try to understand. I'm not in the mood right now. I've got nothing against . . ."

His sobbing cut me off. I glanced in the mirror. The big ape's fat lips were quivering and tears rolled down his cheeks. I turned and faced him. I felt so sorry for him because his eyes were so piteous and he was so black and ugly standing there crying like a baby.

I put my hands on his and said, "Please, Lovee, don't cry. You're making me feel terrible. Come on. Let's go have a drink and dance some more."

He jerked his hands away and blubbered petulantly, "Tilly, you ain't no nasty stinking whore, are you?"

I said, "No sweetie, I give it up for free if I go for a guy. I just met you. But I like you a little bit already."

He pushed his neck down between his shoulders and hunched them.

He almost whispered, "No, that's all right, Tilly. I dig you. You just like most yellow nigger sissies. You don't fuck nothing but paddies and half-white niggers. That's all right, Tilly. I'm too black for you. That what's happening. So take your cute yellow self on about your business. But don't forget that old saying, 'What goes around comes around.'"

He had hit me a bad one below the belt with that crack about his blackness. I felt spasms of pity and sympathy for him. I hugged him around the waist and turned my face up with my mouth half open.

He whimpered and crushed me to him. His big wet mouth descended and rained sucking kisses all over my flaming face, neck and ears. His hand was doing madly marvelous things between my wide-open thighs. I was giddy with passion. I really was. I rolled my belly against his hard-on, and looked up into his tearstained face, so utterly ugly I thought it was one of the strongest and most beautiful faces I'd ever seen.

He said, "You gonna' go to my pad and have Big Lovee, pretty baby?"

I said, "Yes! Yes! I'm so hot. I haven't had a man in a year."

We went down the stairs to the bar holding hands. Lucy was tonguing a young white guy with a whippet face who sported a yellow Nehru suit and a necklace of shiny beads.

Lovee went to the jukebox. Stel brought me a drink and leaned across the bar. She ran blunt fingers through her blond crew cut and darted her electric blue eyes toward the jukebox. Her masculine face was furrowed with concern.

She said, "Tilly, be careful. That bird gives me the creeps. He's funny. Not ha-ha funny, but cuckoo funny. He's a stranger. Mickey brought him here and dumped him early. He looks like a goddamn ass kicker to me, and a stud that ugly can have terrible noggin problems. You get what I mean?"

My stupid head was fouled up but good, afloat in a swishy sea of pills and booze.

So I snickered and said, "Stel, you're all wrong. He's just a lovable country bumpkin with his balls bursting for me. I need him in the most desperate way this morning. He's so sweet and adoring. He's going to beat the hell out of me with his tongue."

Stel shrugged and walked away as Lovee took my hand and danced me across the floor. I drank and danced for another hour.

Then Lucy staggered to me and said, "Tilly, Stel hasn't got a vacant bed, so I'm going to rip off that creamy sonuvabitch at a hotel. I'll be at home in a couple of hours. Drop by and change clothes anytime today, but be careful not to mention the party. My old man will beat the holy shit out of me."

I watched Lucy and whippet face go up the stairs. I went behind the bar and helped Stel tidy up, and in another half hour Lovee was at the wheel of my Plymouth driving me to his place.

He drove down the driveway of a gloomy old two-story house on Taylor Street near Sacramento Boulevard to the backyard almost filled with cars and parked. It was in a rough section of the Westside.

I raised my head from his shoulder and said, "Lovee, that isn't a very cheerful house. Please, let's don't go in there. I'd rather go to a hotel. I'll pay."

His face tightened, then he grinned and said, "I'm glad to hear you got some bread, baby. Ain't no use to blow it since I got a pad. You gonna' think you in a Gold Coast crib when I turn you on. Now git out of the car, pretty butt, so I can bust that rear cherry you got wide open."

I waited for him to come around to open the car door for me. He came and stood there sneering and motioning for me to get out.

I let myself out and said sharply, "Lovee, you're losing your sweet ways. I'm not going in that dreadful house with you. Now give me my car key. I'll drive us to a hotel or it's good-bye here and now.

"Hurry and make up your mind before I call off the whole damn thing. Lovee, you're no raving beauty, you know. I can pick up lots of good-looking guys who will treat me like a human being."

I held out my hand for the ignition key. The brute snarled and punched me hard in the stomach. I threw up and fell to the ground, doubled up.

He kicked me in the butt and shouted, "You better git up, freak. I'm gonna' stomp your half-white ass into the ground."

I struggled up to my feet and leaned over the fender and hood of the Plymouth. The metal felt cool and refreshing against my churning belly and burning face.

I mumbled. "Please don't beat me any more."

I dipped into my bosom and pulled out a roll of bills. I started to turn toward him.

I said, "I've got over a hundred dollars here. It's yours. Please let me go!"

He snatched the money and hammered his fist against my spine. The pain cut off my breath. My legs slid from under me. I lay there on the ground gasping.

He was silhouetted against the dark careening sky like a gigantic creature from a horror movie. He stooped and picked me up and slung me across his shoulder like a sack of potatoes.

I sobbed, "Let me go. What are you going to do?"

He laughed and stabbed stiff fingers into my crotch. I almost fainted from the shock as I bit the back of his topcoat to keep from screaming.

Like from a great distance I heard him say, "Shut up, yellow nigger. You're right. I ain't good looking. But you're gonna' remember me, sissy, 'til you die. I'm gonna' fuck your guts out through your mouth."

I didn't struggle. I was afraid he would bash me against the ground and stomp me. I was hurting and sober as he walked toward the back door.

He knocked lightly on the door.

I heard it rasp open and a whiskey voice said, "What the hell is that, a stiff you got?"

Before Lovell could step inside or answer, a brilliant beam of light illuminated his legs and shoe heels.

A stentorian voice hollered from the alley, "Halt! Police!"

Car doors slammed. I raised my head, but all I could see was a blinding burst of light before I was spun away when Lovell whirled around.

I felt like crying in relief. I was so sure that I was going to escape. I looked up into the casual eyes of an old black man on a tall stool near the door looking toward the alley. Beyond the old doorman I heard cursing and the rattle of dice and the clink of silver money.

I heard pounding steps, and then very close the same loud voice, "You black sonuvabitch, put that white woman down and raise your hands."

Lovell pulled me off his shoulder and stood me on my feet.

He raised his hands and in a tremulous voice said "Officers, you know me. Big Lovee. I work in this gambling joint for Fat Roscoe. I'm off tonight. I pad upstairs.

"You oughta' know this ain't no white lady. You know I got better sense than that. This ain't even a woman. This is my high sissy, drunk as a skunk. Look at him and see for yourselves."

One of the cops holstered his gun and snatched off the wig, and then slapped it back on.

I stepped over beside the police and blurted out, "Officers, please make him give me the key to my car so I can go home. Please help me! I don't know anything about this guy. He beat me and robbed me of over a hundred dollars. I just met him tonight at a party. I'll sign a complaint against him."

The cop ignored me and said to the doorman, "Rabbit, does this boy still work for Roscoe?"

The doorman said, "Yeah, he's still bouncing the shit-heels outta' the joint. He's the best Roscoe ever had."

The other cop said, "And what's the rundown on the faggot?"

Rabbit pursed his lips, blinked his eyes and said, "That sissy been sniffing Lovell like a bitch dog in heart for weeks. Just one of them things, Officers, a lovers' hassle, that's all.

"Ain't nothing to what that sissy said about that dough. It wasn't no C-note. It was only about a coupla' double sawbucks. I saw them blow that together across the crap table."

I screamed, "He's lying! He's lying! Come back and arrest me. I'm in drag. Come back. Please!"

I heard one of the cops laugh and say as they walked to the police car, "OO–EE! Did you notice the keister on that faggot?"

Lovell punched me in the back of the neck and kneed me in the kidney. I half fell into the house.

The air was fouled by the stink of feet and sweaty bodies.

Lovell shoved me past Rabbit down a dim hallway. We passed a brightly lit room jammed with shabby men and rough-looking women, cursing and quarreling around a long green felt-covered craps table. I tried desperately to spot a face I knew, but they were all strange to me.

Several feet past the room Lovell pushed me to a narrow stairway. I balked and started to turn around to plead with him to let me go. The fiend pinched me up and down my back and butt. I felt like he was using red-hot pliers. I wailed and scrambled up the stairs to the second floor.

He was laughing and chanting in a falsetto voice, "I'll sign a complaint against him. I'll sign a complaint against him."

I was shaking as he forced me down the hallway to a steep dusty stairway at the rear of the house. We went up creaky stairs to a padlocked door.

Lovell unlocked it, and we stepped into a musty attic. Ragged spikes of dawn light punctured a soot-blackened octagonal window. He pulled a string and a naked light bulb flashed on a battered brass bed with tangled dirty covers and an old lopsided chest of drawers beside a small, blistered table.

I stood trembling in the center of the dreary room. He doubled his six-feet-six frame to avoid the low-beamed ceiling and went to the table. He picked up a quart bottle of Old Taylor whiskey and guzzled a big belt. He came and leaned close to me. His wild eyes were bloodshot and oscillating.

I said, "I wasn't really going to sign a complaint against you. Let me go and I'll forget I ever met you. I'm not in the mood to sex you."

He backhanded me across the eyes. I fell to the floor curled in a knot, blinded with pain.

He roared, "Git them clothes off, freak, and git in that bed before I stomp you into a puddle of yellow shit."

I crawled to the bed and sat on the side of it. I tried to focus my eyes, but he was just a triple shadow stripping off his clothes. I got my clothes off somehow, and then he came into focus.

He was standing right in front of me naked and hard. I stared at it and cringed away. It was terrifying—horselike—monstrous—deformed—impossible!

He stooped down and sank his teeth into my chest. I screamed and rolled across the bed.

He pressed himself against me and whispered, "I'm going to croak you, sissy, if you holler again. Now git on your knees and break down like a double-barreled shotgun."

I blubbered, "Christ! Jesus! Please, Lovell, don't, don't. I'm too tight and close built. I can't let you do it. I'll do anything but that."

He laughed and started grinding my flesh, from my face to my feet, between his teeth and saying, "Git on your knees like I told you."

The pain was so bad, but I was afraid to scream. I got to my hands and knees. I was trapped with my head against the wall. Then horrible rending pain exploded through the raw core of my being like I had been halved by an axe. I screamed and a merciful bludgeon smashed down on the back of my neck. I jetted into blackness.

3

BACK TO THE WEB

Lovell was grinning as he held a long switchblade knife above his head. It was a gleaming blur as it plunged toward my throat. I scuttled away and heard the whoomp of the blade hit the pillow.

I screamed and opened my eyes. I was sure my head and the back of my neck were encased in fiery lead. I slapped the top of my head to find out if I was wearing the wig. I wasn't. A jolting fist of pain clouted my insides.

There was no beamed ceiling! There was familiar robin's egg blue paint spangled with golden early-afternoon sunshine. I was lying in a fresh clean bed, and I heard the bellow of a truck.

I panicked. Where was Dorcas? Had she seen the female clothes I had borrowed from Lucy? I listened for movement in Dorcas's bedroom next door. I couldn't hear a sound.

I inched my aching body off the bed and went to the closet. The gray suit I had left at Lucy's was hanging there. I patted the suit pockets for my ring of keys. I glanced at the dresser top. The ring was there, and I felt relieved.

I caught a flash of white in the inside pocket of the suit jacket. I pulled out the sealed envelope and saw Tilly scrawled across it in

Mike's handwriting. I slid the letter back in the pocket, and fuzzy bits and pieces started to blizzard my mind.

I remembered the attic and how Lovell punched me into unconsciousness each time I came to and screamed under his torture. Then he had forced me to empty that quart bottle of whiskey with him.

At some hazy time Rabbit had banged on the door and Lovell had gone down the stairs to bounce a bad craps loser. I had been too punished and drunk to try escape.

Much later I had stood reeling with my clothes on. I had stood and looked down at Lovell's ugly face—mouth gaped open—snoring.

I had searched his pockets and found my wad of money and my keys and his switchblade knife. I had gone back to the side of the bed and stood there above him with the deadly point of the blade almost touching the leapy heart pulse in his chest.

I sobbed and shook. I had wanted so much to drive the knife into his rotten heart. I really had. But then I remembered that Reverend Martin Luther King had said, "Black folks have got to stop killing each other," and I just couldn't do it.

I remembered Lucy giving me the letter from Mike and telling me how he had waited for hours at her place for me to show. He had missed me at Stel's by ten minutes.

Then I remembered driving home to the mortuary, and I had thought about turning head-on into the traffic whizzing by me. I had felt so stupid and hopeless, and not really caring about anything except dumping the treacherous bitch, Sally, once and for all.

When I reached the mortuary Dorcas was pulling the hearse from the curb carrying the remains of M. Phleps with a caravan of cars following. I had completely forgotten, under Sally's influence, that his funeral had been scheduled for April 4. I had put Dorcas in one hell of a spot and made a star ass out of myself.

Dorcas had given me a solid glare of angry disgust. I looked in the dresser mirror at my bruised, puffy face. I looked like I had been drunk for a month.

I stood on a chair and turned my back to the mirror. I looked over my shoulder and pulled myself apart. I got nauseated at the sight of my body pocked with ugly bite and pinch wounds.

I knew I needed medical attention for sure. I heard the faint whoosh of the garage door opening to the electronic beam inside the hearse.

I went across the hall to the bathroom and stood there behind the locked door, ashamed to face Dorcas. I heard her come down the hall and go into her bedroom next to mine.

I sat on the toilet. It felt like I was passing my entrails. I almost cried out with the pain. I rose and saw that my stool was bloody. I drew a tub of water and took a bath. I eased the door open and went to my bedroom. I put on pajamas and sat at the window looking out on State Street.

Finally Dorcas came to the doorway and said, "Welcome home, playboy. That call I got from you last night saying you were on the way home must have come from New York. Or maybe you decided not to tear yourself away from Miss whoever she is. What does she look like, Otis? Does she have a lovely slender figure? Go on tell me about her. I won't be hurt. It will be wonderful to know where we stand."

I turned and faced her. "Hon, I'm sorry I broke my word and you had to drive the hearse. For the last time, I'm saying there is no other woman in my life. I got into trouble, real trouble that had nothing to do with a woman. It's the truth, Dorcas. It won't happen again. But I won't tell you what happened. So stop quizzing me."

She came and sat on the bed and said softly, "Otis, please don't lie to me. I checked all the jails and hospitals. Where have you been? I want to know what happened. I love you, but you have to clear up things for me. Whatever it is, I'll understand."

I felt suffocated like under Mama's pressure. My palms were gluey.

I said sharply, "Goddamnit, Dorcas, I told you I'm not telling you what happened. It's too personal, and no woman except Mama could understand it. You'd despise me. Now leave me alone. I want to think."

I got up and went to the dresser. I stood there brushing my hair and watching her in the mirror. She sat there nervously raking her fingers through her long black hair and staring at the floor.

She stood up and came to stand behind me. The big eyes in the furious black face were angry and accusing. I turned and tried to embrace her.

She backed up and spat out, "Don't touch me, liar. You've been cheating on me with one of these Westside chippies. Daddy always told me fellows with your background were dangerous risks. Now you've betrayed me, lied to me. Please don't be a tramp."

She'd smashed the control on my rage machine with the crack about her father. I opened my mouth to shout at her. A pain grenade detonated in my rectum and reared me back on my heels.

I hung there like a corpse from an invisible hangman's noose with my tongue lolling out. I crumbled backward on the foot of the bed like a sweaty rag doll.

Dorcas brought a cold towel to my brow and crooned "You see, Otis, it's ridiculous to carouse with that chippie all night and get hung over like this. What does she look like?"

I lay there looking up at her agonized face.

I cut her off quietly. "Dorcas, I can't stand pressure, so I'm going to tell you what happened, and then I'm going to get out of your sight and give you a chance to get yourself a real man. I haven't been out with a woman. I've been . . ."

She sobbed and threw herself across me and pressed her lips against mine.

She pleaded, "Don't tell me, Otis. Don't tell me if you're going to leave me. I don't want to know. You're my man. I know that, and I love you."

I pushed her away and stood up. I looked into her eyes for a long moment.

Then I said softly, "Hon, that's the problem exactly. You're in love all right, but not with a man. Dorcas, I'm a low-life faggot. A big, black, ugly nigger with a deformed dick fucked me in a filthy attic until he passed out."

Her mouth popped open. She froze like she was having a stroke. I saw the shock anguish in her eyes and knew I was going to break down. I went to the closet and got my suitcase and threw it on the bed.

She shook the bed in convulsions of weeping. My tears blinded me as I packed the bag and slipped the gray suit over my pajamas. I took my car key and Mama's door key from the ring of mortuary keys and touched Dorcas on the shoulder. She sat up on the side of the bed and rocked as she held my hands against her face.

She wailed, "Oh! Otis, don't go. You were wrong about my despising you. I'm just confused and forgive me for saying it, but I'm so relieved that it wasn't another woman. Otis, darling, that was the only time with a man in the year we've been together, wasn't it?"

I pulled my hands away and picked up my suitcase.

I said gently, "Dorcas, last night was the only time since I've been with you. But I've had guys on the brain all along, even when we sexed, so I could stay hard. I love you, Hon. But I can't stay knowing that you know how sick and weak I am. Since we were kids, something has always turned up to keep us apart. I guess we shouldn't be together."

I kissed her on the cheek and turned away. She followed me down the hallway to the door. She hugged me around the waist and pressed her face between my shoulder blades.

She pleaded, "Stay here with me. I won't ever again ask you to marry me. I love you enough to help you get well. You weren't born that way. Together we can . . ."

I pried her arms loose and faced her.

I said tenderly, "I wish I was good enough to marry you. You're still pretty. Some high-class guy will come along to make you happy."

I started down the stairs to the street door.

She said sorrowfully, "I'll never want anybody but you. Otis, I'm going to wait for you. Please promise you'll come back to me."

I opened the door and said, "You're breaking my heart, but I can't promise you that. I have to get my mind together. Dorcas, you can't know how terrible it is to be the way I am. No matter what happens, I'll never forget how sweet and wonderful you've been to me."

I slowly shut the door to her crying and went down the sidewalk to the Plymouth in a storm of tears.

I drove to a medical building at Sixty-first Street and Cottage Grove Avenue on the Southside. I went up a flight of stairs to the office of an old doctor who had formerly practiced on the Westside.

He examined me and found a ripped anus and a traumatized sphincter. He injected a local anesthetic and took four stitches. He gave me pills for pain and sleep and told me to come back in several days.

I went to the Plymouth and sat there confused, not knowing what to do or where to go.

I drove across the intersection and parked in front of the Evans Hotel at Sixty-first Street and Evans Avenue. I went to the desk and checked into a fourth-floor room facing Sixty-first Street.

I sat in a chair by the window in deep depression until twilight lit its lavender lamp. I called room service for vegetable soup and a Denver sandwich. I felt better after I had eaten.

I got pajamas and a small transistor radio from my bag. I took a pain pill and lay across the bed and tried to untangle the snarl of my life. I stared at the ceiling and listened to sentimental music for quite a while.

Then a newscaster started a recap of the day's news. I couldn't believe his words. I leaped off the bed and stood holding my breath.

He said it again loud and clear, "Reverend Martin Luther King Jr. has been murdered by a sniper on the balcony of the Lorraine Motel in Memphis."

I understood why the streets were so quiet and black faces were so solemn and angry. The shock of the terrible news was just too much for my already chaotic mind. I cried and ran blindly in the darkness crashing myself into the furniture like a stricken animal.

I listened to the radio pouring out the sorrow and anger of America. Dozens of times during the lonely night I went to the window and tried to argue myself across the sill to the concrete four stories down. Each time I could feel some frightful force inside me pulling to propel me through the window. It was a deadly struggle to snatch myself away. I knew that if I didn't stop going to that window I would certainly give in to the horrible impulse that got stronger and stronger.

Finally at daybreak I took two sleeping pills. I certainly had a desperate need for sleep because it was late afternoon when I woke up to a news bulletin that burning and looting had started on the Westside.

I was no longer confused. Mama was alone over there. It was true that she could become unbearable with her possessiveness, but she needed me, and I loved her. The least I could do was stay with her until the rioting was over. Besides, I knew I'd be better off with Mama than keeping company with that magnetized window.

I called Mama twice, but her line was busy. It was dusk when I checked out. As I drove toward the Westside, I thought how heartless and stupid it was for the rioters to dishonor the philosophy and death of our leader.

I drove slowly along the 3200 block of West Madison Street. The keening scream of distant fire engines and the hoarse ecstasy of the looters and burners was like baleful music.

Twisting fat flames hula-danced from the tops of gutted buildings. Uneasy policemen stood in the bursts of red light with phony indifference on their faces as the looters crawled through the black window frames into the murky interiors of stores and came out with stacks of flashy finery.

Kinky-topped infants, some no more than five years old, skipped merrily from the sacked stores with their parents. Their tiny black faces lit up in the excitement and joy of the shiny baubles they clutched.

Just ahead in the 3300 block, I saw a fire engine straddling the street pumping streams of water into a flaming building and heard the pop of rioters' pistols sniping at firemen.

I turned off Madison Street into an alley. I came out on Spaulding Avenue, and there, twenty feet away, was a lone white policeman in the middle of the street.

I parked and walked to the outer edge of a crowd spotlighted by the headlights of a police car. The cop was in the center of the horde cut off from his cruiser.

The revolving red dome light flashed eerily on the cop's starch white face paralyzed in fear and shock. His mouth gaped open stupidly, and his sea blue eyes spun crazily.

The leader of the cursing mob was larger than Big Lovell, and his kinky hair seemed to stand on end as he thrust his angry black face to within inches of the cop's face. The whites of his black eyes glowed in released madness, and his wide nostrils dilated in hatred.

I goose pimpled and stood there fascinated.

The heavy blue black lips pulled back from the brown teeth in a grinning snarl. He slapped the slack mouth and shouted into the face of his enemy. "You got a gun, chickenhearted motherfucker. Use it. All you bastards are cunts when the odds ain't in your favor."

The cop just stood there with that awed look of fear on his face. Then the black giant in a deft rapid stroke snaked the cop's gun from its holster. He palmed it in his massive right hand. He twisted his wrist to a backhand and brought his muscular arm back and slammed the blue steel against the side of the cop's head.

The vicious blow landed with a hollow crunching sound. A spatter of scarlet dotted the giant's shirtfront. The cop's legs gave way, and he slipped to the asphalt.

Black fingers clawed at the blue cloth and shredded it. The white figure moaned as the mob kicked at it. Finally, they moved away from the insensible heap lying in the glare of the cruiser's headlights.

The silver badge, a worthless charm, glittered inches away from a ghost white hand.

As I drove away toward Mama I began to feel bad. I couldn't get it out of my mind that he hadn't been born a cop, so maybe he had once been a human being. He could have a wife, children and a mother who cared about him, even though he was a treacherous cop.

I just couldn't stand the thought that he was lying there helpless and without medical aid, so I stopped at a phone booth and called the district police station. I pointed out that the cop was unconscious and the odds were that some black passerby he had brutalized was certain to come along and cut his throat or blow his brains out if they didn't hurry to him.

Homan Avenue was quiet except for shadowy figures darting down the sidewalk heavily laden with booty. I parked in front of Mama's building and hurried down the walk carrying my suitcase.

Mama met me in the vestibule, spidery arms crushing the hell out of me as usual and with a radiant smile of welcome like I had just gotten back from Viet Nam. I didn't have the heart to tell her that I hadn't come home to stay permanently.

4

FORTY CENTS A HUNDRED
AIN'T A PRECIOUS GIFT

I lay alone in the dark rear bedroom remembering Frank, Carol and Bessie, my older brother and sisters, and how we all shared the bedroom until deadly forces within the family and in the treacherous streets cut them down.

I listened to the radio rundown on the savage rioting, and for some strange reason, I couldn't forget that fearful awe on the cop's face before he had been smashed to the ground.

That expression on his face was somehow familiar. But I couldn't remember why.

My thoughts swung to Papa and the smelly one-room sharecropper's shack in Mississippi with the foul holes in the floor that the tenants before us had used as toilets. Papa had built a privy a hundred yards from the shack and dumped quicklime or something down the holes and sealed them. But the rotten stench seemed to come back with full power in hot weather.

Papa and Mama had a battered old bed. Papa couldn't get his hands on lumber to build beds for us. Many steamy nights I'd lie sleepless on the rough pine floor. I'd hear and smell Mama and Papa kissing and sexing behind a potato sack curtain in the corner of the room. I'd get a peculiar excited feeling.

I would crawl across my sleeping brother and sisters and tiptoe from the shack. I'd stand there gulping the fresh air that rippled the stark white sea of cotton plants.

I'd often gaze at the alabaster house of the plantation owner gleaming in the sapphire starlight and wonder how much cotton would a sharecropper have to pick at forty cents a hundred to own a house like it.

At the flash of dawn we would eat a breakfast of biscuits, fat back, grits and gravy before going to the fields. At supper we'd have hog maws and turnip greens or maybe black-eyed peas with hot water cornbread.

It was a hard life and coarse food, but we were never hungry because Papa could always get supplies from Mr. Wilkerson, the plantation owner, on tab against the cotton money our family earned.

Our family never had more than a few dollars in cold cash, but Papa had a big pride in knowing he was all-man, one of the best pickers on the plantation. We loved and respected Papa back there in the South, and Papa respected himself.

It was a huge plantation in the country outside Meridian, Mississippi, that worked many families like ours beneath the blistering sun.

I was frail and prone to sunstroke. I collapsed a half-dozen times in the two years I worked the cotton. When I was eight years old I started staying at the shack, helping Mama sew and wash our clothes when she didn't go to the fields.

The big cast-iron tub Mama used to wash our clothes in was also our bathtub. I'd watch Papa strip off his sweaty clothes when he came in from the fields. I'd admire his muscles that writhed like golden snakes when he bathed.

In the off months of cotton my brother and sisters and I went to a one-room schoolhouse two miles away. Carol and I would often take our reading and writing to a patch of moonlight on the floor after the kerosene lamp had been blown out and Frank Jr. and Bessie were sound asleep.

Papa and my older brother, Frank Jr., and I were real buddies down South. We'd go fishing and hiking together. Papa and Frank Jr. would wrestle each other until they panted. Frank Jr. was taller than Papa and almost as big, but he was no match for Papa's wiry strength.

Sunday afternoon Papa would deck himself out in starched and creased overalls and gleaming brogans ordered from a Sears and Roebuck catalogue. He'd preach beneath a clump of cottonwood trees to his amening congregation. He sure stood proud and beautiful out there giving Satan hell with his booming rich voice.

Papa had some importance and a sense of worth down South, even though living conditions were subhuman. Up North, poor Papa would become a zero, unimportant to everyone, even to his wife and children.

Mama wasn't a bit fire and brimstone like Papa. And when she went to church I could feel that she didn't go because she was religious. Mama and Papa were completely different from each other in habit and desires and morals. But Papa tried because he was a good man and he loved her and his children. I really doubt that Mama ever loved Papa. Small wonder that the Tilsons were doomed to tears and sorrow.

Mama had an obsession to escape the South and go to Chicago where her cousin Bunny lived like white folks with running water, in-the-house privy and a sitting room and electric lights.

Papa was content in the South and would just sit silently with a worried look on his face when Mama read Bunny's letters and got all excited and starry eyed about the wondrous North.

Mama and Papa were unlike peas in a pod in other ways too. They met and married in Vicksburg, Mississippi, in 1919. Papa was twenty-eight and had come in from the country with his father on a Saturday night to bring the gospel to the grog heads, whoremongers and craps shooters.

Papa was taking his preaching turn on a sinful street corner when Mama and cousin Bunny passed him, and then came back for a second long look at the extremely handsome high yellow preacher.

Mama told us she had lived with cousin Bunny since she was ten years old. She was mysterious and vague about her parents and her life before she lived with Bunny. I found out why one terrible day years later.

I found out from arguments between Mama and Papa that cousin Bunny had been a fast twenty-five-year-old hustler who was operating a blind pig and poker trap in Vicksburg's sin district that night that Mama saw Papa for the first time.

I don't know whether Bunny had used bright-eyed, curvaceous Mama as a shill, or worse, in her joint. But I'll always believe that Mama was hurt morally by those years with Bunny in her blind pig. And perhaps what Mama revealed when Bessie left home to whore could explain the cold-blooded things Mama did up North.

Papa rescued Mama from Bunny's den of iniquity and took her for better or for worse a month after they met. Papa took her to Meridian, Mississippi, shortly after that, perhaps to escape cousin Bunny's scarlet charisma and the outraged condemnation of Grandpa Tilson.

Papa shoed horses and mules in Meridian and fathered his first child, Frank Jr. The livery stable burned down, and Papa took his small family to Wilkerson's plantation.

In the spring of 1936 (the same year we went to the Promised Land), Mrs. Wilkerson borrowed half a dozen teenage boys from the fields for the annual scrubbing and wall washing in the big house. Frank Jr. was among them. Mr. and Mrs. Wilkerson had gone to Meridian, and her eldest son was in charge of the workers.

I was helping Mama peel potatoes for supper when Frank Jr. got back from the big house. Papa and the twins hadn't come in from the fields. Frank Jr. acted strangely from the moment he set foot in the shack. His eyes were flashing excitement as he tossed a small paper sack of raw sugar in front of me. I thought he had lost his mind, because as far back as I could remember, he'd always slunk off somewhere alone and devoured his goodies from the big house.

He flung himself to the floor in front of Mama's chair and with his head on her lap stared at her with a radiant look on his dirty face.

Mama said, "Yu sho looks funny. Ah hope yu ain't ben nippin' th' Wilkerson's applejack. Yu ain't no baby; git yo' haid offen mah lap an git kindlin' fer th' cook stove."

He got to his feet and ran to the door. He shaded his eyes with his hand and looked down the path that Papa and the twins used coming from the fields.

He rushed back to Mama and shot a suspicious look at me and said, "Mama, sen thet lil' niggah outdoes. Ah got uh secret tu tell yu thet Ah don' want him blabbin' tu Papa or nobody."

Mama looked sternly at him and said, "Sweet Pea don' blab nuthin'. An' tell him not tu. Now, stop ackin' lak uh star natal fool an' say whut yu goin' ta say."

He stooped and pulled up a trouser leg. He had a red bandana handkerchief tied around his leg. He walled his eyes at the open door as he plucked a roll of bills from beneath the bandana.

In a speedy flow he said, "Now, Mama, Ah ain't stole nuthin'. Ah wuz sweatin' an' slavin' up there en th' big house. Ah wuz thinkin' 'bout mah one an' only dear Mama achin' fer thet train goin' North when dis forgot money fell at mah feet jes' as Ah moved thet ole grandfather clock frum th' wall.

"Nah, ma'm, Ah ain't stole nuthin'. See how dusty these green-backs is. It's sho 'nuff forgot money. Ah found it fer ye, Mama. Count it."

He held out the bills toward Mama's lap as if to drop them there. Mama's mouth flew open, and she spun her lap away like the money was a water moccasin. She gasped and held her hands up as if to ward him off. She got to her feet sputtering and pointing to the big house.

She cuffed him against the side of his head and words came out, "Yu crazy rascul, git them white folks' money back there en thet same spot quick as yu rusty laigs kin go."

Frank's bare feet drummed the floor as he fled the shack. Mama stood in the doorway biting her lip and staring at Frank Jr. sprinting toward the big house. She turned her head and looked down the path leading to the fields.

She screamed, "Boy, come back heah."

In a moment Junior ran back out of breath with a puzzled look on his face.

Mama squeezed his sweaty brow with the edge of her hand and said softly, "Now think hard, an' tell Mama, duz eny uv them lil' niggahs thet wurked up at th' big house know yu found thet forgot money?"

Junior pressed the bills in Mama's hand and said loudly, "Nah, ma'm. Nah ma'm! Wuzn't nobody pee-pin'."

Mama's hand was trembling violently as she counted the tens and twenties. Junior went outside and stood revolving his head from the path to Mama.

Junior hissed like a snake and stuck his head inside the shack and stage whispered, "Papa is cumin'."

Mama balled a fist at me and laid an index finger across her pursed lips. She shoved the bills in her bosom and started to hum a spiritual.

Junior came in with kindling and was starting a fire in the cook stove when Papa and the twins got to the shack. Collard greens with slat pork and potato patties were on our supper table when I heard the Wilkerson's Ford pickup coming home from Meridian.

Mama and Junior ate like innocents. I could only swallow a few bites. I was worried about the Wilkerson money in Mama's bosom that Papa might find out about, and said a silent prayer that it was real "forgot" money and that the beet red sheriff wouldn't come and take us all to jail.

I almost fainted when Papa looked across the table at me and said, "Otis, whut's th' matter yu playin' wid them vittles? Iffen yu ailin' en the belly, Ah have ole vet tu dose yu up good wid croton oil when he cum tumurrah."

Out of the corner of my eye I saw Mama giving me the evil eye.

I said, "No sir, I'm not sick. I been messing with the treat bag that Junior brought from the big house, that's all."

He grunted and went back to the mountain of food on his plate.

It was a balmy, brilliant night after supper, and the next day was Sunday. So we kids played hide-and-seek, and Mama and Papa brought kitchen chairs and sat quietly relaxing (at least Papa was) beneath the starry sky.

We had all gone in to go to bed when Papa said, "Ah'll be Satan's imp iffen old man Wilkerson ain't out prowlin' dis time uv night. Mayhaps uh mule is ailin' so bad Mr. Wilkerson got tu drive an' fetch th' vet. Ah hope Naomi's asthma ain't got no wurse."

We all clustered around Papa at the window and watched the jouncing glow of a lantern move down the hill from the big house to a shack in the irregular line that ended with our shack.

One of the cleanup boys lived in that first shack where they had stopped. I shivered when I thought it hadn't been "forgot" money after all.

Papa lit a lantern and said, "Best Ah go. Sumbody mayhaps need mah prayers."

The twins went to bed after a while. But Mama, Frank Jr. and I stood silently there at the window and watched the accusing orbs of the lanterns moving through the night, stopping at four more innocent shacks on the way to our guilty one.

Finally after what seemed like endless hours, the lanterns stopped at the fifth shack. I felt Mama's fingernails dig into my collarbone. I turned and looked up at her face drawn with tension.

She whispered hoarsely, "We got tu hit th' bed now, an' we don know nuthin' 'bout them white folk's money. Remember, ain't no pruf or nuthin' nohow 'bout Junior."

I lay wrapped in my quilt and had chills. I was afraid Papa would drop dead or something if he found out that Junior was the thief.

Something touched my shoulder.

Carol whispered, "Ah heard Mama. Junior is en terrible truble, ain't he?"

Before I could answer, the flash of lanterns streaked through a window. Carol scooted back to her section of the floor. I closed my eyes tightly and turned my back to the door.

I felt the flooring vibrate under the clump of brogans. I smelled Mr. Wilkerson's distinctive musk and corn whiskey. I turned over and peeped through a hole in the quilt.

Mr. Wilkerson's corrugated face was flaming red in the glow of his lantern as he stooped close to Junior and prodded his chest with gnarled finger. Papa squatted down on Junior's other side. Junior fluttered his eyes open and looked up at Mr. Wilkerson in sham surprise.

Mr. Wilkerson jogged his fingers across Junior's scalp and said affably, "Lil' Frank, you woke?"

Junior cut his wide eyes at Papa and murmured sleepily, "Yes, suh, Mr. Wilkerson."

Mr. Wilkerson said, "Laddie, one of them crew with you at the big house stole Miz Wilkerson's big stash of money, near 'bout or more four hundred dollars. Did you see the sneaking scamp that done it?"

Junior swallowed hard, raised himself to his elbows and croaked, "Nah, suh, nah, suh. Papa an' me alike. Ah sees uh smidget of crookedness on th' plantashun, Ah tells th' news right now.

"Nah, suh, Ah ain't seen nobody fiddlin' wid th' big iron safe. Even when we finish th' wurk an' foot race frum th' big house, Ah don' hear no silver dollars rattlin' nobody's pocket. Nah, suh, Ah ain't seen or heared nuthin'."

Mr. Wilkerson and Papa stood up. Mr. Wilkerson stroked his chin and said, "Laddie, it weren't no silver money. It were in green-backs stashed agin the grandfather clock.

"Mah ole woman's madder than a smoked out hornet. She had a powerful mind to fetch the sheriff tonight to cull out the criminal. But Ah'm a merciful man, and Ah ain't fer that bloodthirsty sheriff whuppin' heads and kickin' asses of the whole damn crew. Ain't but one guilty."

He paused and watched Junior's spastic tongue irrigate his gray lips.

Papa shut his eyes and said, "Lawd, draw th' thief forth fer pur-gin' uv his sin an' returnin' Miz Wilkerson's greenbacks."

Mr. Wilkerson stroked his hooked nose and impaled Junior on sharp blue eyes for a lone moment before he said, "Lissen, Lil' Frank, we gonna' root out the criminal before Miz Wilkerson get that mean sheriff on the place at noon tomorrow. Since Ah knows you innocent and cleverer than them others, Ah'm pintin' you mah secret investigator.

"Ah want you up at daybreak rousing them suspecs and stand-ing the guilty one before me no later than noon. Ain't gonna' be no penitentiary and crool treatment. Jes a fair and honest whupping with a piece of horse harness at the punishing spot. You understand me, boy?"

Too quickly Junior almost shouted, "Sho do, Mr. Wilkerson, sho do, an' ah be up at 'em early, early, sho will."

Mr. Wilkerson's face had a cunning look as he picked up his lan-tern. He patted Papa affectionately on the shoulder and walked away into the salubrious and innocent night.

Papa walked the floor and prayed until daybreak. Mama's face looked awful with the strain and pressure she was under. She fixed biscuits and hash for breakfast that everybody just picked at. Junior kept his eyes riveted to Mama's face like he desperately needed guidance.

Right after breakfast Papa sighed and said to Mama, "Sedalia, Ah best go an' help Junior hunt out Miz Wilkerson's greenbacks."

Mama squeezed her brow between her palms like she was treating a bad headache.

Her vacant eyes looked past Papa out to the backbreaking green oceans of early cotton plants when she said, "Frank, Ah tell yu true, it ain't nuthin' but uh low-down dirty shame thet po' niggahs got tu shag down money fer them rich white folks. Ah swear iffen Ah wuz Miz Wilkerson Ah wouldn't make no commotion. Since Ah ain't payin' but forty cents uh hundard no how."

Papa turned crimson and hollered, "Sedalia, yu stop thet devilish talk. Wikerson's don' pay but uh cent uh hundard, ain't nobody got uh right tu steal frum 'em. Come on, Junior, let's git 'bout our biz-ness. It be noon 'fore we know it."

Suddenly there was a burst of sobbing. Everybody in the shack turned toward Carol in a corner. Papa rushed to her and lifted her into his arms.

He pressed her close and crooned, "Papa ain't gonna' let nobody harm his baby girl. Now yu shet off them tears."

Carol hugged Papa tightly around the neck and blubbered, "Papa, Ah ain't scairt fer me. Ah'm scairt cause Ah know thet sheriff is cumin' at noon time."

Mama and Junior stood frozen, staring at Carol and Bessie.

Papa patted her and said, "Ain't no sheriff cumin'. Me an' Junior gonna' dig up th' thief an' take him tu the big house fer his justiz on th' punish spot. Mr. Wilkerson don' welcome no law on his place iffen he kin help it."

Carol wailed, "Oh, Papa, the sheriff got tu come, 'cause thet money ain't out there en sumbody else's shack. It's right en this shack! Junior took th' money frum the big house! Papa, please don' let th' sheriff take Junior tu th' pen."

The big vein at Papa's temple ballooned out lividly like his head was going to explode. He roughly stood Carol on her feet and turned and seized Junior by the shoulders. He thrust his face close and moved his eyes up and down Junior's face like he was reading a printed page.

Junior's eyes were bucked wide and his lips trembled to speak.

Papa shook him hard, and he sobbed piteously, "Papa, God en his Heaven knows Ah ain't stole nuthin' en mah heart. Ah found forgot money, Ah thought. Ah figured we all ketch th' Chicago train. Papa, whut you gonna' do?"

Papa embraced him for a long moment, and tears rolled down Papa's cheeks.

Then Papa flung him away and said very quietly, "Ah'm takin' yu tu th' big house so's Mr. Wilkerson knows Ah ain't hidin' th' thief's face 'cause he mah flesh an' blood. Yu goin' tu git justiz on the punish spot fer stealin'. Where them greenbacks?"

Junior moaned, "Mama got 'em. Please, Papa, don' take me! Don' take me!"

Mama took the bills from her bosom and stepped between them.

Her words were rapid and impassioned. "Frank, ain't no need tu take mah chile up there fer white folks tu tear his hide off. Fact is, ain't even no wiz reasun tu take this money back. Ole man Wilkerson were bull scarin' us 'bout ole Miz fetchin' the sheriff en tuday. Ain't no way fer him not tu smell thet funky still stinkin' up th' place.

"An' sumthin' else. How we know Wilkerson ain't ben robbin' us wid his pencil all these years? How we know, Frank? Remember whut thet niggah tole us en Meridian even 'fore we cum tu wurk here. We ain't cumalated nuthin'. Don' be no fool, Frank. We keep this money an' tuff it out. Few months we ease off this plantashun an' ketch th' fust thing smokin' tu Cheecogo."

Papa had been standing with an unbelieving expression on his face.

He snatched the bills from Mama's hands and said carefully, "Sedalia, Lawd have mercy on yo' soul. Ah ain't nevah gittin' off this plantashun iffen Ah got tu steal to git off. Yu done fergot th' Lawd said, 'Thou shalt not steal.'"

Papa took a firm hold on Junior's wrist and led him out the door.

Mama went to the doorway and cried out to Papa's back, "Niggah, yu ah uh star natal fool tu take thet money back tu them cheatin' white folks. Forty cents uh hundard ain't uh precious gift no way yu look at it. Ah'm gonna' quit yu, niggah, iffen yu don bring mah chile an' thet money back heah. Fool, forty cents uh hundard ain't uh precious gift."

Papa didn't even turn his head. He just kept marching Junior to the big house. We all went to the window and watched them go up the hill to the big house followed by people from the shacks who sensed that Junior was the thief, and they were eager to break their awful boredom at the punishment spot.

The twins and Mama sprawled on the floor and bawled. Carol was pitiful the way she told Mama over and over how sorry she was that she told Papa the secret.

Mama cried bitterly and shouted over and over, "Ah hate white folks. Oh, how Ah hate white folks."

I stood at the window remembering what the punishment spot looked like and cried for Junior. In the days of slavery it had been a hut where recaptured runaway slaves and troublemaking slaves had been beaten and tortured under the supervision of Mr. Wilkerson's grandfather.

It no longer had sides or a roof, just a rotted floor of bloodstained planking with four iron stakes in the center making a square roughly the size of a man's spread-eagled body.

I stood at the window until I saw people drifting down the hill to the shacks. Then I saw Papa and Junior. Junior's chin seemed to be resting on his chest, and Papa had his arm around Junior's waist as they came down the hill.

I raced out of the shack and met them.

Junior's back was covered with ropey welts, and he kept mumbling, "Papa, don' touch me. Papa, don' touch me."

It was more than a week before Mama's lard-based ointment took the soreness out of Junior's back. It was longer than that before Papa and Junior exchanged whole sentences.

Something sweet and important had soured and died between them. They didn't tussle or horseplay together any more, and I'd often see Junior looking at Papa with cold eyes when Papa wasn't noticing.

For more than a month after Papa took Junior to the punishment spot, Mama communicated with Papa by grunts and head nods and head shaking.

And then one night the moon filtered through the potato sack curtain and I saw Papa's naked shadow humping and thrusting and finally quivering with Mama's legs and arms locked around him.

On November 1, 1936, the day I reached my eighth birthday, a miracle happened. Mama's cousin Bunny's husband died, and there had been enough money left from his insurance policy after funeral expenses to send Mama money for five tickets to Chicago and a furnished apartment with rent paid up two months across the hall from Cousin Bunny.

The letter with the money said, "Please hurry, because I have lung cancer bad, and I need someone to look in on me."

Everybody except Papa was thrilled and excited at the prospect of going to the enchanted North. Papa hassled with Wilkerson about our cotton account and got a fabulous sixteen dollars.

Three days after Mama got the money we were on the train wearing our hand-me-down and homemade clothes. But I didn't give it a thought. There would be bales of money waiting for us up North and store-bought clothes by the piles.

I remember how sad Papa's face looked when the train crossed the Mason-Dixon line. Poor Papa couldn't know that his brawny back and strong hands would become counterfeit as exchange in the Promised Land where cotton didn't grow and the trade unions locked out black men.

Papa couldn't know that hope, self-respect, manhood and dignity would die inside him in the brutally repressive North. How could he know that Mama would become like the man of the family and he would become like the woman?

After what seemed like weeks, our train pulled into Chicago. It was all so shocking. The street sounds exploded like a bomb. Hordes of insane-looking people with twisted, tense faces moved at breakneck speed down the dim sidewalks, shadowed by ominous buildings that seemed to be teetering in the heavens.

We all crowded into a taxicab. I looked at Papa on our way to the Westside. He was staring at the desolate concrete wilderness, and he had a look of fearful awe on his face that I would see many years later on the face of a white cop trapped by a mob of blacks.

I looked at Papa's work-scarred hands, and I felt like crying when I remembered Mama crying out to Papa's back, "Fool, forty cents a hundred ain't a precious gift."

5

THE PROMISED LAND AIN'T

The apartment supplied by Cousin Bunny was in a six-unit building. It was located on Homan Avenue, on the Westside. Faint indentations in the concrete facade of the weather-battered structure read: Regal Arms Apartment. Roaches crawled about even in daylight, and at night, huge rats squeaked and scampered about the flat.

The first night I turned on the light in the kitchen and saw a large rat about the size of a squirrel on the sink drainboard staring at me with tiny malevolent eyes. He had only three feet. The stump was ragged, like a trap had backed off the foot, or perhaps the old crip had chewed it off in a valorous escape from the trap. He outstared me. I forgot I wanted a drink of water and went back to bed.

The apartment was furnished with old but sturdy stuff moved from Cousin Bunny's apartment a week before our arrival. She had decided to furnish her own apartment with new stuff.

The instant water taps, the magic blue gas flames for cooking and heating and the bright odorless electric lights were exciting novelties. Only Papa was unimpressed and unhappy. He spent most of his time pacing the floor and gazing out the window at pinched-faced figures in flimsy overcoats shuddering against the blasting winds.

At the end of our first week in Chicago a snowstorm hid the grimy bleakness beneath three feet of glamorous whiteness. Cousin Bunny made Papa smile for the first time in Chicago. She gave him a pile of winter work clothes that her dead husband had worn to work sewers and to collect city garbage for twenty years. Then she had Soldier Boy, an acquaintance of hers who was a snow scuffler, pick up Papa to help shovel snow from the sidewalks of commercial businesses for a fee.

Mama and we kids crowded the frosty front window looking at Papa going down the walk turning to wave to us. His face was glowing with happiness, because he was going to earn some money for us.

Papa was a slight, but sturdy, five feet nine, and he looked so comical struggling into the snow scuffler's battered pickup truck. Cousin Bunny's husband had been a large man, and his clothes made Papa look like a child masquerading in his father's storm coat and boots.

Later I followed Mama across the hall to look in on Cousin Bunny. Her door was open, and she was sitting on a purple sofa, and she sipped whiskey from a double shot glass.

Drab patches of tarnished silver fouled her shoulder-length auburn hair. Her tiny figure was skeletal, and the big-eyed yellow face was gray tinged and saggy. A flicker of fire in the brown eyes and curves in the sexy lips were the last reminders that she had once been the belle of Vicksburg's black sin streets.

Mama frowned and scolded, "Bunny, why yu mixin' cansur with hooch? Yu gonna' die."

Bunny quickly drained the shot glass and said thickly, "Honey, you're sweet to remind me. But I don't really give a goddamn."

She refilled her glass from a pint bottle on a table beside her at the end of the sofa. She stared for a long moment at a paper-framed photograph of a good-looking black man on the table.

Mama said, "Oh, Bunny, yu got nice things, an' yu ain't much mo' than forty. Why yu stay down en th' dumps? Shoot, Ah wish we git yu an' Joe's luck up here."

Bunny laughed mirthlessly and said, "Sedalia, bless your dumb little heart. Poor Joe must have flipped-flopped in his grave when you said good luck. Sedalia, I loved Joe so much. He made me respectable.

"He died in his sleep at forty-two, and the coroner, with all his knives and education, could only say that Joe died a natural death. It wasn't a natural death for Joe. He was intelligent, ambitious and a high school graduate.

"But he was black in the white folks' hateful world, where a nigger is like a mop head or toilet brush. The white folks used him to clean up their puking and droppings until he wears out. Then they simply press another hungry nigger into service. They never really see him or realize he is a human unless he steals from them or kills one of them. Then they drop the full weight of their double standard law and bury him in prison or barbecue him in the electric chair.

"No, Joe didn't die a natural death. He was proud and fit for better, and he hated the filthy garbage and the slimy sewers he worked. He just lay down that night and died of hopelessness and a broken heart."

Mama jut sat there with a pained look on her face like she was hurting to hear the North wasn't paradise after all. Bunny fingered a policy slip on the table and looked at it wryly.

Mama said, "Bunny, yu bin frum down South a long time. An' yu ain't nevah done no share croppin' an' raisin' younguns. Ah knows up heahs bettern down South. We havin' good luck up heah. Frank's workin' a'ready, an' we ain't jammed up in no one room hearin' one anuther breakin' win', thanks tu yu, uv cose.

"Ain't nuthin' real wrong up heah. A day don' pass, ah ain't seen big shot niggers drivin' great long cahs pas' this buildin'. Up heah a po' nigger got a hope tu hol a big 'mount uv money. Yu jes' drinkin' an' missin' Joe, an' it got yu en th' dumps."

Bunny waved a flesh bare hand through the air and said, "Sedalia, I'm funky drunk, and there's no doubt the North is better for some spooks than the big foot country. Only time will tell whether or not it's better for you and Frank.

"Those dapper niggers didn't get those pretty cars shoveling snow or shining shoes. They are policy wheelmen, pimps, dope peddlers and hustlers. All of nigger Chicago is lousy with policy stations, gambling joints and whore cribs. So Sugar, stop dreaming and play policy. It's the only way a poor honest nigger can hope to get big money."

Mama got up and headed for Bunny's carpet sweeper.

Mama laughed halfheartedly and said, "Oh, Heifer, save thet breath. Ah ain't takin' yur jinky talk serious."

Bunny squealed and jerked her feet in the air as Mama raced the sweeper past the sofa. I got a rag and dusted. Mama was massaging Bunny's scalp when the sound of loud quarreling came from the hall.

A guttural female voice shouted, "Get the hell off my property! I've changed my mind. I don't want to rent to you. You better get the hell out. I've called the police. Now go on! Get out! Get out!"

A man's trembling voice protested, "Miss, Ah ain't movin' a peg 'til yu gimme back mah thurty dollars deposit. Ah be gladder than yu tu see th' law come. They gonna' tel yu yu ain't actin' legul latchin' on tu mah money th' way yu is. Yu ain't mah woman. Ah ain't got nutin' tu give yu. Now gimme back mah money, lady."

The woman laughed contemptuously and said, "Baloney, the law says I don't have to give a refund without return of a receipt."

The man said, "Shit, lady, don' jive me. Cose ah ain't got no piece a paper. Yu an' me know yu ain't give me none. But me and yu damn sho know yu got mah money. Ah don wanta' get mad so unass mah money, lady."

There was a frantic scrape of feet and the hysterical voice of the landlady screamed, "Don't you speak to me that way. Stay away from me. Don't you touch me, you nigger sonuvabitch."

Cousin Bunny and Mama went to the half-open door. I followed and lay on the floor looking out between Mama's ankles into the hall. The twins and Junior were standing in the doorway of our apartment across the hall staring at the tense scene.

A small black man in a leaky blue overcoat held out his demanding palm toward the rigid figure of the landlady glaring down at him like a curved beak bird of prey, vivid blue eyes round and cold and unblinking.

There was the screech of brakes in the street. The vulture's eyes lifted from the excited face of the little black man and looked through the glass of the vestibule door. Her mean little mouth shaped a sick smile. The black guy read the smile and spun around big eyed toward the door.

Two burly white cops in blue police overcoats stormed into the hall. The black guy snatched out his wallet and held several pieces of ID in his shaking palm.

He skinned back his fat lips in a wary smile and blurted, "Ofcers, Ah'm so glad yu done come. Ah' Woodrow Spears, an' Ah want yu tu make thet lady gimmee back mah thurty dollars down pay on thet flat upstairs since she ain't gonna' rent it tu me."

They ignored him and looked at the landlady with odd grins on their hard red faces.

The taller one winked and said, "Connie, is this the nut that you called in about?"

She plunged her splotchy hands into the pockets of her monkey fur jacket and said, "Carl, this crazy shrimp has bugged me all afternoon. He's followed me from this building to my home down the street a half-dozen times. He has the hallucination that he gave me a deposit on an apartment several days ago. He didn't, of course, and . . ."

Woodrow Spears sprang forth and shouted, "Lady, why yu say sumpin' lak thet? Ah give yu mah money an' yu promis tu paint up an' clean up thet greasy flat so me an' mah famli ken mov in tuday. Ah ain't lyin', Ofcers. Thet ole broad thinks she slick, an' Ah ain't holdin' stil—"

One of the cops hooked a fat paw into the coat collar of the bantam victim and flung him violently away against the wall. The vulture's round blue eyes glowed with pleasure.

She said, "Carl, as God is my judge, I swear none such occurred. I did show this fellow an apartment several days ago. He had been drinking and was critical of the color scheme and all. I was relieved when he told me he'd get his paycheck and be back later to give me a deposit.

"I rented the apartment an hour after he left to a clean-cut religious man. You can imagine how afraid I was when this bird turned up today trying to extort refund of a deposit he never gave me. Carl, I should make a complaint against this crook, but if you can persuade him to leave me alone, I'll forget the whole affair."

The victim's mouth was gaped open about to speak.

Carl grinned and poked his club hard against the little guy's belly and said, "Boy, show me a deposit receipt or get your black ass out of my sight fast."

Woodrow's face faded to gray. His throat made a choking sound as his head revolved from the cops to the landlady. Tears rolled down his face. He gave the white trio a hateful look and opened the door to the vestibule.

He stood in the doorway like an ugly child and blubbered, "Thet's all right. Thet's all right. Ah ain't nuthin' but a fool. Ah ain't holdin' no piece of paper. Yu all right tu bump mah head, but yu dirty paddies will git yourn down th' line."

He turned and took a step through the doorway. Carl, the cop, bared his teeth and raised his club high. The twins screamed across the hall when the club sledged down on the back of Woodrow's bare head.

He shivered and reeled back into the hallway. An eerie thing was that the loose metal fasteners on his galoshes jingled merrily.

He clapped his hands over the sudden red spurting from his skull and bleated pitifully, "Oh Lawd, hav mercy, Ofcers. Ah ain't don nuthin'. Don whup me no mo'."

Both cops bludgeoned his head and shoulders with their clubs like he was some ferocious wild animal or poisonous viper they had to smash.

Awful shiny scarlet covered his face and head. As he fell to the floor he clutched the front of Carl's overcoat. Brass buttons bounced on the tile. The vulture held the door open as the cops each grabbed a leg and dragged the little black guy to the vestibule.

I heard his skull clunking against the vestibule's stone steps. Junior's face was a hard mask of hatred as he pushed our apartment door shut.

I followed Mama and Bunny to the front window. It was snowing hard, but I could see the cops drag Woodrow to their car at the curb.

Carl, the cop, had the burlap feet wiper from the vestibule under his arm. He stooped down and wrapped the sack around Woodrow's bloody head before he flung him onto the rear floor of the police car. The three of us squeezed ourselves together and watched the police car speed away.

It was the first really horrible sight I'd ever seen. It really was.

Bunny called the district station and complained about the bloodletting. A captain told her to mind her own fucking business.

The terror and excitement of what the landlady and the cops had done to the little black guy really upset Mama and me. Mama gave Bunny some soup, put her to bed and we went home.

Junior and the twins were huddled silently at the front window staring out at the snowy dusk. Mama and Carol went to the kitchen to fix supper. Bessie turned on the living-room lamp and stretched out on the floor with a dog-eared high fashion magazine.

Junior and I were playing checkers on the sofa when I saw Papa and Soldier Boy trudging down the snow-clogged walk. I shouted Papa's coming and ran to unlock the front door.

After Papa and Soldier Boy had washed up they sat down at the kitchen table and destroyed Mama's smoked neck bones, navy beans, and cornbread.

The fresh memory of the bloody little black guy had killed the appetites of the rest of us. Later in the living room, Soldier Boy entertained us by acting out some of his exciting battlefield adventures as a foot soldier in World War I.

He had to be at least forty, but he pantomimed his lean six-feet-two inches across the floor like a twenty-year-old. Soldier's face had a powerful American Indian cast with its high cheekbones, lustrous piercing black eyes, buffalo nickel Indian nose, a full but delicately shaped mouth. The deep red in the velvet brown complexion and the luxuriant mop of curly blue black hair completed the strikingly handsome effect of African and Indian bloodlines coalesced.

I watched fascinated as he lost himself in vicious hand-to-hand combat with an imagined German soldier. The friendly face twisted in hate as he straddled his enemy and bayoneted the phantom soldier.

Papa shook Soldier's shoulder. Soldier shifted his enormous black eyes to Papa.

Papa said loudly, "Sojer, yu don kilt him an' the wah bin over."

Soldier's snarl softened to a grin. He and Papa sat down on the sofa beside Mama. There was a long silence.

Finally Mama said, "Two white law wuz heah an' beat a lil' man's head tu jelly out en the vestabul."

Papa frowned and said, "Whut he don?"

Mama replied, "He ain't did nuthin' Ah seen but deman his rightful money from thet ole crooked lanlady he put on thet flat upstairs. Ah wish cullud law had come en place uv white."

Soldier's hearing had been damaged in the war. He leaned forward intently as Mama spoke.

He shook his head and said in a loud bass voice, "Mrs. Tilson, please don't ever wish for nigger cops. They're worse than the gangster white cops."

Papa blinked his eyes and looked at Mama.

Mama laughed nervously and said, "Frank, lissen tu Sojer talkin'."

Soldier said, "I wish it was a lie, but every black soul in Chicago knows it's true. I was born and educated here, and I want to tell you nice folks about this big funky town and the police department.

"Sometimes fairly decent human beings join the force. They don't stay long after they find out they're a part of a vicious system that has a license to maim and murder black people in the street.

"But too many white cops in the ghetto are just thugs. They try to kill hope in black people so that the black man especially is niggerized and becomes a drunken bum in the ghetto.

"Now you take the nigger cops. They're so mean and brutal because they are ashamed of their uniform and they know how much they are despised by their own kind.

"A lot of them don't let their neighbors see them in uniform. They change at the station. The maniacs help the white hoodlum cops to suppress and humiliate their black brothers imprisoned in the ghetto.

"There are only a few cops black or white who don't go on duty in the ghetto with a thirst for blood or their hands out for a bribe or shakedown. One of these days black people will crawl out of their ratty tenements and destroy the hoodlum cops in the streets. I'm going to soil myself in joy when it happens."

Mama looked embarrassed and bluntly changed the subject.

She said, "Sojer, yu know 'bout rats?"

Soldier said, "I have lived with them all my life. They carry diseases like typhoid, typhus and jaundice. This is the season when rats desert the alleys and dumps to get in out of the cold.

"It's almost impossible to keep them out of these old buildings.

They gnaw and tunnel through wood, plaster and even decaying cement. A female rat can get pregnant several times a year and have up to two dozen young.

"Many city rats, especially the older ones, are too cunning to fall for traps and poison. The best you can do is keep all food away from them and your sink and drain boards wiped dry because they can live on only crumbs and drops of water each day.

"That way you will force them to go elsewhere where pickings are better. Does that cover the rat question for you, Mrs. Tilson?"

Mama smiled and said, "It sho do. Ah got roaches too."

Soldier said, "Powdered borax spread along the woodwork and under the sink in the kitchen is the only way a poor person can deal with them. The only sure-shot remedy for roaches and rats in these old buildings is to burn them to the ground."

Mama said, "Thank yu, Sojer. Yu sho is smart."

Papa had started to say something when there was a knock on the door. Carol opened the door. It was Cousin Bunny in a pink housecoat and matching fluffy slippers. She staggered into the living room and plopped down on Soldier's lap.

Papa frowned and waved us from the room. We went to bed. The twins and I slept in the bed. Junior slept on a pallet on the floor. But none of us could sleep.

We listened to Bunny's crying about the little black guy, and then her cursing of the police. And then she wailed about how guilty she felt because she hadn't blown the white cops' heads off with her dead husband's shotgun since she was dying anyway.

I heard Papa go into the bedroom across the hall. For what seemed like hours I heard Soldier and Bunny briefing Mama about the treacherous black ghetto.

Finally Mama let them out and I heard her slow steps to her bedroom. I lay there with my heart raging, and I was trembling all over in fear for my family.

Just before I fell into nightmarish sleep larded with murderous police, thieving and horny black preachers and dope fiend pimps enslaving my innocent sisters, I heard Papa say, "Sedalia, Ah got eight dollars' snow money. Mayhaps Ah git uh sho nuff job an' ketch snow wuk tu. Come a nice seasun, we git frum this hellhole an' mayhaps go somewhar's else, an' even th' big foot country."

Mama said, "Oh, shoot, Frank, ain't no use tu rabbit outta' heah. Bunny an' Sojer both tol' me ain't no town up heah gud fer niggers. They's all bad an' Ah ain't goin' South, Frank. We just got tu tuff it out an' keep th' younguns an' us hin' pahts frum eny law truble."

6

MERRY CHRISTMAS IN HELL

Papa and Soldier were lucky together. When there was no snow-fall, they found a few store windows to clean or small hauling and moving jobs to do with Soldier's truck. Papa managed to keep our stomachs filled with chitterlings and hog balls. The butcher called them hog maws. Every penny not spent for food was put in a lard can toward the sixty-dollar monthly rent.

Soldier had no relatives in Chicago, and he was lonesome. He was so sweet and kind and generous that all of us couldn't help loving him and treating him like one of the family.

He wasn't the least perfect. He had his faults, like constantly nipping from a whiskey bottle he always kept in his smelly sheepskin coat. Whiskey was legal, but he drank bootleg stuff. He was loud and cussed a lot when he talked about cops and highfalutin middle-class niggers. But it wasn't a filthy kind of cussing, and he did it almost charmingly.

He was the smartest man we had ever met. He knew something about everything. Many evenings he brought Papa home and after staying for supper he would be too tired or tipsy to drive to his furnished room on the Southside. Mama would make a bed for him on the living-room sofa.

Soldier gave me the feeling that he felt something extra for me. He called me "Little Brother," and bought me treats when I went with him in the truck to get groceries for Mama. When we saw a cop I would grit my teeth and put a mean look on my face. Soldier would laugh tears in his eyes. I was crazy about Soldier. I really was.

About a month and a half after we had come North (around December 19), Papa came home with our first Christmas tree. Mama trimmed the tree with dyed cotton balls and stars made from cigarette package tin foil she salvaged from the trash bin.

Christmas morning was so exciting and beautiful with the presents wrapped in colorful paper lying beneath the red, green and silver tree.

I got a black leather jacket lined with fleece and a handsome pair of gray woolen trousers and a pair of shiny high top boots. The twins and Junior also got warm clothing and shoes. It was all used Salvation Army stuff, but we couldn't have been happier if it had been new.

Bunny and Soldier really helped Mama and Papa to give us kids a very merry Christmas. Mama roasted two fat hens with dressing and candied sweet potatoes topped with pineapple slices and baked biscuits so light and airy they seemed to melt in the mouth.

After dinner, Soldier and the twins sang and danced. Bunny brought her portable Victrola and played Bessie Smith's blues records. It was the happiest, brightest Christmas our family ever had together. We were never to have another like it.

Mama had decided that we should wait until September to enroll in school. She wanted to be sure we'd be able to afford books and other materials.

On the second floor just above our apartment lived a Mrs. Greene with eight stair-step kids. Only two of them had the same father, and they had it rough on relief.

Two teenage girls, Denise and Sally, came to visit Carol and Bessie a day or so before the end of December.

Sally was golden brown, curvaceous and pretty. Denise was runty and thin with a bad case of acne. But Denise had poise and a large vocabulary. Sally was shallow and giggly, and all she talked about was clothes and boys.

Junior was dazed. He stayed his distance with a worshipful look on his face. Carol and Denise hit it off as pals right away; Sally and Bessie had almost matching temperaments and identical interests.

Denise brought Carol two of her high school books, an English text and the other math. I could tell Carol was puzzled and upset by the nervous way she flipped the pages of the English book.

Soldier and Papa came in just as the Greene sisters were leaving. Sally rolled her hot hazel eyes sexily at Soldier. He gave her an icy look and strode past her.

After supper, Soldier gave the twins and Junior tests in reading, spelling and math. Then he sadly shook his head and told them they would almost certainly have to enroll in the fourth and fifth grade in grammar school instead of high school.

Carol ran from the living room. Bessie and Junior just sat dumbly on the floor. Mama and Papa darted glances at each other, and then quickly dropped their eyes away.

I felt like crying when I imagined how pitifully comical the buxom twins and strapping Junior would look in grammar school with little kids like me.

I played a lot in the hallways of our building with Mrs. Greene's younger children. Several times we sneaked into the large shed in the backyard. Connie used it to store the shabby almost worthless goods she had impounded that had belonged to tenants who had fallen hopelessly behind in rent payments.

Connie had a big brass padlock on the front of the shed, but she didn't know about the rotted boards fallen away in the rear of the shed. We'd slip through the opening and prowl the musty gloom.

Lopsided floor lamps, a headless dressmaker's type dummy and a tall rough carving of a tobacco store Indian cast spooky shadows across the clutter of mildewed clothing and dusty old chairs and sofas.

When Connie, the landlady, snooped around, we'd have to stay inside and suffer the dreary winter days.

Junior spent most of his time with Railhead Cox. He was a tall husky guy about eighteen who lived on the second floor just above Bunny's apartment. He lived there with his parents and a skinny older brother called Rajah fresh out of Joliet prison for dope peddling. He had a normal length head and a sharp featured tan face.

Railhead had dark brown skin and thick blurry features and a horribly long head. He also had a fancy prancy hip walk. He was the image of Mrs. Cox, his brawny mother.

She suppressed poor Mr. Cox and her sons with her stentorian voice and inventive profanity. Haggard Mr. Cox, a graduate of a Southern agricultural college, had put in twenty years of stoop labor as a bootblack in a Loop hotel barbershop. He was a drunk who moved about with glazed eyes and a slow shuffle like a withered zombie.

Mama started to get the "country" out of herself that first winter in Chicago. Bunny taught her some slick makeup tricks. She gave Mama some dressy clothes that no longer fit Bunny's wasted frame.

Mrs. Greene pressed and curled Mama's hair. In those early years Mama was sexy and beautiful when she got herself together. Satiny black skin stretched tautly across her bold African features and fine body.

Several Sundays when Bunny felt like it, Bunny, Mama and I and sometimes Carol would walk the three blocks to Bunny's independent church. Papa was unshakably Baptist, so he stayed at home and read his Bible on Sunday. The goo on Mama's face really distressed him. He'd look at her sternly and turn his face away from her goodbye kiss.

The preacher at Bunny's church was a dapper slick-haired guy with gem quality false teeth and a debauched yellow face that had once been pretty.

One of the deacons that sat behind the preacher on the pulpit platform was a chubby black guy about forty with a wide drooly mouth, pug nose and slanted eyes that gave his comical face a harlequin look. He was the guy that lived in the third-floor apartment above Railhead 's flat. His was the same apartment that the little black guy got his head caved in about.

Across the hall from the deacon lived an old man and his son who looked at least seventy years old. Bunny told us she had seen the old man just once, and he was at least a hundred and had been a slave. The son was a cook in a Loop restaurant.

The preacher's congregation for the most part consisted of broken-down ex-whores, old snuff-dipping crones and a goodly number of that tired army of mop heads and toilet brushes who kept the white folks' world free of funk and stink.

A seedy mob of starving fornicators winked and grinned at the cow-eyed sisters to latch onto a cinch source of shelter, sex and hog balls.

Almost all of the women leaped in the air and shouted from the ecstatic gut. They quivered their crotches in fits of obscene joy when the bombastic bantam bombed them with fire and brimstone.

When it came time to pass the collection baskets, the crafty extortionist would lean forward in his pulpit with slit eyes and intone in a deadly voice, "Now, Brothers and Sisters, the Lord demands you to share with the Lord what the Lord has let you get.

"Let me tell you children there's no sin worse than stealing from the Lord what he needs for his work and church. You got to strain and dig deep because the Lord loves you and keeps you lucky.

"I can't stop you from cheating the Lord if you just want to do something dangerous. Go ON! Hold out on him. But watch it! He's sure to strike you blind, deaf or dead."

Then the coldhearted slicker would stand there in the pulpit chanting Amen as the poor suckers stuffed the baskets with paper money.

I remember how angry and nervous I'd get after the services were over. What would almost make me wet my pants was the simpering eye-fluttering way Mama handled the bumptious bastards.

And that goddamn freakish Reverend Rexford was no inducement to serenity. He'd walk right up to Mama acrobating his tongue across his sensual lips, advertising right there in the house of the Lord that he ate cunt.

Looking back at that Sunday torment, I guess I must have been defending and feeling for Papa. The reverend finally persuaded Mama to join the church.

Dear generous Bunny passed away in the middle of March. Her insurance was just enough to bury her. She had spent her savings helping us and on her illness.

The store repossessed Bunny's new furniture after she died. We just didn't have the money to pay the two delinquent installments. Mama got Bunny's clothes, cooking utensils and several old appliances. We were covered with sorrow and missed her very much.

Bunny's death increased the already terrible pressure on Papa to feed us all and pay the sixty a month rent. He had other more deadly pressure put on him by Mama. She started speaking harshly to him and criticizing his dress and screaming at him for wearing a belt with suspenders when he had done it all his life.

I guess the preacher's sharp clothes and Cadillac limousine had made her see Papa for the first time as a sloppy dresser from the big foot country who couldn't even spell Cadillac.

Many times that first winter I got the feeling that if it hadn't been for her children Mama would have packed Bunny's flashy clothes and got in the wind.

Bessie's pal Sally Greene was still in school. Carol had reading material that Denise brought her, and I had Mrs. Greene's younger children to frolic with in the halls. Junior had Railhead.

Bessie was like a bored cat in a cage. She spent most of her time looking at clothes in the catalogues and gazing out the front window at the racketeers and pimps cruising in long shiny Buicks and Cadillacs. Some days she'd do nothing but play old records by Bessie Smith, the blues singer, on Bunny's phonograph.

One day about ten days after Bunny had passed, Bessie, Mama and I were sitting on the sofa at the front window. Mama was trying to remove a splinter from my thumb.

Bessie sucked in a loud deep breath and shouted, "Look at Sally! Oh! Look at Sally n' thet cute fella an' thet gorgus cah."

Mama and I forgot about the splinter and looked out at the curb. A brilliant sky blue La Salle was there. A short cruel-looking guy in a blue Chesterfield overcoat was gazing into Sally's face. He had his hands on her shoulders, and he was talking so fast his white teeth flashed like blinkers in his black satanic face. His processed hair was completely white.

Mama moaned, "Thet fool chile."

She pounded her fist against the windowpane. Sally spun around. Mama waved her toward the building. Sally came down the walk. The guy sneered at Mama and got into his machine and pulled away.

Sally knocked on our door. I let her in. She came into the living room with a puzzled look on her face.

She said, "You want me, Mrs. Tilson?"

Mama pounded a palm against her thigh and hollered, "Chile, ain't yu got no sense? Pore Cousin Bunny pinted out thet rat en pants tu me. He's uh nasty dopehead pimp.

"Bunny tol me th' pimps an' whores call him Grampy Dick 'cause he ain't got no normul natchur. All he do is use his mouf on wimmen. Do Hattie know yu battin' round wif him?"

Sally giggled and said, "Mrs. Tilson, you just got here from the big foot country. You don't understand. That's a lie. He's called Grampy Dick because his first name is Richard and he has that gorgeous white hair. Grampy Dick is so sweet. Mama wouldn't care that a rich guy drove me home from school.

"He told me I'm the prettiest chick he's ever seen, and he wants to marry me. He said he'll get rid of all his girls and go to work if I say yes.

"Say, Mrs. Tilson, are you sure you're not turning a little green because Grampy Dick wouldn't spit on old married women like you?"

Mama just looked at her for a long moment.

Then she waved Sally away and said sternly, "Heifer, yu ah star natal fool an' don' darken mah door agin. Yu ain't gonna mount tu uh jar uh rooster droopins, an' Ah don' want yu pizenin' mah twins. Ah'm gonna tel Hattie whut Ah tol yu. Now git goin', heifer."

Sally tossed her head arrogantly and wiggled her way out the front door. Tears welled in Bessie's eyes.

Mama put an arm around her shoulder and said softly, "Ain't no need tu bawl. Thet pore chile jes' ain't no gud. Yu fin anuthur fren whut ain't mixin' wif low-down niggah pimps en big cahs."

Bessie shook herself loose from Mama and screamed, "Mama, yu wuz wrong tu hurt Sally's feelins. Ah don' need no other fren. An' also Ah wish Ah wuz sweetheartin' wif a cute rich fella lak thet Grampy, have a fine cah tu ride me en an' buy me a red satin dress."

I heard a shoulder seam rip in Mama's gingham dress when she backhanded Bessie hard across the mouth. Bessie tumbled off the sofa and bounced on the floor. She drew herself into an agonized knot and moaned in high pitch as she pressed her palms tightly against her face.

Mama sat on the sofa staring at her. Finally Bessie got up, dry sobbing, and glared at Mama with reddened, cold eyes. She patted her lips that were swollen fat and went down the hall to the bedroom.

Mama went upstairs to see Hattie Greene. I went to Bessie and hugged her and cried with her until I felt like a firebomb had exploded in my chest.

The last week in March an element of deadly fate popped up in the circumstance that Jonnie Mae Hudson moved into Bunny's old flat.

Jonnie Mae was a jolly hulk of black jelly in a size forty dress. She had a wide snoutish nose that coalesced with her fat face and spacious mouth. Her hippolike tiny ears were carelessly pinned toward the rear of a small round head, cockleburred with short kinky hair.

Peewee embers of maroon fire flared in sunken sockets whenever she laughed or was angry. There was nothing deadly about Jonnie Mae herself. In fact, she was likeable. She and Mama hit it off friendly like right away.

It turned out that it was a deadly circumstance that Jonnie Mae was a tool for and sister to Lockjaw Hudson. He was a policy racketeer who had installed Jonnie Mae in the apartment to use it as a policy game check-in station.

In the early evening of April 4, Jonnie Mae brought Mama a big yellow birthday cake that she had baked. Soldier, and then Jonnie Mae, would slip in and out of the bathroom with a quart bottle of Soldier's colored bootleg whiskey.

We were in the living room having cocoa and cake and laughing at Soldier's antics when someone knocked on the front door. Carol stopped on her way down the hall and swung the door open.

I saw her stiffen as she looked up into the face of Lockjaw, hideous in a bright spot of living-room light. He had a body and face shaped remarkably like Jonnie Mae's except that the right side of his face had been crushed in from eyebrow to jawbone. His maimed right orb was crimson and unblinking. It protruded from its mangled socket like a bloody gut.

Carol finally stammered, "Howdy do."

He stood there staring his live eye down at her. He was breathing hard and fast and cocking his ugly head from side to side like some monstrous dog in heat. The terrible quiet was broken by Jonnie Mae's flushing of the toilet down the hall.

Papa had risen from the sofa to break up the weird tableau when the monster croaked, "Jonnie Mae here?"

Jonnie Mae came to the doorway and looked at her brother. She smiled and took his arm and led him to the living room. A tough-looking red-haired guy with psychotic yellowish eyes and a battered bulldog face followed on his heels. She introduced him to everyone; everyone except Soldier who was acquainted with him.

His right hand was infested with diamonds, and when his left hand moved, a fantastic cluster ring on his pinkie burst colors like a swarm of pastel fireflies.

As the Hudsons went out the front door, Lockjaw turned and crawled his live eye over Carol's curves. Carol shut the door and came to sit beside me on the floor. She squeezed my hand. Her palm was wet, and she was shaking.

Soldier said, "That bird gets uglier and uglier every time I run into him. And that bulldog with him is Cockoo Red. He's done at least five murders for Lockjaw and countless mayhems. He knows Lockjaw will spring him."

Mama said, "Is them dimons sho nuff?"

Soldier said, "As real as bedbugs. He's the operator of the Eldo-rado policy wheel on the Westside and the Lucky Tiger wheel on the Southside. He's rich as cream. I can't understand why he don't spend a few grand and get his face fixed and replace that pukey right eye with a clean-looking fake."

Papa said, "Ah don' want thet ol' ugly niggah sniffin' 'round mah babee gul iffen he holin' all th' money en th' wurl."

Junior said, "He git his face messed up en th' Fust Wurl Wah?"

Soldier smiled bitterly and said, "No, Little Frank, he's almost seventy. He was too old for that war. He got it in another kind of war.

"I heard a gang of heroic cops in East St. Louis, during the 1917 race riots, handcuffed him and smashed his face in a police quiz room.

"A pal of Lockjaw's had fought a gun duel with the police and killed one of them. They picked up Lockjaw to make him put the finger on his pal's hiding place. At first he tried to con the cops he didn't know where his pal was hiding. The cops punched him around and made him mad so he boasted that he knew but he wouldn't tell. He never told so the police smashed his face. The underworld rewarded him with the 'Lockjaw' moniker."

I said, "What's a policy wheel?"

Soldier grinned and said, "Little Brother, it's a slick joker like Lockjaw with a big bankroll backing him against the nickel-and-dime bets of thousands of half-starved chumps who sucker for odds countless thousands to one against them.

"It's the prospect of the big payoff that hooks them. A dime played on a gig that hits brings eighty-six dollars. A buck on a lucky gig or bet pays eight hundred and sixty dollars.

"They believe they can dream up numbers that will make them nigger rich when thay appear on a slip of paper with a double line of numbers 'pulled' in some secret place by the wheel."

Mama said, "Pulled, whut thet? Thet mus' be whut Jonnie Mae's doin' en her flat, all them men en an' out."

Soldier shook his head vigorously and said, "Sedalia, I don't think Jaw is pulling numbers over there. I think the flat is a check-in station for so-called runners or writers who turn in their bet books and cash, less their earned twenty percent.

"Those books have to be in before ninety-nine numbered balls are pulled from a hopper and those numbers mimeographed on thousands of slips of paper and passed out to the bettors. Jaw is got a sweet racket with the police practically in his hip pocket."

Bessie said, "Thet wuz some fine purfum' he had on him. Ah wish ah had some."

Mama said, "Shet up, heifer, an' pull thet dress down."

Soldier said, "Old Jaw pays top dollar for everything, including broads. With them, he gets more than he pays for. One of my old army buddies who used to bodyguard him told me Jaw is a freak for using mental torture on his women and keeping them under guard like convicts.

"Rumor has it that he brutally uses his women in every sexual way. I guess he really hates broads because he's so ugly he's got to buy them. They say he always gets what he wants and nothing is so low and dirty that he won't do it to keep his score perfect. Old man Lockjaw is a dangerous and powerful man."

I saw Papa picking at bumps under his chin. I got a sewing needle and sat on his lap and raised the ingrown hairs. The conversation went on and on about Lockjaw and the policy racket. And so did Soldier's visits to the bathroom with the hooch.

The party broke up around 10 P.M. Soldier was loaded, but he wouldn't take Mama's advice to sleep on the sofa and not try to drive to the Southside.

Everybody was asleep by midnight except me. I was at the kitchen sink getting a drink of water. I glanced out of the window. In the moonlight I saw Railhead Cox sprint across the backyard and dart behind the storage shed.

I saw a feeble flicker of light flash through the sooty shed window. I got my coat and dashed out the back door. I stood on a box and tried to see what was going on. I couldn't, so I eased behind the shed and peeped through the opening.

Railhead was kneeling at a far corner with a flaming match in one hand and he was shoving something into the end of an old rolled up carpet with his other hand. His match went out, and I sped silently back to my kitchen window on the balls of my bare feet.

I watched Railhead walk casually toward the back door of the building. I heard his big feet pounding up the rear stairway. I counted to twenty-five and went back to the shed. I struck a kitchen match and walked over to the stash rug.

I pushed my arm into the end of it. I didn't touch anything. I pushed to my armpit. My fingertips touched something cold and metallic. My match sputtered out. I put my hand in my coat pocket for another. I froze and felt an electric tremor vibrate the pit of my stomach. I heard feet and voices at the rear of the shed!

Somehow my wobbly legs took me behind an old icebox at the empty end of the stash carpet. I crouched there and heard the muffled voices of Railhead and his big brother, Rajah.

I thought I was going to faint. I wondered if they had seen the flare of the match I had lit. But they walked directly to the other end of the carpet. I stuck an eye around the side of the icebox and saw Railhead light a candle and ram his arm up the carpet.

Rajah squatted beside him. Railhead pulled out a blue steel pistol, and then a roll of greenbacks and a shiny package wrapped in black cloth. Rajah undid the package and smelled the contents. He wet an index finger and stuck it into the contents and licked his finger.

Railhead frowned his impatience and said, "Raj, what have I got?"

Rajah put a pinch of the white substance on his thumbnail and sniffed it up his nostrils. He closed his eyes and moaned rapturously, "You got maybe half a pound of cocaine and also pure, is what you got."

Then suddenly he popped his eyes wide and vised Railhead's arm. He hollered, "You dumb chump, you've went and put the heist on some big shot dealer. Haven't you? You're gonna wind up in an alley with the rats squabbling over your stupid brains. Tell me, sucker, who did you sting?"

Railhead snatched his arm away.

He had a pained look on his face as he begged, "Please, Raj, don't call me a chump and sucker. You could motherfuck me and it woudn't hurt as bad. I stung Little Hat up in the next block.

"The rats ain't gonna' chew up my brains because Little Hat ain't hip it was me that took him off. I jimmied a window at his pad to beat him for any frog skins I could latch onto and maybe for his table Philco and record player.

"I was prowling the joint when he stuck his key in the door. When he came in I coldcocked him with an iron pipe and took the heater, a grand in foreskin and the dope out of his pockets. Hell,

Raj, I ain't stupid. I'm slick to take off a score like this with a chickenshit piece of pipe."

Rajah sniffed another nail load of cocaine and said, "Yeah, it was pretty clean considering there was no deep casing our outlay for the caper."

Then Rajah leaned close to Railhead.

He had a serious look on his sharp cunning face when he said, "Chuck, look me dead in the eye. You're gonna need me to unload this dope on the Southside. Now tell me, have you cracked to that square-ass country nigger, Junior Tilson, about this score, or anybody about it?"

Railhead gazed into his brother's eyes and energetically shook his head no. He started pushing the pistol and money into the carpet. Rajah stood up and put the package of dope in his robe pocket.

He said, "Chuck, gimme that stuff. I'm going to lock everything in my trunk."

Railhead stood up and dropped the pistol and money into Rajah's other robe pocket. Railhead snuffed out the candle when they reached the opening at the back of the shed.

I heard Railhead say, "Raj, how much can you get for the dope?"

Rajah said, "Don't worry about it, Chuck. I'll get what I can. It's a cinch I ain't gonna' burn my own baby brother."

I sat there behind the icebox for what seemed like hours. I was so stunned that Junior's best friend was a criminal. I really was.

Finally I left the shed and went to bed. But my sweaty sleep was one long nightmare. I kept seeing Railhead and Junior sprawled side by side in an alley with millions of slobbering rats devouring their blasted out brains.

Next morning I had a hard time forcing down my grits and biscuits for two reasons. The other reason was that everybody was upset because Soldier hadn't come to pick up Papa for several trash-hauling jobs they had scheduled.

At 11 A.M. Papa left to take the streetcar to Soldier's Southside rooming house. Junior and the twins got out a deck of cards the minute Papa left the flat. They went to the living room to play dirty hearts.

Mama gathered up some dirty clothes and put them in the bathroom tub to rub clean on a washboard. I followed and was at the point of telling her about Railhead when I heard the front door open and Hattie Greene came down the hall to the open bathroom door.

She was a short, tan double for actress Marlene Dietrich, and the still pretty face stuck there on the lumpy body made her look like she'd had an ill-advised head transplant. Tears streaked her haunting face, and one of her fat tits had almost escaped the torn bodice of her faded housedress.

Mama said, "Hattie, whut's don happen?"

Hattie's heavy bosom heaved with her sobbing. She opened her mouth to say something, but she was so upset only whiney, choking sounds came out.

Mama rubbed her sympathetically across the back and said, "Hattie, is Sally got en tu sumthin'?"

Hattie shook her head and said in her sharp yappy voice, "You got a gun, Sedalia?"

Mama said, "Nuthin' but thet ole shotgun uh Bunny's passed husban'. Why yu huntin' uh weapun?"

Hattie's damp eyes widened hopefully as she held her hands out toward Mama and said, "Oh, please, Sedalia! Let me have it. My caseworker tore my dress and slapped me. That black burly bitch slapped me. Please give me the gun, Sedalia. I don't want to kill her. I just want to set her funky ass on fire. Please, Sedalia, let me have it before she leaves the building across the street."

Mama backed up and said, "Hol on, ah said ah had uh gun. But ah ain't got no bullits. Why she slap you 'roun?"

Hattie said loudly, "She told me right in front of my boyfriend and kids that she had heard from one of her stool pigeons that I was screwing four or five guys on the QT.

"The bitch told me I should stop giving it away and sell it, and then I wouldn't have to be a parasite on relief. I told her to get out, but she wouldn't. So then I tried to shove her out.

"She slapped me and grabbed my dress and threw me against the wall. These rotten-hearted workers act biggity, like it's their money the poor people get. The bastards are always snooping around us to find something wrong so they can cut us off from relief. White people on relief don't never see them."

Mama took her arm and said, "Thet dirty niggah is got powful white folks back uh her, an' yu do sumthin' tu her, them white folks sen yu tu th' pen. Whut them younguns yu got do then? Yu bes' cool off an' lemme brew us up some coffee."

An hour later I watched her go out the front door, dry-eyed. Hattie had bandy legs that were wide apart, and she had a wiggly, grindy walk like she was riding an invisible penis.

I went to the front window and waited for Papa to come back from the Southside. I thought he'd never come. It was 6 P.M. when I saw him come down the street. He was a sad sight with his shoulders drooping as he walked slowly down the front walk with his head low.

I went to the door and let him in. I took his coat and hung it on a nail in the hall. He walked slowly to the sofa. We all followed him. I sat beside him and put my head on his lap. His voice broke many times as he told us about Soldier's bad break.

Soldier had driven to the Southside without incident. Then at Thirty-fifth and State Streets he parked the truck and started across the street to a greasy spoon for black coffee. He was struck by a hit-and-run driver.

Papa found Soldier at County Hospital with a compound fracture of the hip and back and chest injuries. Papa got the key to the truck and went to get it off the street. He was shocked to find that it had been stripped of battery and tires.

I couldn't help crying at Papa's emotional account. Junior and the twins left to visit the Cox and Greene flats. Mama sat silently beside Papa and me for a long time. I looked up at Papa. He was working his jaw muscles like he always did when he was worried.

Mama sighed deeply and said softly, "Ole Cheecogo gonna' whup th' Tilson famli iffen we ain't kerful. Sojer an' th' truck laid up an' Ah got fawty singuls en th' lard can. Ole landlady be at thet do' sticken her han' out tu git thet big sixty ten days away. An' also, we ain' got no vittles 'roun heah tu las' tu even nex' week.

"Ah ain't cryin' mah joy tu do it, but it 'pears thet Ah oughta put mah pride en storage an' be uh mop haid an' tolet brush fo' the paddies 'til we git on solid groun'. Ah don' see no way but thet. Ah sho ain't gonna' kiss th' behin' uh no niggah chaity wukur. Whut yu gonna' say 'bout thet, Frank?"

Papa swung himself so quickly and violently to face Mama that I almost tumbled from his lap.

He said in a tight voice, "Sedalia, ain't yu los' yo' mine? Ahma man. Don' need mah woman tu go frum home tu clean th' white folks filt up. Don' worry, th' Lawd ain't gonna' let us stahv or git put outdos.

"Ah got uh Triboon newspapur tu try tu git me uh steady job. Ah ain't no fool. Ah ken cahpentur an' plastur an' paint an' lay bricks. Sedalia, Ah luv yu an' th' younguns, an' Ah ain't gonna' fail mah famli.

"Sedalia, Ah ain't lyin' tu yu. Iffen Ah did fail, Ah would dig uh ditch an' pull the groun en on top uh me. Ah knows Ah couldn't stan tu see yu makin' th' livin' an' waring mah pants. So don' worry 'bout nuthin', Sweethaht. Ah'm gonna' have happy news by th' fust uh nex' week. An' mayhaps tumorra."

7

POOR PAPA STRUCK OUT

Poor naive Papa wasn't able to keep his "happy news" promise. He went into the streets and joined the multitudes of desperate men seeking jobs. From sunup to sundown, rain, sleet or shine, Papa was out chasing down even second- and thirdhand rumors of job openings with heartbreaking results.

He'd go all day on a sandwich of cold collard greens and corn bread. Papa made me cry when he told us about the vicious building trade unions those offices and halls he haunted.

He told every white man he saw wearing a business suit and tie how his daddy down South had made him a master carpenter and brick layer, and how single-handedly he had built a wing to the big house for Mr. Wilkerson on the plantation.

He was a "character" to them, so they played the cruel game "string out" for laughs. Finally, a sympathetic official told Papa the union didn't accept blacks as members or apprentices. He patted Papa on the back. He told him it was a pity that Papa was so near white and yet so far with too much yellow in his complexion to pass.

I guess the crookedness and bigotry of Chicago was just too much for an honest and fair man. Rebuff and aching failure had

broken the spine of hope that he could find a steady job to support
his family.

If it hadn't been for Jonnie Mae Hudson's money loans to
Mama, we wouldn't have had food or a roof over our heads.

I remember that first week in May when Mama started scrubbing and cleaning for the white folks. Papa acted so strangely.
When he would come back from sweeping out a store on Madison
Street he'd go straight to the bedroom, pull down the shades and
sit in half darkness.

I tried several times to go in and keep him company. He'd act like
a stranger, waving his arms and speaking sharply to drive me away.

The second week in May I saw him sneak to the trash bin in the
backyard to dispose of a wine bottle. When he came back to the
bedroom I darted in behind him and shut the door. He spun around
with a hostile look in his eyes.

I smiled and said, "Papa, please don't drive me away. Can I talk
to you please? Huh?"

He grunted and sat down heavily on the side of the bed with his
face in his palms.

I sat down beside him and blurted out childishly, "Papa, why
don't we have fun like we used to? Did I do or say something to
make you hate me? Papa, if I did, I'm sorry, and please don't be a
nasty wino. I love you, Papa."

He looked at me with stricken eyes that slowly brimmed with
tears, and then with a high-pitched animal outcry of raw agony, he
squeezed me to his chest and sobbed, "Cose Ah luv yu, mah babee.
Ain't no resun tu luv me an' Ah ain't nuthin'. Ah ain't 'nuff man to
foot mah bills."

We clung together for an hour before he told me someone
very important wanted to be alone with him. I went out and
closed the door.

Moments later Carol and I heard him praying, "Lawd, yu ain't
gonna' turn yo bac on me, an' Ah ain't don nuthin' sinful. Is yu,

Lawd? Yu ain't mad, Lawd, coz Ah drink uh lil' wine to sofen mah trubles, is yu? Lawd, whut is yu doin' tessin' mah faith? Lawd, iffen yu is, ken yu change 'roun an' bles me wif uh sho nuff job an' tess anuther way. Lawd, is yu fergit Ah ain't stol nuthin' an' ain't 'buse nobody en mah life? Lawd, hep me fo' Ah git niggahized lak Sojer say."

Carol and I couldn't stand anymore of it so we hid in the shed (in case Bessie and Junior would come home and laugh at us) and cried our hearts out.

Many women like Mama were so desperate they were forced to buy their pathetic domestic jobs from employment sharks who took a big bite from their pitiful wages.

Mama did general cleaning, including wall and window washing, in the homes of middle-class whites living in the suburbs surrounding Chicago.

She'd leave before dawn and get home after dark. I don't remember that she made more than two or three dollars a day after carfare, except when she got a couple of dollars extra for serving a party until midnight or later.

She was slaving, but we weren't eating as much or as well as when Papa and Soldier were working together. Papa had often made four to six dollars a day and sometimes eight dollars.

The competition between us kids at mealtime was really rough. We wolfed down the sparse food and stayed alert to keep Junior from spearing a prize morsel from our plates. We quarreled over food at the table like starved animals.

Papa had lost his appetite, and he never ate with us anymore. So overburdened Mama had to worry with the discipline and order in the house. Papa became completely indifferent to what went on around him. He spent most of his time in the gloom of the bedroom.

Sometimes I'd go in the bedroom to visit him, and he wouldn't drive me away. He'd sit silently with me on his lap and hug me so tightly I could hardly breathe.

By the middle of steamy July Papa had become a mere shadow of himself. His grief and the poisonous wine had made him look like a hollow-eyed scarecrow. His once smooth yellow skin was bumpy and sickly looking.

His delicately chiseled features seemed indistinct in the puffy framework of his face. His once proud athletic stride became a stooped shuffle.

Mama kept clean clothes for him, but he wouldn't change into the fresh things. He grew a tangled beard. The garbage wine and his trampled nerves made his voice trembly and hoarse. New dirty gray sprouted at the roots of his curly jet hair.

But it was his eyes, his tragic, hurt eyes that I tried to avoid. All their fire was gone, and when he was spoken to, his response was tardy, like he had a short in his brain. He was only forty-six, but he acted and looked like sixty-six. Mama at thirty-two looked like his daughter.

No matter how deep and black the circles under Mama's eyes, she never missed church on Sunday. She'd blot out the circles with makeup and put on one of Bunny's freaky frocks and undulate away to the ministry of the horny little spellbinder. The last Sunday in July Mama started going to church without me.

Soldier had been transferred to the Veterans Hospital for hip therapy and general recuperation. Papa had become acquainted with a guy across the street who often visited his brother at the Vet Hospital. Papa had it all fixed with the old guy that all of our family could make the trip with him as soon as Mama got back from church, which was usually around one thirty, and no later than 2 P.M.

The old guy was parked in front of our building in his big black Dodge at 2:30 P.M. He and Papa were irritated as hell because Mama hadn't come back from church. We all piled in, and the old guy drove past the church. It was locked.

Papa shook his head slowly, and I noticed how bad his hands were trembling. The old guy drove to the hospital without Mama.

Soldier was in a ward that looked like it had a thousand beds. He was thin and looked pooped out, but he managed a smile when he saw us. He got almost radiant when he saw the sweet potato pie we brought him.

As we were leaving, Papa asked him how long he expected to be in the hospital. Always the clown, Soldier rolled his eyes to the top of his head, and then raised himself on an elbow. He swiveled his head and looked furtively in every direction.

He stage whispered, "Frank, old pal, the finance company got what was left of the truck. The croakers tell me I've got a forever game leg. I slaughtered Krauts and suffered in the funky trenches for this white man's country. I'm gonna chisel the government like the slick white folks and stay here and rest my crippled ass like a lousy pimp. I got a buddy down the way with dough and a hooch connection."

Mama wasn't at home when we got back. Carol made macaroni with cheese and heated some weiners for supper. Papa didn't eat. He sat on the sofa looking out the front window with his face in his hands.

After supper Junior opened the front door to go out.

Papa turned and said, "Come heah, Boy."

Junior frowned and moped into the living room.

Papa said, "Yu bes stay 'roun 'til Sedalia git heah. Mayhaps Ah need yu tu call th' law uh sumpthin'."

Junior tossed his head arrogantly and said, "Oh helly, ain't nuthin' happen. Mama's all right. Besides, Ah ain't goin' no whar but upstairs."

Junior turned and walked away. Papa started to rise, and his mouth opened to probably order Junior not to leave. The door slammed behind Junior, and Papa sank back on the sofa.

For the first time I noticed something strange and yet familiar about the way Junior's legs took him through the door. Then it hit me. Junior had perfected Railhead's fancy prancy walk and lifted his "helly" expression too. I wondered if he'd get stupid enough to imitate Railhead's finess with an iron pipe.

I sat on the sofa with Papa and the twins waiting for Mama. Around 8 P.M., I saw a black shiny Cadillac stop way down the block. Papa noticed me craning out the window, so he stuck his head out the window.

I recognized the huge black guy who got out on the driver's side as a flunkey for the jazzy minister. He went around and opened the passenger door. Mama's orange satin dress blazed like a torch as she stepped out under a street lamp.

I heard Papa draw a deep breath. I looked at him. There was no anger on his face, just slack-jaw shock and awful anguish.

Carol and I put an arm around his shoulders. He was shivering like a naked man in a blizzard. He rose and walked jerkily toward the front door like a robot. He opened the door and looked back at us with heart wrenching eyes.

Carol screamed, "Papa, please don't leave. Papa, where yu goin'?"

Tears glistened in Papa's eyes.

His mouth worked silently, and his lips said, "I'll be back."

And he was gone. We saw Mama and Papa nod at each other as they met on the sidewalk like they were only slightly acquainted. We raced to the door. Carol won and opened the door. Mama's eyes were bright, and when she kissed us, I got a fragrant whiff of wine. She kicked off her shoes and dropped onto the sofa.

Bessie had unbelievable nerve. She really did.

She got right in Mama's face and said peevishly, "Papa wuz worried an' Ah thot yu wuz gonna' stay out all night. Whut yu been doin', Mama? Huh?"

Mama shoved hard against Bessie's chest and said angrily, "Heifer, don' ast 'bout mah bizness. Ah'm th' onlyess wuk hoss 'roun heah, an' Ah'm gonna pleshu mahself lak Ah don at uh bankit afta chuch. Is Junior home?"

Carol said, "Junior's up at Railhead's. I'll bring him home."

Carol went out.

Mama said, "Sweet Pea, yu an' Bessie hol' them feet up so Ah ken see them shoes."

Mama took a quick look and clapped her palms against her temples in playful condemnation. She shot a swift glance at the street and pulled a twenty dollar bill from her stocking top just as Junior and Carol came in.

Junior's eyes popped wide.

He said, "A Jackson frogskin! Whr'd yu git it, Mama?"

Mama stuck the bill in his shirt pocket and said, "Shet yo mouf, fool, and don' worry 'bout th' mule goin' blin'. An' lissen, yu take the twins an' Sweet Pea an' git bran'-new shoes tuhmorra. An' don' none uv yu blab mah bizness 'roun th' hous."

We went to bed around 10 P.M. I couldn't sleep. It wasn't that I was that excited about new shoes. I was worried about that look in Papa's eyes.

I was confused. I couldn't understand what Mama was up to sneaking around in the preacher's Cadillac and hurting Papa the way she was.

Mama wasn't worried. I heard her snoring blissfully. I lay there for a long time thinking angry thoughts about Mama, and then I heard Papa's key fumbling in the lock. I almost cried out in relief. I heard him stumble down the hall to the bedroom and soon his shoes hit the floor, kerplop. I fell asleep right away.

Next morning Carol didn't fix breakfast because nobody was hungry. I took a cup of coffee to Papa's bedroom, but he was gone. I had forgotten he swept out a pawnshop on Madison Street every Monday morning for a buck and a half fee.

It was a warm and brilliant July day. We took a streetcar to the Loop. The boom and the bustle of traffic, and the grim-faced white people made me clutch Junior's arm like I was going to drown in the sea of sound.

We stood entranced gazing at the opulent merchandise that seemed touchable behind the almost invisible plate glass.

We found a shoe store near State and Madison streets. Brand-new shoes were displayed in the luxurious window like burnished treasure.

We went and sat down gingerly for fittings on purple velvet chairs. A young blond white guy with a movie star face and gleaming teeth and clothes came to serve us.

Bessie giggled and looked down at the fuchsia carpet. Carol called out the numbers for the shoes we'd liked in the window. The clerk took our measurements, all except Junior's. He hadn't seen what he wanted in the window.

I got a pair of black Buster Brown oxfords. Carol got a pair of black sandals. Bessie got a pair of gaudy red sports shoes.

The clerk turned to Junior and said, "Now sir, may I help you?"

Junior gave him a hip sneer and said, "Yu ain't got nuthin' but square junk, Jack. Ah'm goin' to th' Southside and score fer some tan knob-toed kicks."

We decided to wear our new shoes.

When the clerk said he'd wrap our old shoes, Bessie drew herself up and flung her hand through the air like a shabby countess and commanded, "Throw 'em away, sweety. Burn them raggity ole shoes."

Carol frowned and led us from the store. We caught a south-bound streetcar on State Street. A pleasant freedom from tension happened as the streetcar rattled away from the Loop's dizzying human whirlpool.

It really felt wonderful to cross the border of solid black town at 188th Street. I had felt so unclean and ragged down there in the Loop among the crisply dressed white people.

I knew I wasn't really dirty and my secondhand clothes weren't torn or tattered or anything. But still I had felt so alien and uncomfortable.

We left the streetcar at Thirty-fifth and walked toward Indiana Avenue. Shop doors gaped open in the sticky heat. The ecstatic voice of Pat Flanagan, the Cub's baseball team announcer, blared from the dingy bars, pawnshops, beauty and barbershops.

Gaudy secondhand suits hung limply under the furnace sun like faded swatches of rainbow. Black guys in silk shirts and sailor straws strutted in and out of the womblike bars with high yellow strumpets tossing awesome rear ends inside loud tight dresses.

White pitchmen in front of jewelry and furniture stores cajoled and clutched at passing black mothers. Their skeletal children had horribly old faces and puslike yellow matter in the corners of their sunken eyes.

A white-haired black guy with insane eyes sprawled drunkenly in front of a vacant store in a puddle of piss. He was slobbering and shouting, "I'm a man, motherfuckers. Come on, fuck with me and go to the cemetery, motherfuckers."

Ben Hur perfume, the cloying odor of hair pomade, stale beer and whiskey odors, and the greasy smell of cooking chitterlings coasted heavily on the humid air.

A sweaty black guy in a bloody white jacket snatched a squawking chicken from a crate on the sidewalk. He stood talking with a trio while the chicken shrieked in terror.

I heard the butcher say as we passed him, "Cocksucker, don't say that no more. Is you crazy? Ain't a peckerwood on the planet can whip Joe Louis. He's gonna' knock the shit outta' every white pussy that's fool enough to get in the ring with him."

At Wabash Avenue a frowzy housewife type slashing the air with a butcher knife held a thickly rouged whore-type woman at bay in a doorway. Her mascaraed eyes were glittery with fear, and she flinched with each pass of the knife.

The protector of her husband's sexual boredom screamed again and again, "You nasty dick-sucking bitch, stay away from my husband. You hear me, bitch?"

I can remember distinctly the peculiar laughter (almost all of it identical) that I heard that first day spent in the ghetto streets.

The wild laugher was on all sides as we walked to the corner of Indiana Avenue and Thirty-fifth Street. It was strident laughter, unemotional and without mirth, like perhaps the treacherous laughter of a madman before he goes berserk.

We stopped at a sidewalk stand and got pig ear sandwiches and bottles of Nehi soda. We had almost finished when we missed Bessie. We found her in a bar down the street chatting gaily with a slick-haired black guy draped out in a sharp white suit.

Junior strode in and jerked her out. The dapper buy grinned like a Cheshire all the while and flicked open a switchblade and held it casually at his side.

Junior kept looking back over his shoulder until we went into a shoe store near Calumet Avenue. Junior let the store dispose of his old shoes and pranced to the sidewalk in his new tan knob-toes. I suddenly remembered that Railhead Cox wore nothing but tan knob-toed "kicks."

We walked back down Thirty-fifth Street toward the car line at State Street. Near Michigan Avenue we paused at a vacant lot. A wiry black guy with a savage face stood in the bed of a battered pickup truck and hoarsely exhorted thirty to forty poorly dressed black people.

His strange grey eyes glowed as he pointed his index finger like a pistol. He was hypnotic crouching there and baring his teeth like a snarling black leopard.

He was saying, "Mr. and Mrs. Niggers, I ain't speaking nothing but the truth when I tell you the flag and national anthem shouldn't mean and ain't worth a pint of dog shit to black people.

"Now lemme tell you about the Constitution. It was created for white people by the slave-holding criminal Founding Fathers of this country. I wanta tell you about the corrupt bastards that call the rotten shots behind the scenes and mold the laws and the government to keep themselves rich and powerful and us poor and suppressed.

"They're the cynical clique of conning sonsuvbitches who have a death grip on the important money in this country and use it to buy the elections and the candidates."

He paused and mopped sweat from his face and bald head. There was recognition on his face as he glared at an impressive-looking brown skin guy who got out of a shiny Lincoln sedan and came to stand on the fringe of the crowd.

The exhorter gave the rich-looking guy a venomous look and shouted, "I'm gonna get back to the big shot white crooks controlling the government and strangling free enterprise with their monopolies.

"But lemme tell you about the sick sadiddy niggers with pus on the brain who strive to be white. Don't worry, the police will always bust their nappy heads wide open just like they do mine and yours,

"Lemme say this. You remember the race war we had here in 1918. Well, Mr. and Mrs. Niggers, there's gonna be a big countrywide race war one of these days. Lemme tell you what's gonna happen to the pus head middle-class niggers who have forgotten their blackness. They are gonna be marooned out there, grinning and suck assing in white neighborhoods. The treacherous paddies are gonna cut off their peckers and ram them up their . . ."

Carol took my hand and led me down the sidewalk. We had walked almost to State Street before Junior and Bessie tore themselves away from the fanatical exhorter and caught up with us.

Junior and I sat across the aisle from the twins on the westbound streetcar. Bessie was rolling her eyes up at a sleek-looking Mexican in a dusty purple suit standing beside her in the crowded car.

I noticed how much the twins looked alike and yet how unalike they were under close scrutiny. Carol's mouth was tiny and seductive like mine. Her face was round and her tip-tilted nose was delicate, and her light hazel eyes were large and curly lashed like mine and Papa's.

Bessie's face was angular like Mama's and Junior's. Her mouth was large, and her eyes were small like Mama's. Bessie's teeth had a slight overbite, and her feet were a size larger than Carol's. Bessie had long auburn hair like Carol's, but she put oil on it that gave it a greasy shine. Bessie was bold and flighty. Carol was soft and sensitive and demure. Bessie was simply a coarse version of Carol.

When we got home Papa was too tipsy to notice our new shoes. Mama came home around seven. She was silent and edgy during supper. Later while massaging her feet in the living room I asked her if she was sick.

She sighed and said, "Not en mah body, Sweet Pea. Ah let thet devlish white heifer whup mah spirit tuday. Ah started tu knock her head off follin' me 'roun lak Ah wuz uh chile an' finin' mah wuk wrong, an' she wuz low nuff tu plant uh fity-cent piece on the cahpet tu tess mah honessness."

Carol said excitedly, "Mama, did yu give it tu her an' tell her yu don' steal?"

Mama smiled and said, "Shoot, Ah didn't say nuthin' tu her 'bout thet foolishment. Ah jes' put down uh quatah, two dimes an' uh nickul en place uv thet fity-cent piece. Wen fo-thurty come, Ah tol' her Ah wuzn't comin' back no mo."

We all rolled on the floor laughing because Mama had been so clever. All but Papa. He grunted and went out the front door muttering.

That first summer in Chicago passed quickly. During the first part of August, radio and newspapers covered an electrifying event for black people. Jesse Owens won four gold medals at the Olympics in Berlin, and Hitler almost wet his pants.

Papa was a doddering shadow of himself. Slop wine and frustration had killed his ambition and energy. Mama's big pride, high temper and dislike for the white women she worked for caused her to often walk off jobs. This meant scraps of food on our table.

Mama had to scratch desperately to pay the rent. Many days hunger growled our stomachs, but Mama didn't give up or complain about being hungry. None of us could know that she was full, glutted with cunning schemes.

Toward the end of that first summer, I remember sticking my head out the front window watching her crawl home from the humiliation of cleaning for the despised white folks. I'd see her start way down the block to set her shoulders proud as the devil and quicken away the lag in her walk.

She'd come down the walk and into our ratty flat with an air that all was well and tomorrow would be marvelous. Her pitiful act was so sad because her eyes always mirrored the stark naked hate, hurt and horror of her blackness that rotted her soul.

In September, Mama took me to Hayes Grammar School, and I was enrolled in the first grade. I was small for my age so I fit right in with the kids in my class.

The twins and Junior didn't start school. The country school down South had prepared them for nothing higher than grade school up North. They simply couldn't face the embarrassment. And Mama didn't force them to.

Carol got a waitress job at a cafe on Madison Street. The twins had turned sixteen on June 25.

I liked school except for a bunch of teenage rowdies who called me Bustle Butt because I had an unusually fat behind for a small kid. I'd burst out crying and run home fast as I could with my palms clapped over my ears. I hated those loud-mouthed bums. I really did.

Soldier was evicted from the Vet's Hospital the last of September. Papa would get up enough energy on weekends to go to the Southside and help Soldier wash and wax cars under the El at Forty-seventh Street.

Papa bought a few groceries, but most of the little that he made with Soldier was spent on wine. Carol gave Mama most of her salary to apply on rent and utilities. As a result, Mama was able to start paying back the money she'd borrowed from Lockjaw Hudson's sister, Jonnie Mae.

Bessie spent her time with Sally Greene who had dropped out of school. Junior and Railhead were real tight, and Junior stuck to him like his shadow.

I remember how awfully lonesome I'd get with Mama and Carol working all day. Papa was home a lot, but he wanted to be left alone.

One sleety October afternoon I strayed to the third floor of our building. I saw Deacon Davis dumping his wastebasket into the big barrel on the rear landing. He was wearing yellow pajamas and a skullcap made from a woman's black silk stocking.

He turned and stepped from the landing into the hallway and walked toward the open door of his flat. He was whistling "Joshua Fought the Battle of Jericho." He saw me, and the pyramid of husky lips collapsed. He came and stooped down in front of me.

He grinned and said in a West Indian accent, "Hello! Hello! You frightened me, sweetheart."

I said, "I'm sorry. I was only playing."

His friendly clown face fascinated me as he examined every feature of my face with slumberous brown eyes.

Suddenly he stood up and took my hand and said, "Come with me, precious. I want to show you something pretty."

I followed him into his living room and sat on a flaming red sofa waiting for him to bring the pretty thing. He came back smiling mysteriously and holding his hands behind his back.

He sat down beside me and said, "Now, dear little boy, sit on my lap and close your eyes."

I got on his lap and closed my eyes. He was breathing like he had just run a record hundred yard dash, and his lap was pulsating.

He held me close against his chest and placed something smooth and round in my hand. I opened my eyes and looked down at the magical sphere.

Lacy snowflakes were falling lazily down on a tiny Santa Claus seated on a sleigh hitched to a cute reindeer that seemed alive inside the vivid crystal ball. I was so excited and thrilled. It was the prettiest thing I'd ever seen. It really was.

I sat there on the deacon's lap gazing at the wondrous ball that came to life each time I shook it. I was only half aware of his fingertips stroking me from earlobe to ankle.

He crooned in my ear, "Do you like the pretty ball, sweetheart?"

I said, "OH! Yes, yes."

He said, "Do you like me?"

I said, "I don't know you real good, but I think I like you."

He put his face very close to mine and said, "I love you so much, darling. I'll give you the ball if you give me some sugar and promise to keep a secret with me."

I couldn't believe for a long moment that I'd heard him right. Then it dawned on me, and I was wild with joy. I put an arm around his neck and turned my cheek toward him.

He slid his big wet mouth across my face and pressed it against my nose and lips. I couldn't breathe. I pulled my face away and felt his hand unbutton my fly.

I tried to slip off his lap, but his arm was like a vise around my shoulders. I felt his hot hand between my legs, caressing away my resistance. Then he dropped his head down, and I felt a voluptuous thunder of blood explode in my head.

And then we were naked, and I saw it. I was flabbergasted at the length of it.

His voice was hoarse with excitement. "Kiss it and lick it, you dear little boy, like I did yours. Mine is a magic wand to make any wish come true when you make it cry tears of joy."

I put the long crooked thing in my mouth until it spat its slimy tears. I cheated the wand and made two wishes, that poor Papa found a steady job and that Mama wouldn't be so cruel to Papa anymore so that look in his eyes would go away.

After I put my clothes on, he gave me a bowl of ice cream and said, "Now, darling, you want to keep the pretty ball, don't you?"

I nodded yes.

"Well, you must promise not to tell Mama, Papa or anyone about coming up here to visit me and what we did. And precious, don't tell that I gave you the ball. Say an old woman passing on the sidewalk gave it to you. Do you promise to keep our secret and get not only the ball but lots of other beautiful things as time goes on?"

I gripped the ball tightly and as I ran toward the door I shouted, "I promise! I promise!"

I never told the secret to anyone. I guess I was too ashamed. Time went on and on and I got many flashy toys from the phantom old lady on the sidewalk.

Things got worse between Mama and Papa, and Papa never got the steady job I had wished for him. When I complained that his wand wasn't working, the deacon would grin and say, "Dear boy, I know what's wrong. The wand must cry deep in your bunger, and then the wishes will come true."

I was a stupid little kid so I went on sneaking upstairs to the deacon's flat and letting him use me like a woman. The first few times going in, it hurt like holy fire. But then after that, not at all. It felt good. It really did.

He moved to the Southside the last of October in 1931, a couple of weeks past a year since that sleety afternoon when he first used me.

During 1937, nothing really tragic happened to our family. But we were marked. Papa's hair turned almost white, and he got stinko more often, and he was a little more stooped.

Junior and Railhead drank gin and smoked reefers in the shed a lot. Hattie Greene's daughter Sally got looped in the shed several times and joyfully screwed all the guys in the block. Hattie got the news, but she was drinking so heavily she did nothing to stop Sally from being a community bangee.

Carol's friend Denise Greene got a one-way ticket to New York from an aunt. And Railhead Cox got a big red Buick.

The apartment on the third floor occupied by the ex-slave and his chef son was vacated in the summer of 1931. Connie, the landlady, used the cops twice to back up her swindle of two black suckers who didn't get deposit receipts.

There had been wild joy and dancing in the streets on June 22, because Joe Louis whipped Braddock for the world's heavyweight boxing title.

Lockjaw often would bolt from the policy flat across the hall when Carol came down the walk. He'd confront her and practically force her to speak to him. He never got rough or anything. He'd just step aside and caress his hungry orb over her body. We didn't know he'd start shooting for her in his all-out deadly way soon.

Carol still worked at the cafe on Madison Street. There was a sweet and secret thing growing between her and a young German guy who hung around the spot.

Carol was so happy that excitement laced her voice even in casual conversation. But it was the dreamy rapture in her eyes that made me so afraid that Mama would notice and probe out the secret. It was terrifying because I knew how much Mama hated white people. But I guess Mama was just too tired to notice anything when she left the white people.

Bessie and Junior gave Mama a million headaches during 1937. Mama couldn't keep Bessie away from Sally and cute monsters with cool cars and cold hearts and glossy triple A shoes.

Junior seldom got off the streets before 2 A.M. or later, and sometimes he'd sleep in his clothes. It was always a bad scene when Papa heard Junior stumble in and would confront him in the hall.

Many times I was awakened by their angry voices. Papa would threaten to whip Junior. He'd taunt Papa until Mama came storming out of her bedroom flailing hell out of Junior with the first thing she could lay a hand on. I guess she felt that the abuse of Papa was her private privilege.

One midnight, a week or so after 1938 had come around, Mama snuffed out the last spark of Papa's manhood. I woke up drenched in sweat. The twins were awake and rigid with tension. Junior was on his floor pallet, propped on an elbow listening intently.

Mama's sharp voice had pierced my sleep and translated into the nightmare that she had discovered Carol was weak for the German guy and was berating her.

Mama was saying, "Lemme uhlone, niggah. Ah'm sick uh yo' pawin'. Ah'm tared, and yu drunk."

Papa said thickly, "Ah ain't drunk, Sedalia. Mah luv jes' come down fer yu, sugah. Whut's wrong wif uh man pattin' whut's his'n. Yu ain't nuthin' but tared an' evul eny mo. Ah'm uh man, Sedalia. Ah'm yu man. Now loose up."

Mama laughed contemptuously and said harshly, "Niggah, git you paws offen me. Ah ain't gappin' mah laigs fer yu. Uh man foots th' bills fer whuts his'n. Mabbe yu is uh drunkard, and mabbe you uh tramp. You sumpthin', but for sho you ain't no man."

There was long, heart sledging silence.

Then I heard Papa's voice choking with hurt and anger say, "Ole Saten got yu an' pushin' at me tu beat an' cuss yu, but Ah ain't. Whutevuh Ah is now Ah sho ain't fergit mah paw an' me wuz preachin' 'roun nuthin' 'cept whores an' crooks when Ah fust seen yu, an' thet jint yu an' Bunny lived at warn't no temple uv the Lawd. What wuz yu, Sedalia? Whut is yu?"

There was another long painful silence in the bedroom across the hall. Carol was crying into her pillow. I felt my own tears burst forth.

Then Mama struck the killing blow.

In a slow, icy voice, she said, "Ole funky gray-ass niggah, Ah don' want yu. Ah hate yu, wino. Ah dream thet yu die or git kilt. Git yo' stinkin' feet an' breath outta' mah bed, niggah, an' don' git en no mo."

The twins and I lay there stricken in the silence. Then in the utter quiet of that terrible moment, Junior did something so insane it haunts me still. He giggled gaily.

Finally, I heard the bed springs creak and Papa shuffle down the hall. I went to the kitchen for a drink of water. I had drained the glass and was just going to put out the kitchen light when I noticed an old acquaintance staring up at me from the corner,

I was the elderly rat with the hacked off foot. I stomped the floor to frighten him, but the crip glared venomously at me and bared yellowed fangs.

As I flipped the light switch I got a silly, but really hateful thought about Mama. I wished that I had made a pal of the crip way back when we first met so he'd do me a favor and scamper right in and bite the blood out of Mama for hurting Papa so bad.

Then sudden remorse and alarm struck me when I remembered that Mama hadn't uttered a sound since she'd spewed her brutal tirade. Had she goaded gentle Papa to stab his pocketknife into her heart?

I rushed frantically to the doorway of her bedroom. I almost fainted with relief as I saw her in the dimness turn on her side and heard her belch.

Then a new fear stiffened me. Had Papa in his grief wandered into the subzero night? I walked down the hall to the living room, and there he was. He was sitting on the sofa in long underwear with his head down, furiously working his jaw muscles and staring at the floor.

I went to him, and as I put my arms around his shoulders, I whispered, "Papa, don't feel bad. Mama didn't mean what she said."

Papa pushed me away and backhanded me against the side of the head. I fell flat on my back. I was more bewildered than hurt, because it was the first time that Papa had ever struck me.

I was struggling to my feet when Papa leaned down and tenderly helped me into his arms. He cried and begged me to forgive him. I fell asleep on his lap and dreamed about how proud and powerful Papa had been on Sunday mornings down South on the plantation preaching under the cottonwood trees.

8

MAMA'S NEW PANTS

Papa knew that his children had overheard Mama's raw rejection of him in the bedroom, and he withdrew even more from us in his shame and misery. He still managed to sweep out and mop a store or two to support his wine habit. He ate haphazardly, and when he did, he usually had sweet potatoes or navy beans cooked with salt pork.

He started the strange practice of pouring sorghum molasses over his beans and whipping it into a gluey mess before gulping it down. He never touched a morsel of food that Mama had bought or cooked. He bought and prepared his own food.

He and Mama didn't exchange a smile or a pleasant word after that last night they slept together. At least once a week Papa would visit Soldier.

I guess it was more than coincidence that he always left early Sunday morning before Mama got painted up and freaky in Bunny's clothes for church.

She couldn't hurt him when she didn't return until midnight or later as she often did because Papa always stayed on the Southside with Soldier until at least Monday noon.

Soldier visited us, but seldom when Mama was at home.

Soldier was visiting us, and Mama was home and so were the twins the blustery March night in 1938 when Lockjaw Hudson started his destructive strategy to capture Carol for his bed.

He had been patient and observant. Cunningly, his first shot was aimed so that overshooting Carol for the moment would sit Mama on bull's-eye and furnish him with (as it turned out) an ally and booster.

Mama answered Lockjaw's knock on her way from the kitchen. I heard him speaking in that creepy breathy way of his about a possible message from his sister who apparently wasn't home. Anyway his whole pitch was phony, because that live orb of his glittered as it swept over the top of Mama's head searching frantically for a glimpse of Carol who was out of range.

Then I heard Lockjaw ask how Papa was doing and Mama invited him in. I mean *them* in. "She" and Cuckoo Red followed Lockjaw into the living room.

She was about twenty-five years old with deeply troubled sable eyes that matched the luxuriant fur that encased her tiny brown frame from shapely calf to heart-shaped diamond earrings.

Lockjaw stood there in the middle of the floor making extremely small talk with Papa and Soldier, and stealing glances at Carol and Mama to perhaps gauge their reactions to the show he was staging.

The girl kept her eyes downcast when she was introduced. She seemed completely preoccupied with gazing at a monstrous solitaire diamond ring on her left hand. She apparently didn't hear Soldier pay her an indirect compliment. She didn't look up or smile or anything when Soldier told Lockjaw he had a pretty girlfriend. She looked unearthly with the thick, much too light colored makeup on her drawn face.

She didn't give a flicker of reaction when Lockjaw looked seriously at Mama but said jocularly, "Soldier, she's pretty awright, but hell, I ain't gonna' marry a hoofer I yanked out of the Grand Terrace cabaret."

Then the torturer paused and switched his live eye rapidly from Carol to Mama and said, "I got a secret love I'm gonna' marry. And ain't nothing gonna' keep us apart. I'm gonna' put her in the lap of luxury, and everybody she knows in good shape."

His companion looked up at him piteously, and then her eyes fell back to her hand. Ceiling light ricocheted off the diamond, and her blank, chalky face was ghastly in the speckled flash of blue white fire.

Lockjaw strutted and bragged and dramatized until Carol cracked that she had a headache and went to bed. Mama sat like she was in a daze for a long time after they left.

Finally in the middle of Soldier's conversation about gangster cops, Mama asked in a dreamy voice, "Sojer, how much thet gal's ring sit Mistah Lockjaw back?"

Soldier gave her a hard look and said, "Eight, nine thousand. But you ought to ask her what she's paying for it."

Around the last of April in 1938, Papa developed an almost unquenchable thirst. Each day he drank six to eight gallons of ice water from two-gallon jugs in the icebox that I constantly refilled. He'd go to the bathroom every half hour or so.

Night and day the cycle went on. Carol brought his meals from the cafe. Strangely, he had a ravenous appetite, but barely the energy to clean himself up.

By the middle of May he was spending most of his time reading the Bible and dozing on the sofa. Sometimes I'd almost panic when it took maybe three or four minutes to shake him awake.

Then at the end of May Papa's vision became so blurred he couldn't read his Bible. His legs ached, and the ends of his toes were numb.

The twins and I begged Papa to see a doctor. Even Mama showed concern and sat on the sofa beside him and spoke kindly to him about the logic of seeing a doctor.

Junior avoided Papa like Papa had TB. Carol borrowed five dollars from her boss to send Papa to the doctor. Papa spent the money for wine. The pain in his legs at times became so intense that I stayed out of school to look after him. He got relief when I rubbed and massaged his legs until I felt my arms would drop off.

The first part of June, on a Saturday night, I left Papa and Bessie about 7 P.M. to walk Carol home from the cafe in case Frederick, her boyfriend, was apprenticing late with pumpernickel and strudel in the kitchen of his family's bakery shop on Kedsie Avenue.

Frederick was a blond, blue-eyed guy with a round soft face and body, and a gentle voice that sometimes stuttered. When I got to the cafe I saw Frederick's old Model A Ford was parked at the curb.

This meant that he would drop her off around the corner from home. Carol had told me that they could never risk walking together at any time because someone acquainted with our family or his might report it. The sad truth was his parents hated blacks like Mama hated whites.

Carol's shift was over, and she was sitting in a dim corner booth with her love. I stood on the sidewalk peering through the window hoping that Carol would notice me so I could wave and get back to Papa.

I didn't move to go through the door. I was held there at the window watching the pudgy white guy romancing my sister. I'd seen them together a dozen times before, but I couldn't get used to it.

In Frederick's presence I'd start remembering how the white women worked Mama nearly to death for a pittance and humiliated her. I could never forget the grisly job the white cops did on Woodrow Spears, the little black guy in the vestibule of our building. And also how the white bastards who controlled the trades unions had rejected Papa because of his blackness.

Childishly, I felt a twinge of resentment toward Carol that she was ignoring these sound reasons for hating all white people and could sit there in the booth snuggled on the enemy's shoulder with eyes closed in trusting contentment.

I always felt so uncomfortable and frustrated whenever I'd had close range contact with him, like the few times I'd sat in a booth with him and Carol. He was so goddamn sincere, kind, jolly and real, and he adored Carol so much, that hard as I tried, I couldn't hate him. It was a helluva mess for a kid ten years old to work out in his head alone.

I saw Carol open her eyes. She said something to Frederick. Then I saw them looking at me with big smiles on their faces. I waved quickly and turned away before they could signal me to join them.

I sprinted madly down the sidewalk and cut abruptly across Madison Street. I peeked from behind two parked cars at the cafe. Frederick was out front down the sidewalk. Finally he went inside the cafe.

I leaned against a car fender out of breath, but relieved that I'd avoided that terrible feeling I got in the company of the white guy I couldn't hate.

When I got home Papa was gone. Bessie said he had been feeling fair, and he told her he was going for a walk and that he might go to the Southside to visit Soldier.

Shortly we heard Mama talking to someone outside our front door, and when she walked into the flat, Lockjaw's sister, Jonnie Mae, came in with her.

Mama's face was more tense and haggard than usual. She sat down heavily on the sofa and held a hand over her heart. My own heart was leaping at the thought that she had found out about Carol and the German guy.

I slipped off her shoes and rubbed her feet.

Jonnie Mae screwed up her friendly hippo face in concern and said, "Sedalia, what's wrong? You need a doctor?"

Mama gritted her teeth and said, "Ah jes' hate white folks so much, Ah'm gonna' bus mah haht opun iffen Ah don' bile en th' 'leckrik chair. Ah got tu git way frum white folks, an' stay way."

Jonnie Mae stroked Mama's temple and said, "Girl, what happened to upset you like this?"

Mama said, "Un dirty low-down skunk lickin' suck-ass dog white bitch wuz th' honor gues' at uh dinnah Ah wuz gonna serve. Ah come tu th' table an' she seen th' servin' tray en mah black hans an' turn flour white. She raised uh ruckus an' tol' th' table thet her appatite had went. Thet no-good white heifer Ah wuz wuking fer got th' white choffer tu serve, an' Ah quit. Ah'm sho glad Ah missed white law truble an' bloodshed."

Jonnie Mae sat and talked sympathetically to Mama until she was calm. Jonnie Mae left, and Mama and Bessie went to bed. I stayed at the open window watching the kids clowning on the stoops in the balmy June weather.

Carol came down the walk with the usual food in a paper sack for Papa. About half an hour after Carol had joined me on the sofa we saw Railhead Cox driving his red Buick down the street toward our building.

And then a door opened and Junior and Rajah leaped to the pavement from the moving car that went on down the block. Junior glared at us when he came in, and his eyes had a strange glassiness.

Fifteen minutes later Railhead walked into the building. I wondered why he hadn't used one of the parking spaces near the building, and if Junior was heisting hustlers with the Cox brothers. And would Junior, in the words of Rajah, "wind up in an alley with the rats squabbling over his brains."

I stopped expecting Papa to come down the walk. I was sure he had gone to visit Soldier. I brushed my teeth and took a bath and went to bed. But sleep came late and ragged. Junior thrashed about on his pallet and in a terrible nightmare cried out and whimpered in fear.

I awoke next morning, which was Sunday, and got a whiff of a rare smell, frying ham. I heard Mama in the kitchen emotionally telling Junior about the white woman who had refused to let Mama serve her. There was a long silence when she finished.

Then Junior said rapidly and loudly, "Mama, dahlin', 'spose Ah

tol' yu them goodies Ah got at th' markit ain't don nuthin' tu mah
bankroll. An' Ah ken bribe yu tu res' an' stay way frum them dirty
white folks uh few days. Mama, why yu lookin' at me lak thet? Ah
ain't shuckin' and jivin' an' Ah ain't stol nuthin'. Looka head! Ah
got moren . . ."

There was a violent hissing sound, and then I heard only faint
whispering come from the kitchen.

Bessie was asleep, but Carol's eyes were bright as we lay there
tensely and strained to hear more.

Finally the whispering stopped and Mama said, "Honey Pie, git
Sweet Pea an' th' twins up."

Carol and I feigned sleep and let Junior shake us a bit before we
reopened our eyes. After breakfast, Mama and Junior went to her
bedroom and talked until Railhead knocked on the front door for
Junior half an hour later.

Mama came from the bedroom with a satisfied look on her face,
and Junior went whistling upstairs with Railhead. Mama got pretty
for church and had Jonnie Mae call a cab.

The twins and I just looked at each other open mouthed as the
cab scooted away from the curb. Carol was off at the cafe on Sunday, and she usually met Frederick in the balcony of a Loop theater
showing a picture they wanted to see.

At least that's where Carol led me to believe they spent their Sunday afternoons and early evenings. Carol prepared vegetables and a
roast for dinner before she left.

I was at the front window around 4 P.M. and saw Rajah park
Railhead's Buick at the curb. It had been painted jet-black. My heart
fluttered when a police car eased to the curb behind the Buick and a
burly white cop followed Rajah down the walk toward the building.

Rajah's face was grim, but he didn't falter. I was certain the white
cop was coming to beat Junior bloody about the money he had
boasted about in the kitchen. I was shaking on the sofa when the
booming knock smashed against the door.

I couldn't shout, "Who is it?"

It happened again. I couldn't move. I heard Bessie at the door, and the cop ask for Sedalia Tilson. Then I heard him say that Papa had gone to sleep on a streetcar Saturday night and the motor man couldn't wake him at the end of the line.

Bessie and I bumbled about the flat in shock and confusion for a few minutes. And then Bessie used Jonnie Mae's phone to call the hospital, and I started to get ready for a trip to the Southside to get Soldier's help.

Bessie was telling me that the hospital told her Papa was just rundown and had arthritis and had been discharged and was waiting for someone to bring him home when Soldier knocked on the door.

We blurted, "Papa's in the County Hospital."

He looked down the hall toward Mama's bedroom and shouted, "And what idiot sent him there? The white beasts out there let black people rot and die in their own waste."

After Soldier realized that Mama wasn't at home and she hadn't sent Papa away he cooled off and hired the old guy who lived across the street that owned the black Dodge to drive us to get Papa.

He had been discharged and was sitting on the curb resting his head against a fire hydrant. It was really heartbreaking to see him looking so shabby and sick and thrown away. It really was.

I jumped from the car and ran to him. His eyes were closed.

I touched his shoulder and said, "Papa, it's Sweet Pea. Let's go home."

He didn't hear me. He was asleep. I glanced up and saw Soldier and Bessie pushing through a knot of gawkers. Soldier stooped down and shook him hard and shouted his name.

Papa's eyes stayed closed, but his throat made a guttural sound. Frantically Soldier slapped his face and pinched him for a few seconds. Papa's eyelids finally opened in slow motion and recognition. He focused his glazed eyes. With our support he walked to the car.

Inside the car Soldier said gently, "Buddy, why didn't you wait inside the hospital until we came?"

Papa chuckled bitterly and said, "Ain't no resun tu linguh en hell iffen mah laigs ain't cut off or broke. Them mean white folks beats on them po' sick black peoples an' says black bastid an' niggah more'n Ah heered en th' big foot Ian. Ah jes' thank th' Lawd Ah ain't got nuthin' 'cept uh tech uh artharitus an' Ah need uh bildin' tonick."

Soldier said, "Frank, that's what they told you at County Hospital, but I don't trust them because I know they don't care. The pain in your legs could be arthritis, but it worries me that you fall into deep sleep the way you do. It could be sleeping sickness. Suppose you drop off with me on the Southside and let's try a good black doctor. All right?"

Papa nodded his head.

Junior and Carol were at home when we got there, and surprisingly, Mama too. Bessie and I gave them a complete rundown on Papa, and by 10 P.M., we all had gone to bed, even Junior.

I lay there wide eyed for a long time and thought about Papa and Carol and Frederick and how horrible if Mama found out about them. I thought about the expensive groceries Junior had bought and the whispering in the kitchen, and the terror of his nightmare. I cried quietly to sleep.

I was surprised to see Mama at home the next morning. I guess I was really trying hard not to face the truth about her pitiful weakness for money, any kind.

Soldier brought Papa home around 3 P.M. They were grim faced as they sat on the sofa and told us about Papa's diabetes, which, at the time, was a horrendous disease to have because of limited research and haphazard treatment.

Soldier's voice shook when he explained that when we found Papa asleep against the hydrant the hospital had been criminally negligent in discharging Papa in his condition. Soldier told us the black doctor said he was in mild coma.

Papa had a list of recommended foods, and he had been

instructed in the use of the insulin and hypodermic needles Soldier had made possible. Soldier told Mama right in front of Papa the doctor had told him that Papa had a disease for which there was no cure. And if he continued to drink alcohol or missed his dosage of insulin or took too much, he'd die.

Soldier looked at Papa and shook his head and told him how lucky it had been for him that he hadn't been drinking before he boarded the streetcar. The police would have hauled him to a drunk tank when he went into coma. Finally Soldier lapsed into silence, and I could feel the tension between him and Mama.

And then Hattie Greene came in, and her eyes blinked nervously when she saw Soldier. She was a little tipsy and a lot optimistic because she squeezed in beside him on the sofa and hiked her skirt above her lumpy knees. Soldier shifted uneasily and smiled stonily in the absolute hush.

Hattie stared blearily at his smooth brown-skinned profile and blurted, "Soldier, you handsome thing. Have you ever been married?"

Soldier slowly turned his head and looked at her through half-closed eyes for a long moment.

Finally he said, "No, Hattie, I have never been married. In fact, I have never lived with a woman for more than three months. Like legions of black men, I just never found a black woman who inspired and helped me to set free my inner power and strength and to achieve the glory of my manhood in this hellish white man's world."

Hattie drew back with a frown and yapped, "All right, nigger, I'm waiting. Say it. All black women are turds, and white women are great."

Soldier fixed level eyes on Mama sitting tensely across the room and said, "No, I won't say that. There are many black women who understand that black men living in this hellhole life where the white man has a stranglehold on the lifeline, goods and services, need their black women fighting the enemy with them, not unwittingly helping the enemy to uproot the black family. Black women who don't understand this and crush their men are pathetic fools.

"Oh yes, about white women. I have never tried any. All I know about them is what I have learned from black women who ape them.

"I have also learned the bitter truth that great numbers of black women today stomp on the manhood and dreams of trapped black men just as their arrogant and ignorant sisters, drunk with freedom, did at the end of slavery. Like them, certain misguided black women still ruthlessly and criminally help the white man to deball and destroy black men.

"This is happening on a mass scale, and so long as it continues, the lowly masses of black men must go on blundering and hobbling about in the white man's complex world mentally maimed and crippled by white haters and unthinking black women. The positive black woman uses her glory and strength and power to inspire her man toward self-improvement and leadership so that her children might have a strong pattern image."

Soldier's hard stare softened as he continued to look at Mama fidgeting uneasily.

Soldier went on, "The negative black woman dominates the home like a despot or she covets the role. In both cases, during the lunatic strife, these pitiful black women are never aware of the terror and hurt on their children's faces as papa crumbles. The negative black woman fears and hates the white woman because ill-advised or not, black men in droves are defecting to the promise of sympathetic white arms."

Soldier saw that Papa was asleep beside him. He stood up. Mama sat there in her chair staring coldly at Soldier.

Hattie sighed and said, "Soldier, you oughta be a lawyer."

Mama snorted and mumbled something that sounded like, "Sojer been drinkin'!"

Soldier ignored her and started to turn toward the front door.

Hattie said, "Tell me, Soldier, have you ever been in love?"

He paused and looked wistful for a moment.

Then he said, "Hasn't everybody at least once? I fell hard for her a week after I got out of the army in 1918. We shacked up at Thirty-fifth and State streets for those three months I mentioned. We couldn't live apart until her divorce became final.

"I was a young dreamer with the idea I was going to invent something and get rich and famous.

"One hot night in July I left to get cold suds. Something or other triggered what I thought was a brilliant idea for an invention so terrific the white man would be forced by public demand to put black Edward Cato's name in his Jim Crow history books.

"Well, anyway, I rushed back to her without the suds. I tossed her in the air and blurted out my brainstorm. Then I noticed she had a sour look on her pretty face and she demanded that I put her down.

"I stood there with my mouth open in shock when she said, 'Nigger, are you crazy? Stop dreaming. Don't you know that if one of your silly ideas was worth a good goddamn, a white man would have thought of it already? Now hurry back with our beer. I'm dying of thirst.'

"I don't remember what the invention idea was, but I do remember that I turned and walked out that door and never came back.

"And I have never since given another woman a chance to stomp on even an impossible dream of mine."

Soldier opened the front door and limped away on his game leg into the night.

I don't know how much money Junior gave Mama in the kitchen that Sunday morning when he bought the expensive groceries. I do know she didn't go to work for a week. When Connie the landlady picked up the rent Mama gave her all paper money. It was one of the rare times that she didn't scramble frantically about searching out every nickel and dime to pay the rent.

The strange and worrisome thing I couldn't figure out was why Junior and the Cox brothers didn't leave the building until two weeks after Rajah parked Railhead's Buick out front.

Papa was like a vacant-eyed robot as from day to day he injected his insulin and forced down the bland but nutritious fish and vegetables Carol brought home from the cafe. He visited Soldier and the doctor once during the two weeks and got a fresh supply of insulin, at Soldier's expense.

The first week in July an odd couple of guys moved into the flat above Railhead's on the third floor. I don't mean they looked odd. They were Pullman porters and looked like ordinary human beings coming in and out of the building.

One was tall and husky and black, and the other was tall, willowy and yellow. Both were in their early twenties and wore jazzy clothes.

I noticed when the movers brought their stuff in how fancy and glossy it all was. I mentioned that they were odd because at the end of July little nosey me peeked on them and found out they were.

I remember the date, July 26, 1938. Nineteen thirty-eight. I can't forget it. It was the humid afternoon that Sally Greene led Bessie to her debut as a whore. And perhaps it was the first time that Sally didn't lay for free.

We were alone in the flat sitting on the sofa at the open window when Sally came excitedly through the front door that was open to snare breezes that stirred when the vestibule door was used.

She waggled her head, and Bessie went down the hall a bit with her. I tuned my ears up high and heard Sally's voice say something in praise of Pullman porters, cold champagne and ten dollars. Then I heard Bessie mumble something that had a sour tone of dissent. Sally said something in a scolding way, and I heard their footsteps go down the hall and into the bathroom.

I listened to the faucets run for a long time and wondered what they were doing. Finally I tiptoed down the hall and the keyhole thrust itself before my eyes.

Mama would have gone to the electric chair for sure if she had seen what was going on. Sally apparently had taken a bath and was naked sitting on the commode with Mama's douche bag hanging on a nail above her and the nozzle buried in a fat bush of jet-black crotch hair.

Bessie was wallowing in the tub. I went back to the sofa. I heard them come out of the bathroom, and I smelled Mama's perfume as they wiggled through the front doorway and up the stairs to the Pullman porters.

I sat at the window for a half hour or so watching Connie the landlady having a heated, arm-slinging argument on the sidewalk in front of her house with her lanky, expensively dressed son. As I had seen her do several times before, she took a checkbook from her bosom and made out a check on the gleaming fender of her son's Lincoln sedan. Then he pecked her on the forehead and zoomed away in his machine.

I guess he only came to visit Connie when he ran short of cash. Maybe like the black people she abused and cheated, he hated her too.

Curiosity nipped hard at me about Sally and Bessie and what was happening with the Pullman porters. I locked the flat and eased up on the third floor in bare feet.

The porters' door was open about four inches, and I saw a length of chain lock stretched across the gap above my head. I could hear the whirring of an electric fan and Bessie giggling against the muted background of a bass-toned phonograph.

I knew from the sounds that the party was in the living room. I stretched out on the floor and almost twisted my neck out of whack trying to get just a tiny peek into that damn living room.

It was no use. I was sweating and dizzy and really ill with frustration. I really was. I was afraid I might pass out and be discovered, so I went back to the flat and fell onto the sofa exhausted.

Then a thrilly idea shot through me. I raced into Mama's bedroom and got a tiny hand mirror from a purse and sped back to my position on the floor outside the freaky flat.

Slowly I stuck the mirror past the doorjamb. I was shocked and excited at the sight of Bessie and the others naked and freaking off on couch cushions in the middle of the floor.

It was really hard to believe it was my big dumb country sister groaning in ecstasy with her face pushed into Sally's bush. Sally lay there on her back like a bitch dog between the knees of the yellow porter and licked his balls as the black porter knelt behind him and sodomized him with a huge stiff black dick.

I was mesmerized as Sally and Bessie paired off and did a sixty-nine while the porters called them filthy names. I was so angry and hurt when Bessie sucked off both guys.

Then the yellow guy started fucking Sally from the rear as they lay on their sides watching the black guy lock Bessie's legs over his shoulders. I held my breath when Bessie cried out as he poked his gigantic whang into her.

And then as he pounded into her violently with long brutal strokes, the bitch Sally lay there listening to Bessie scream, and hollered, "Oh shit, your dick is beautiful going in and out of that sweet cunt of hers. Fuck her! Fuck her harder. Oh, you gorgeous mule dick sonuvabitch. Tear that bitch up. Oh! Goddamn, fuck me, you pretty yellow cocksucker. OOEE I'm coming, sissy bastard."

I felt faint and queasy, so I struggled to my feet and managed to get downstairs to the flat. I rushed to the bathroom drenched with sweat and sudden diarrhea and my heart felt like it might knock a hole in my chest. I was sick enough to die for fifteen minutes sitting on that stool. I really was.

I started to feel better and my heart gentled down. I was thinking about getting Jonnie Mae or somebody to go upstairs with me to rescue Bessie before the black guy killed her with his outrageous dick when I heard Bessie call my name.

I cleaned myself up and went to the bedroom. She was stretched across the bed with her clothes on. She didn't look funny or different or anything except maybe too bright eyed from the champagne. And the raw odor of "come" wafted from her.

I must have been looking strange because she said, "Why yu squenchin' up yo' nos an' lookin' mean at me, Sweet Pea? Ah buy us ice cream, yu git it."

I lowered my eyes and said, "I don't feel good. Not now, maybe later. You want to use the bathroom?"

I went down the hall and out the front door to the shady stoop. I sat there getting my head together and trying to decide if I should tell Papa or Mama about Bessie and the Pullman porters.

Papa came home at sunset, drunk. I sat on the stoop until Mama came home at 9 P.M. One look at her haggard, tense face and I knew the white folks had been shooting her through hot grease again. I couldn't heap Bessie's mess on top of it all. I guess the Tilson family was doomed to have horrible things happen to it.

Everybody except Junior was home and in bed by 11 P.M. The excitement and shock of peeking on Bessie's freak off sure played havoc with my bowels. I had to get up and go to the bathroom every half hour or so.

A bad rain and thunderstorm started around midnight. In fact, I was on the stool when I heard Junior slam the front door and clump noisily down the hall. I heard him stop in front of Mama's door and knock urgently. I didn't hear Mama answer or open her door.

He knocked again and said petulantly and thickly, "Ain't yu uh blip, Mama, dahlin'? Heah ah am fatern uh goose wif frogskins an' kickin' yo' doe down whilst yu playin' possum lak Ah'm shuckin' an' jivin' out heah. Them dirty white folk ain't gonna see yu fer uh munt. Opun the doe, Mama, dahlin', an' looka heah yu ken . . ."

I came out of the bathroom and walked toward Junior at the same time that Papa reached Junior and placed his hand on Junior's burly shoulder.

He said firmly, "Boy, Ah ain't goin' tu stan no mo' ruckus heah tunight. Why yu beatin' on Sedalia's doe? Whah yu git thet fist uh money?"

Papa almost lost his balance when Junior jerked violently away and stood glaring down at Papa with a crooked grin on his face. Mama opened her door and stood yawning in the doorway and gazing raptly at the sheaf of greenbacks in Junior's hand.

Junior said loudly, "Mama, dahlin', whutsa mattuh wif this crazy niggah? Ah ain't got tu tell him oauh bizness, huh?"

Mama tore her eyes away from the money and patted Papa's cheek.

She said sweetly, "Honey Pie, git on back tu bed an' res'. Ah don' need no hep wif Junior tunight."

Papa drew back from her and frowned.

Papa said, "Yu ain't wukin' an' ain't nobody givin' way no money. Ah ain't gonna have no crooks 'roun mah house. Whah yu get thet money?"

Junior shot a puzzled look at Mama, and then apparently charting his course by her impassive face he lashed out, "Niggah, yu ain't crazy. Thet wine is got yu stupid. Niggah, yu ain't got no wife an' no house."

Papa said in a croaking voice, "Yu crook, don' yu talk tu me lak thet. The Lawd gonna' give me th' strenth tu whup yu."

Junior said, "Fool, Ah ain't no crook, Ah'm uh hustlah. Me an' Railhead an' Rajah play lemon pool. Ast Mama."

Papa turned questioning eyes to Mama's solemnly nodding head.

The twins came to stand trembling beside me as Junior stuck his finger in Papa's face and said slowly, "Niggah, yu ain't th' boss 'roun heah. Mama is, an' Ah don' want yu effing wif me agin. Nex' time Ah'm gonna' kick yo' ole gray—"

Papa clawed the air and lunged at Junior. Junior sidestepped and punched Papa hard between the shoulder blades as he went by. The twins and I screamed together and clutched at Junior. Mama just stood in the doorway looking curiously down at Papa lying on his back gasping for breath.

Junior stood over Papa with us clinging to his arms to restrain him and shouted, "Mama don' want yu, niggah. Yu jes' en th' way. She tol' me so. Ast her, niggah. Ast her."

Papa lay there on the floor and walled his pleading eyes up at Mama begging her with them not to crucify him, to deny she'd said it.

Lightning burst through the living-room window and lit the hallway and Mama's face like a klieg light. And Mama's face was cruel and cold and so sick. She turned and shut her bedroom door behind her.

Junior went to the bathroom, and we helped Papa to the sofa. We heard him break down in racking sobs when we got back to bed.

I couldn't sleep. I lay there too hurt and dazed to really understand it all. The storm seemed to get worse, but somehow, listening to the violent lyrics of the thunder and the furious music of the rain drifted me into half sleep.

I awoke startled. I had a vague notion that I had heard the click of the front-door lock. I heard the storm raging and daylight hadn't come. Then it struck me vividly and hard about Papa and the awful rest of it.

In panic I leapt up and ran to the living room. Papa wasn't on the sofa. I looked behind the sofa for the few articles of clothing he stored there. I saw things, but my panic wouldn't let me take inventory.

I rushed out into the storm in my bare feet and rayon pajamas. The blowing rain chilled and soaked me within seconds as I stood on the sidewalk and tried to spot Papa through the walls of rain.

And then there was a brilliant explosion of lightning and I saw him stooped and bent against the storm at the end of the block. He was wearing the comical great coat that had belonged to Bunny's Joe.

Papa's white hair was gleaming in that flash of light, and he carried his pasteboard suitcase, the same one he brought from down South.

I ran toward him screaming, "Papa! Papa! Come back, Papa!"

My voice died on the wind and beneath the rumble of the

thunder. I walked slowly back. I was afraid to go inside where I knew Mama and Junior were sleeping and helpless. I loved them, and I didn't want to do anything bad to them to pay them back for Papa.

I sat numbly on the stoop of our building. I couldn't feel the rain or anything. I just cried my heart out for Papa.

9

THET PECKAHWOOD VARMINT

Papa went to his one source of shelter and friendship, Soldier. I went to bed with a bad cold and high fever from exposure on the stoop that stormy morning. Carol woke up, missed me and found me out there after two hours in hysterics.

After a week of Mama's searing mustard plasters on my chest, and honey and lemon juice laced with whiskey down my swollen sore throat, I got out of bed and felt fair for a kid with a broken heart. The twins and I pleaded with Mama to go and get Papa.

All she'd say was, "We groun. Yu mine yo' bizness. Ah ain't beggin' Frank tu do nuthin'."

Mama played Junior's irresistible bribe game of "stay away from the dirty white folks" for ten days. Several uncommon events happened during the week I was in bed, or rather, on the sofa.

It was the third morning of my misery, I think, that Junior, feeling guilty about Papa and knowing I was mad at him, stood at the side of the sofa clowning and trying to make up with me. Railhead came through the open front door with clenched teeth and anguished eyes glistening with tears.

Junior whirled around and froze like a stone man as Railhead blubbered, "Junior, they got Raj. Them sneaky motherfuckers got Raj. Poor Raj, them cruel cocksuckers trussed him up like a Christmas goose and shotgunned the back of his head off. They . . ."

Mama had come to stand behind Railhead. He turned and saw her and went swiftly through the front doorway.

Mama stared at Junior coldly until he blurted out under the icy pressure, "Mama, dahlin', Ah sweah Ah ain't en no truble wif nobody."

Mama jerked her head slightly and went down the hall to her bedroom. Junior sighed deeply and followed her. I lay and listened to Junior pitching himself hoarse convincing Mama that Rajah's Southside execution was the result of some private boo-boo, that Junior and Railhead had no part in or of, and knew nothing about.

She bought his tale because she came out of the bedroom with all the ice melted in her eyes. I guess she really couldn't afford not to believe Junior even after overhearing Railhead putting the finger on the guilty "they" to Junior. She really couldn't.

The day before I got out of bed Rajah was buried, and I watched at the front window when brawny Mrs. Cox, stony faced, practically carried grief-shattered Mr. Cox to the funeral home's family car the morning of the funeral.

Hattie Greene, who had been playing the dead man's row of figures since Rajah's death, hit Lockjaw's policy wheel with a buck bet for eight hundred and sixty dollars! She gave a party that lasted until after Mama went back to work.

Mama lost a good friend a day or so before she went back to work. Lockjaw switched his sister, Jonnie Mae, to an operation on the Southside. She was replaced in the check-in station across the hall by an old retired craps hustler called Five Lick Willie.

A day or so before the middle of July, the twins and I went to visit Papa on the Southside. We found him and Soldier washing cars with a garden hose under the elevated train tracks in the rear of their rooming house just off Forty-seventh Street. Papa sure looked much better, and he was moving instead of dragging.

We kicked off our shoes and wiped off the cars inside and out. Later in the afternoon we all went to a chili parlor on Forty-seventh Street.

Just before we started for home we told Papa how much we missed him and we hoped he'd come home soon. We didn't beg him or press him to come back because he looked like he might be getting well and we all knew he would only get torn down at home.

He and Soldier walked us to the car line and while waiting for a streetcar, I said, "Soldier, what is lemon pool?"

He said, "Little Brother, it's cue stick con played by a shark who never lets the sucker know his true ability. He lets the sucker win and lose in a natural way to build him up for the kill, and the shark also knows how to 'skill out' and make it look like he 'lucked out.'"

I had remembered Junior telling Mama that he, Railhead and Rajah had played lemon pool for the money he had flashed.

I frowned and said, "Can three partners play lemon pool together and all make a lot of money?"

Soldier laughed and said, "No, I doubt it, although sometimes two lemon players will pretend to be bitter rivals and play each other while a third and maybe a fourth member of the team will lay bets among the onlookers. Naturally the lemon players with the heavy bets on him to win will lose to his partner.

"It's possible in spots to pick up nice money playing the lemon, but it's a hard hustle and the scores are usually small and far between. I know some crackerjack pool hustlers solo sharking that are starving to death."

A streetcar rattled to a stop, and we climbed aboard. We sat in the rear of the car and watched Papa and Soldier waving at us until twilight dropped her quick lavender curtain and disappeared them.

On the way home, I shivered at the sight of every alley mouth. I couldn't forget Rajah, and I just knew "they" were searching for Junior and Railhead. I really did.

The day before Mama went back to work after her ten-day

vacation Junior gave her, she was sitting in a living-room chair soaking her feet in a pan of warm water to soften her corns and callouses for paring off. Hattie Greene rushed into our flat drunk and jubilant. She waved a section of the *Chicago Defender* (the world's most influential black newspaper) under Mama's nose.

Hattie gurgled drunkenly, "Sedalia, it worked! It worked! He swore it would! He swore it would! I'll never have to take her abuse and see her ugly black mug again. Sedalia, she's gone, gone forever.

"This paper called it an accident, but I 'fixed' her, and it happened to her an hour after she left my flat on her snooping tour. I did it and I can't go to jail for it. Here, read about the dirty black bitch. Now if I could just 'doo-doo' in her casket, I would."

Mama had been looking at Hattie with a puzzled expression on her face throughout the strange monologue. When Hattie paused for air, Mama snatched the section of newspaper with one hand and shook Hattie's shoulder vigorously with the other hand.

She shouted, "Heah, heah, gal, git yosef tugethah. Yu drunk an' crazy tu? Ah ain't got no time fo' no niggah foolishment. Whut yu talkin' 'bout?"

Hattie's haunting face was instantly shocked and incredulous that Mama needed a rundown. Hattie spent at least an emotional half hour doing just that after Mama made her admit that she had not discussed any of the details of the weird affair with Mama before, and that it was Hattie's memory that was faulty, not Mama's.

The basis of Hattie's perverse joy was the death of her despised relief caseworker who had tripped and fallen down a flight of dilapidated tenement steps and broken her obese neck.

Hattie had discovered a black sorcerer in the next block who was known as Prophet Twelve Powers. He dealt in "enemy destruct" powder and "lover stay forever" oil candles, lotion and incense, and other items and services to cover the total spectrum of human desire, frustration and general frailty.

Hattie had treated a chair in her living room with some of

Prophet's "enemy destruct" powder. It was where the caseworker always sat when conducting her humiliating inquisitions.

Perhaps it had been pure coincidence that the unlucky caseworker had left Hattie's flat and had her fatal accident. Hattie believed also that one of the Prophet's "fast luck" candles was why she socked it to the policy wheel for the eight hundred and sixty dollars. Prophet Twelve Powers had gathered unto himself an everlasting disciple.

I was set to wondering after Hattie's rundown, to hear Mama say, "Hattie, gimme thet house numbah. Ah mabbe see th' Prophet one uh these days."

No more than a week after Mama went back to work Railhead started offering his brittle heart to frivolous Bessie. He bought her perfume and huge boxes of chocolates for openers. Mama approved. I guess she was hoping to marry Bessie off before the street claimed her. Junior was in Railhead's corner all the way. But Bessie liked cute guys, not guys with ugly faces and deformed noggins.

Of course, no one except me knew that Sally and Bessie were freaking off with the Pullman porters upstairs and taking sneaky round-the-block joy rides with Grampy Dick and several other notorious pimps and hustlers in their gaudy machines.

But it was Toronto Tony, a white pimp fresh from Canada who had put together a fast stable of black Chicago whores, which made Sally and Bessie gasp and squeal like they were in orgasm.

He'd cruise by in his white Caddie convertible crammed with his stable and his Barrymore-like profile tilted arrogantly toward the sky. And his diamonds were a vulgar riot in the sun. It was tragic that he played for Sally and Bessie, especially Bessie. But then, who can ever know where and how he plots himself toward the end.

Moths and wear all but wiped out the clothes that Bunny had given Mama. One Sunday Mama couldn't go to church because she just didn't have one thing to wear. We had never seen her so depressed. And then like a miracle the following Saturday she went to the Loop and brought back a sparkling array of new finery. And a furniture store delivered bright green new living-room furniture.

She got angry when we asked where she got the money to buy the things. We knew Junior hadn't given her that much money because we heard him ask her if she had hit policy. I found out later that in a way she had.

With Papa gone, Lockjaw started hanging around the flat a lot, especially on weekend evenings. Mama didn't object because he handled her like she was a cream puff. And the choice cuts of meat and fancy pastries he lugged in didn't get him treated like the pompous ass he was. In fact, when he would angrily recoil from Carol's numerous and chilly rebuffs, Mama would lead the monster to her bedroom and soft talk him to gentle him down. She'd shove him out the front door and his live orb would be radiant with revived lust and hope that Carol would one day be his.

Around the first part of August, on a Sunday evening, Junior opened the front door and unveiled a surprise package in the doe-eyed, spectacularly bosomed and bottomed person of Ida Jackson, a penny-toned Westside divorcée, maybe thirty-five to forty years old. Her ruined baby face leered risqué half smiles like the ones on freakish bitches in pornographic movies. And her voice was whiskey contralto.

Mama sat silently and tensely watching Junior paying moon-eyed attention to the battered beauty. And each time Junior called her "Muh Deah," Mama winced. Junior was sauced up and couldn't keep his eyes and hands off Ida's epic chest, and they left after a few minutes. Junior didn't come home until noon the next day.

The following weekend Carol was off Saturday and Sunday because of some redecoration at the cafe. Saturday at noon Carol and I were restless and since she wasn't to see Frederick until Sunday, we decided to visit Papa.

Bessie and Ida were out double dating Railhead and Junior in the Buick. And Mama was working.

We had an exciting visit with Papa and Soldier. And it was wonderful to see Papa looking better each time we saw him. They took us to a Chinese restaurant, and then to the Regal Theatre for a stage show. Comedians Butter Beans and Susie gave me laughing cramps.

Carol and I were chatting gaily on the Madison streetcar when she glanced out the window and stiffened. I leaned over and looked at the street. Frederick's old Model A Ford was halted at a stoplight across the intersection, and as our car rumbled past on the green light, I saw a young white girl with long straw-colored hair in the front seat beside him.

Carol was silent all the way home, and I could tell by the way she chewed her bottom lip that tears were on the brink. The flat was deserted when we got there at seven thirty P.M. Carol didn't cry. She wrote a letter and told me if I hurried I could catch Frederick at the bakery and get back home before Mama arrived at nine P.M.

I took a streetcar to the bakery on Kedsie Avenue. The front store part was closed. I went down an alley to the rear and peered through a barred half-open window.

I rattled a quarter across the bars when I spied Frederick and the girl with the straw-colored hair moving about in crisp white uniforms. He walked over and saw me and let me in the back door.

My mouth flooded as I inhaled the spicy aroma of baking strudel and bread. He frowned as he read Carol's letter and he kicked the side of a brick oven when he had finished.

He stuttered in a low voice, "Carol's wrong about Gretchen. She's my cousin from Wisconsin."

He turned and motioned the girl toward us. She came and stood smiling.

Frederick said, "Gretchen, this is Otis, a friend of mine. Just for fun, say how you're connected to me and where you come from."

She shifted puzzled blue eyes from him to me and said, "You're my cousin Frederick, and I came from Ripon, Wisconsin, yesterday to help with the shop baking, and I'm certain you have been drinking."

She laughed and walked away. He scrawled a message hurriedly on the back of Carol's letter and gave me cab fare and a hot loaf of bread.

Carol was at the front window biting her nails when I got home. She heard what I had to tell her and read the note. I could tell by the way her face relaxed that all was well with her and she'd keep her Sunday date with Frederick as usual.

Mama came in around nine P.M. Carol and I were in the living room when Lockjaw and Cuckoo Red paid another of their oppressive visits. They plopped down on the sofa between me and Carol.

Mama was taking a bath and shampooing her hair for Hattie Greene's pressing and curling irons early next morning for church. Lockjaw had been drinking heavily, and his horny thigh chased Carol to the end of the sofa.

Lockjaw said, "What the hell, you think I'm poison?"

Carol said quietly, "No, it's hot an' stuffy en heah."

He dropped a paw where her escaped knee had been and said, "C'mon, baby, I'll have Red take us for a long cool ride along the lake."

Carol had stood to avid the paw. She yawned and looked past his head at the street and murmured, "No, thank yu, Mistah Lockjaw. Ah'm goin' tu bed."

She turned to go, and he grabbed her wrist and jerked her between his knees and locked them around her legs. I started to rise with the thought of pushing his knees apart.

Cuckoo stabbed a stiff index finger into the soft spot under my earlobe, and a bright galaxy of lopsided stars whirled in the near blackout. I wanted to get Mama, but I was stunned and my legs felt numb.

Lockjaw said, "Girl, you're a joke. You got a run in those forty-nine cent stockings a foot wide. But you got the nerve to nix dough and cold-shoulder me, Lockjaw. I always get what I want, and I'm gonna have you if you walk this earth and stay pretty. Now, c'mon and kiss me good night. You owe me that."

Carol's face was flushed in fury, and she literally leaped from the knee lock and her voice dripped with contempt, "Ah ain't nevah goin' tu be nuthin' tu yu, ole funny-lookin' niggah. Ah ain't swallowed uh moufful uh thet food yu brought heah. Ah'm goin' tu have Mama put yu out fer good when she heah whut yu done tu me an' whut yo' flunkey done tu Sweet Pea."

Carol was walking away when Lockjaw brayed like a jackass, and she froze in her tracks when he said, "She can't throw me out of here unless she returns my down payment on you.

"How the hell do you think your old lady got this fancy furniture and the ritzy clothes from Marshal Fields—with box tops? She got a grand and a half from me with the understanding she'd talk you into giving me some consideration. And if she failed, then she'd pay it back at ten percent.

"She begs me to have patience, but I'm busting loose soon and putting you in my bed gangster style. Go on, ask her about our deal.

"Oh yeah, the way you abuse me and call me names—I better not find out you got some punk. I do, I'm gonna have Red stomp his guts out."

Carol just stood there staring at him in shock with her palms pressing to her temples like she was asleep with her eyes open. Lockjaw and Red stood up, and Carol didn't flinch or anything when Lockjaw kissed her flush on the mouth. Lockjaw and Red walked to the front door and paused.

Lockjaw hollered down the hallway toward the bathroom, "Sedalia, I'll drop in next week."

They went out and I said, "Carol, let's tell Mama what he said about buying you."

Not an eyelash flickered. I said it again. She blinked her eyes.

She stood there for a long time wiping her mouth with the back of her hand before she sighed deeply and said in a breaking voice, "Oh, Sweet Pea! He ain't lyin'. She got th' stuff, ain't she? Ain't no use tu say nuthin'.

"We ain't got tu worry now wheah she got the money to buy th' clothes an' furntchur. Ah got uh headache. Mama put th' hurt tu me. Ah'm sick. Ah'm goin' tu bed."

She went slowly down the hall, and I heard her say a dry hello to Mama coming from the bathroom. Mama came down the hall and stuck her haggard face into the living room.

I opened my mouth to tell her about Lockjaw and Red, but she said, "Sweet Pea, them dirty white folks give me ches' pains agin, an' Ah'm beat so don' let Presadent Roseyvelt hissef bothah me."

I sat at the front window and watched Railhead pull his Buick to the curb. Only he and Bessie got out, which meant Junior was probably going to be adoring Ida's epic chest for the rest of the night.

Bessie came in with rumpled clothes and hair in disarray and gave me a dollar from a thin roll of sweaty bills she dug from her bosom.

I heard Bessie running bathwater, and I couldn't help wondering if Railhead was just another pay-and-lay customer like the Pullman porters. I lay my head on the restful ridge of the new green sofa and closed my eyes against the glare of the street lamp.

My little boy's mind thrashed madly in the frightening web spun from the tangled affairs of Carol and the German and Mama and everything that Lockjaw had said and threatened. Soon my head gentled and felt balloon light and seemed to soar above the spectral tenements and slumber on night's indigo pillow, star embroidered.

And then I saw an old black Model A Ford park behind Railhead's Buick. A pudgy white guy got out. It was Frederick! I raced out the front door into the hall. And there, horror of horrors, was Lockjaw and Cuckoo Red talking to a policy runner. I rushed through the vestibule doors to the sidewalk.

Frederick had started up the walk, and he just grinned stupidly when I screamed, "Don't go in that building! They're waiting to kill you! Don't worry, it's all patched up with Carol and she's meeting you tomorrow."

He shoved me aside and strode down the walk.

He said over his shoulder, "It's really your mother I'm calling on. I'm sick and tired of ducking and hiding with Carol. I'm going in and tell Mrs. Tilson that we are in love."

I wanted to shout out the warning that Mama would do him great bodily harm, but I was paralyzed because Lockjaw and Red had come outside and overheard him.

Red walked down to meet him. I saw the glint of brass knuckles on Red's brutish right hand as he gouged a crimson rill along Frederick's jawbone. Frederick dropped moaning to the concrete, and Red stood waiting for orders.

Lockjaw said gleefully, "Stomp his face in and make the peckerwood bastard pretty like me for Carol."

I ran toward them and screamed a dozen times, "Please! Please! Don't do it! Frederick is a good guy. Frederick is a good guy."

And then there was the sudden glare of the street lamp in my eyes and Mama was shaking me and saying, "Yu wringin' wet, Sweet Pea. Who thet name yu callin'?"

I stammered, "Wh, who? Oh! A guy at school, I guess."

I took a quick look out the window to make certain that Frederick's Ford wasn't really there and went to bed on shaky legs.

Carol took me with her to a Loop movie house for her date with Frederick. I guess she felt that leaving the building with me would bamboozle any spy that Lockjaw might have had about.

I sat in the balcony several rows behind them. My glimpses of their torrid kissing and petting were few because the picture was taut adventure titled *International Settlement* with debonair George Sanders, my favorite actor, as a soldier of fortune and the heavenly Dolores Del Rio as his costar.

I fell asleep during the second feature because I hadn't slept well the night before, after that Cuckoo Red nightmare. Carol awakened me, and we walked to a side street where Frederick was waiting in the Ford. I was fast asleep on the backseat before we got out of the downtown section.

I felt a jolting of the car and opened my eyes. Frederick had parked with the Ford's engine running. I lay looking at the skyline and realized we were on the Westside several blocks from home. Carol was nestled inside Frederick's arm with her head on his chest.

She said sadly, "Baby, Ah don' want tu leave yu. Ah cain't hahdly stan tu be wifout yu an' Ah'm so scared uh thet evul ole man. Yo Mama and Papa hate black people, and Mama hates white people. Ah jes' know sumpthin' bad goin' tu happen. Whut we goin' tu do, Baby?"

He patted her and squeezed her tightly and crooned, "Now, darling, you promised me you wouldn't worry. I'm just glad for your sake that you don't love and miss me the terrible way I do you.

"Let's go underground a bit in case the dirty old man has a bad case of nose trouble. We will stop seeing each other in the restaurant for a while, and Sweet Pea can see you home from work except on those two nights a week when we go to 'you know where.' And, darling, don't worry about my parents and your mom.

"It won't be long before I won't need permission to marry you, and then we'll never be apart, and we'll have a house full of beautiful kids that will warm their cold hearts and make them proud and happy we found each other and fell in love."

Carol moaned and raised her open mouth to his and they tongued deeply.

He whispered hoarsely, "*Gott en himmel,* I love you with my soul. It was just Friday, remember? Yet I'm burning like it has been forever since we had some. OH! Please, darling, wake up Sweet Pea and go home before I lose control."

I rescued them. I sat up and rubbed my eyes.

It was good that Carol and Frederick "went underground a bit" because Lockjaw and Red haunted the area where Carol worked and often stopped in near the end of her shift to offer her a ride home.

On Tuesday and Friday evenings, when the lovers went to some secret place, Carol would leave the cafe through the rear kitchen door. I'd be waiting to take her through a catacomb of scary alleys to Frederick parked on a side street many blocks away.

Lockjaw must have been putting pressure on Mama, too, because she yakked constantly to Carol about how rich Lockjaw was and how even though he was old and ugly, a smart girl could at least be friendly toward him. And a girl wouldn't exactly be a fool to marry him since he was practically ready to tumble into the grave. And, of course, a girl could think of her mother killing herself slaving for the dirty white folks.

Carol always got nervous and silent under Mama's sales pitch. Then Mama would look at Carol wide-eyed like she couldn't understand why Carol didn't close her eyes and grab Lockjaw and his diamonds, furs and money.

I was sure glad Mama didn't understand it. I really was.

In the middle of November 1938, Carol and I visited Papa and Soldier. Carol tearfully told them all about Mama and Lockjaw and Frederick. Soldier exploded and advised her to leave immediately and get a furnished room in the building with him and Papa until she could marry.

Papa didn't agree and told her to stay with Mama until she was sure that she and Frederick would marry or at least until she turned eighteen on June 25, 1939. Naturally, Papa's advice had more appeal for her despite the Lockjaw threat, because she was very close to the rest of us.

And even though Mama racked Carol's nerves with her Lockjaw heckle she loved Mama dearly. It was a fatal shame that Carol hadn't taken Soldier's advice instead of Papa's. It really was.

Several days before the new year of 1939 arrived, Carol told me she had been having short dizzy spells and often an upset stomach, and that she hadn't told Frederick about it because she thought it would be a passing disturbance.

New Year's night we lay in our bedroom alone because Bessie and Junior were out with Railhead and Ida. Mama was snoring across the hall. Carol's face was radiant in the glow of moonlight, and her eyes were shining.

She embraced me and said softly, "Sweet Pea, Frederick took me tu uh doctah, an' guess whut? Ah'm goin' tu be uh mama en July. Ah'm so happy Ah don' know walkin' frum flyin'."

I leaped to attention on my elbows and sputtered, "Carol, are you nuts? What about Mama?"

She smiled and said dreamily, "Ah bought uh girdal an' mah coat is loose. Ah cain't show til March or April an' Mama don' notice nuthin' no how. An' when Ah cain't hide it, Ahm goin' tu tell her Ah luv Frederick an' we goin' tu git married wif her uhpruvul en May when Frederick turn twenty-one or wifout it on June 25th when Ahm eighteen."

I said, "But, Carol, have you forgotten Mama hates white people? She'll probably go out of her mind when she finds out about Frederick. And the baby, oh boy! And to make it worse, you kept it secret from her. And what about Lockjaw? Carol, I'm scared."

Carol patted me and said, "Ahm tu happy tu be scahed. Frederick goin' tu drive his Papa up tu Minnesota on uh trip after th' wintah thaw, an' Frederick goin' tu look out up theah fer us uh place tu live wheah theah ain't no hate agin skin color.

"We goin' tu wuk tugethah an' opun uh bakry an' git rich an' buy uh fahm biggern th' Wilkerson's an' let Papa run it an' preach on Sunday like he did on th' plantation."

I lay there in her arms and fell asleep listening to her rhapsodizing her dreams.

In February, I was riding on the backseat of Frederick's Ford going west up Madison Street from a Loop horror movie we had seen.

Auto headlights started to burst on in the infant night like the orbs of awakening vampires. Frederick and Carol were laughing and having a ball as Frederick inched the Ford forward in the bumper-to-bumper traffic.

And then suddenly Carol's voice strangled on a high note of

laughter. I jerked erect and leaned forward against the back of the front seat. She pressed her palms tightly against her chest, and her yellow face was white and contorted.

I thought she had been shot or something, and then I followed her wildly staring eyes and the blood seemed to drain from me.

It was Cuckoo Red! He was maybe twenty feet away slowly driving Lockjaw's limousine Cadillac toward us in the heavy traffic going east toward the Loop on the other side of the white center line. The Ford was halted.

From a great distance and above the roaring inside my head, I heard Frederick shouting, "What's wrong? What's going on?"

Carol was mutely staring ahead.

I heard a choking voice that I couldn't be sure was mine say, "Cuckoo Red over there."

Red pulled the Caddie toward us, and he was halted with a front fender no more than three feet from the Ford's fender. If Red had turned his head even slightly, he would have looked right into the Ford's front seat.

Carol and Frederick were like wax figures sitting rigidly and scarcely breathing. I saw Red's lips move. I looked past his face and saw Lockjaw and his chalky-faced sweetheart on the backseat.

I perched stiffly on the edge of the seat for what seemed like forever and trembled waiting for someone in the limousine to look inside the Ford.

Then the OOGAH! OOGAH! of an old car blowing its horn behind us almost sprang the safety on my bowels as Red, attracted to the sudden sound, seemed to look directly at me. Frederick didn't help at all when in his haste to move ahead he killed the Ford's engine.

But luckily it caught on the first grind of the starter, and I fell back onto the seat in limp exhaustion and relief as Frederick was able to put thirty feet between us and the limousine.

It had been a terrible trauma for Carol in her delicate condition because Frederick had to stop twice before we got home so Carol could be ill outside the car. That was the last time they went to the movies together. They went only to the "you know where" on Tuesday and Friday nights.

Winter's freezing winds, snow and ice disappeared under April's warm sun. Frederick drove his father to Minnesota on a business trip around April 10. He told Carol he expected to be back inside of three weeks and that he'd write her every day at the cafe. He advised Carol not to write him since he couldn't be sure he'd be at any location long enough to receive a letter.

Carol started suffering the day after he left. She was an edgy, lovesick female by the weekend after Frederick's leaving.

Lockjaw and Red, heavily laden with packages, came Saturday noon. Mama and I were alone in the flat. Lockjaw and Mama went into her bedroom and squabbled.

The fragments I overheard pointed up the themes of Carol and her callous attitude toward his—Lockjaw's—superb qualifications for suitor and husband. And Lockjaw's mention of the payment of the loan Mama owed him made her squeal a promise she'd see to it that Carol's attitude was revamped.

He preached about how much it meant to him for Carol to be his date at a birthday shindig in his honor at a Southside cabaret. The monster stepped from Mama's bedroom. He grinned and made the insane demand that Mama, in effect, transform Carol's soul just to please him.

He said in deadly tones, "Mrs. Tilson, I've been a friend. Believe me, you don't want me to be your enemy. I've got a gut full of kissing Carol's ass. I'm warning you to have the girl made up and dressed in that grand's worth of glad rags. The shoes and everything are the size you gave me.

"You gotta have her ready by eleven tonight. I don't want no shitty look on her face like she's been giving me. When I come to get her I wanta see her smiling at me like she's overjoyed to see me,

and I wanta see a certain light in her eyes to tip me off you wised her
up that Lockjaw's the biggest nigger on the Westside and she under-
stands I'm due some respect and affection.

"Mrs. Tilson, I didn't deny you what you wanted from me so
don't try to play me for a chump and deny me what I want from
you. You do and I'm gonna turn Red loose in this funky flat with
orders to bust everything to pieces, including asses.

"Oh yeah, if she's fixed up swell and her mind is in the shape I
want, I'm gonna put two C notes between your tiddies. See you at
eleven sharp."

He and Red went out and left Mama standing in the hall with a
fearful trancelike look on her face. I burst into tears, and she winced
like she'd been struck. She put her arm around my shoulders, and
we went to the sofa. I cried on her lap in great racking sobs for a
long time.

Finally I was able to choke out, "Mama, please don't make Carol
go with Lockjaw, huh?"

Mama said sternly, "Mine yo' bizness, Sweet Pea. Thet ole man
ben gud tu th' famli, an' Carol ain't no china plate. She groun as
she ken git, an' ain't no harm en thet party an' doin' her mama uh
favuh."

Mama sat thoughtfully for a while, and then she went to her bedroom. I heard the rustle and rip of packages being opened.

Suddenly it hit me what I had to do to rescue Carol from Lockjaw at eleven P.M. I'd sneak out the back door and race to the cafe
and convince Carol to walk right off the job in case Mama got
jumpy and came to bring her home early.

We would go to the Southside and stay with Soldier and Papa all
night or maybe forever. I soft shoed down the hall past Mama gazing
at herself in the dresser mirror wrapped in a white fox cape. I went
to my bedroom and put on a sweater. I had crept through the back
door and had run across the backyard toward the gangway leading to
the sidewalk when I heard Mama's shrill voice shout, "Sweet Pea!"

I braked hard and turned. Mama was standing in bare feet outside the back door still draped in the gleaming white fur and calling me back with a frantic index finger. I guess she was reading my mind because I got a boff on the head as I went by her, and she never let me get beyond tripping range for the rest of the day.

Bessie dropped in to change clothes around five, but I didn't get a chance to say anything to her. And Junior hadn't come home the night before, and since it was the weekend, he might not tear himself away from Ida until sometime Monday.

Shortly after Bessie left, Mama led me to the kitchen and I watched as she prepared stuffed green peppers and tapioca pudding with caramel sauce for dessert. They were irresistible favorites of Carol's.

At six thirty Mama and I were sitting tensely at the front window when I got an idea and said, "Mama, Carol is going to wait for me to walk her home. Don't you think I'd better hurry up there? She gets off any minute now."

Mama didn't answer. She was staring at the old guy that lived across the street getting out of his Dodge. She raised the window and hailed him. He came to the window, and she gave him a dollar and the address of the restaurant where he was to pick up Carol.

The old Dodge backfired down the street and so had my last bid to warn Carol away. Mama nervously paced the floor and frequently glanced out the front window. Finally the Dodge came, and Carol got out. I will always remember how pure and pretty she looked in her white uniform that very last day.

Mama let her in with a warm hello and a barrage of groundwork chatter like, "Honey Pie, yu don' look uh bit tahed. Yu sho yu ain't gittin' paid fuh ressin' an' lookin' lak uh movie stah?"

Carol came into the living room and hugged me. She sat on the sofa and kicked off her shoes. I gave Mama a mean look and massaged Carol's feet.

We were going down the hall to the kitchen for supper when Mama said casually, "Honey Pie, look whut Mama got on her bed."

Carol stepped into the bedroom and flipped on a wall light switch. She frowned and recoiled at the sight of the luxurious clothing neatly arrayed on the bed.

Mama had a stricken look on her face as Carol said in a breaking voice, "Mama, they nice an' Ah see they come from Marshall Field's agin."

Carol turned and ran down the hall to the bathroom. Mama looked puzzled. I wasn't. I remembered how hurt Carol had been when Lockjaw told her the money Mama had spent on the clothes from Marshall Field's had been something like a down payment on Carol.

And after we passed the bathroom and heard Carol sobbing softly, Mama looked tortured. Mama nervously chewed her bottom lip when she saw the kitchen clock read eight o'clock. Carol joined us at the kitchen table and scarcely touched her food.

Mama said in a sugary voice, "Honey Pie, them clothes ain't mine. They's your'n."

Carol looked Mama straight in the eyes and said evenly, "Mama, wheah yu git th' money?"

Mama said scoldingly, "Carol, Ah don' want no 'who shot John' 'bout them bootiful clothes. Ah ain't bought 'em, an' whut do it mattah tu yu 'bout thet?"

Carol slid her chair back from the table several inches and said, "Mama, it mattahs uh lot. Mama, did ole ugly Lockjaw git them clotes expectin' me tu be his sweethaht?"

Mama said sweetly, "Cose not, Honey Pie, cose not, an' Ah'm so glad yu ast me. Thet ole fool jes' want yu tu git glamus an' ack lak yu sumpthin' tu him enfrunt uh his frens at his birthday pahty tunight.

"Yu ken play uhlong jes' so he cain't worry me to death. Will yu please, Honey Pie, if yu luv me, go long wif me an' git uh bath an' git them clothes on by leven o'clock?"

Carol's face was an incredulous mask as her mouth trembled to answer, and she was shaking her head wildly when she said sharply, "Ah luv yu, Mama, but Ah cain't put them clothes on an' go no place wif thet ole man.

"And Mama, Ah ain't said nuthin' tu yu 'bout it befor', but Lockjaw tole me right on frunt uv Sweet Pea thet he give yu uh down payment on me. Why yu do thet? An' why yu ben beggin' me tu marry up wif thet ole man if yu luv me? Ah don tole yu uh miyun times Ah cain't stan tu look en his ugly face. Mama, Ah reely cain't evun prahten tu be sumpthin' tu ole Lockjaw now cause Ah'm en luv an' Ah promised tu be true."

Mama sat frozen in shocked outrage as fury stormed in her eyes. Carol looked suddenly frightened and slid her chair even farther away and started to rise cautiously as Mama started breathing heavily and pressing her hands over her heart. Mama leaned forward and blurred a hand to Carol's shoulder and shoved her back into the chair.

Mama said coldly and rapidly, "Yu sassy, stinky-butt heifer. Yu tryin' tu bus mah haht opun lak them dirty white folks. Sho Ah luv yu, thet's why Ah'm still beggin' yu tu hitch up wif Lockjaw so yu cain't suffah lak Ah did wif uh po' dumb niggah lak yu Papa an' wuk yo' looks an' juices outta yu frum sunup tu sundown an' don nevah have no luxries or nuthin'.

"Yu marry thet ole man an' Ah don' have tu slave for them white folks anuther day, an' yu owe yo' ole wukhoss Mama thet. Now stop thet foolishment 'bout luvin' some po-ass niggah an' go git yoself glamus fo' thet ole rich fool wif uh foot en th' grave an' th' othah one en ah puddul uh grease."

Carol sat there blinking as if to block tears and biting her bottom lip and shaking her head slowly in the face of Mama's unreasoning pressure.

Then Carol said softly in a little girl's voice that haunts me still, "Mama, Ah ain't goin' tu have nuthin' tu do wif Lockjaw no mattah if yu stay wif th' white folks til yu die, an' Ah don' nevah have no luxries.

"Mah Papa is uh gud man, an' it ain't his blame thet the wurl is hard on black folks. Ah luv uh white man, Mama, an' he ain't goin' tu let me slave fo' no white folks an' live en misery. As soon as we ken, we gon' tu git uh big fahm, an' yu and Papa ken help run it. An' Mama, Ah got yo' fust li'l gran chile inside me. Put yo' han ovah heah an' yu ken feel it movin'."

The expression on Mama's face had become scary. Her eyes appeared to be popping from her head, and her face was hideously gray and twisted out of shape as she ground her teeth together and grimaced like a lunatic taunting herself in a mirror.

Carol threw her hands up and cringed away. I screamed when Mama, with clenched fists, lunged at Carol with a hoarse-throated bellow of anguished frustration and rage. Carol was knocked to the floor flat on her back as she had risen to escape. Mama's knees thudded into Carol's midsection.

Carol cried out in pain, and then she just lay there shielding her face with her arms and whimpering as Mama pounded her fists against Carol's body and shouted over and over, "Who is the peckahwood fuckah, heifer? An' wheah do he live?"

I tugged at Mama and screamed at her begging her to stop. Mama's mind was away that night because she didn't stop until I threw myself down there between Carol's body and her hammering fists. And then she stopped, and she stank of emotion sweat. But her face wasn't twisted anymore, and she looked genuinely surprised to see the three of us sprawled on the floor.

Carol was moaning. We helped her to her feet, and she mumbled something about the bathroom. Mama put an arm around her waist and took her into the bathroom.

I heard Mama say something about "cord" and she didn't have her key. I whispered a fast rundown on what had happened. She went into the bathroom and left the door cracked a couple of inches.

I heard Mama say something about "cord" and "varmint." I tried to see inside, but all I saw was Bessie vomiting into the face bowl near the door.

I heard Mama say in urgent tones, "Bessie, han' me uh razuh blade an' thet alculhull on thet cabnet."

A few minutes later Bessie said, "Mama, thet blood is sho gushin'. We bettah call uh doctah."

Mama said, "Shet up an' git thet douche bag full uv cold watah an' mix thet alum powdah en wif it. We git her en bed an' off her feet she be doin' gud as th' doctah ken do. An gimme uh piece uv thet newspapah undah thet bowl so Ah ken wrap the stinky var-mint up."

They brought Carol out between them wrapped in a towel and put her tenderly to bed. Then Mama went into the bathroom and came out with the tiny fetus wrapped in a crumpled sheet of news-paper. She went out the back door. I watched through the kitchen window as Mama went to the huge steel garbage bin and casually hurled the pathetic package into it.

I went to Carol, and she looked up at Bessie and me and mur-mured over and over in a plaintive voice, "Why Mama kilt mah baby? He didn't do nuthin' tu her. Whut Mama do wif mah baby?"

I heard Mama come in the back door.

I whispered in Carol's ear, "Mama threw him in the garbage box, but I'll get him and bring him to you when she goes to bed."

And there was bald hatred on Bessie's face for Mama when she stuck her head into the bedroom and sweetly asked Carol if she wanted anything.

Mama told Bessie to stay up until Lockjaw came at eleven P.M. Mama was holding her hand over her heart as she went slowly down the hall to her bedroom and shut the door behind her. Bessie stayed in the bedroom with Carol.

I went quietly out the back door to the garbage bin. I climbed in and lit a candle. I poked and searched through the odious heap until my back ached and my arms felt numb. I just couldn't find Carol's baby among the scores of garbage parcels wrapped in newspaper.

I did discover the crushed corpse of an old acquaintance. He had

apparently been beaten to death because he wasn't easily recogniz-
able covered with a mass of dried blood, but I knew by his hacked
off foot it was Crip, the old rat.

Finally I gave up and went to the bathroom and cleaned up. Carol's blood was on the floor, toilet seat and the bathtub. Bessie told
me in the hall that Carol had stopped bleeding and was napping.

I went and watched out the front window for Lockjaw and
Cuckoo Red and shivered as I wondered if Lockjaw would have Red
stomp us all into blobs of gore because Carol wasn't going to his
birthday party.

I went to the back of the house a dozen times to check on Carol
and the time. After the last check I was on my way down the hall
when someone rapped sharply on the front door and I almost
tinkled in my pants.

I stood there shaking until Bessie came to the door. It was Lockjaw and Red dressed to the brass knuckles in tuxedos and velvet-col-
lared Chesterfield overcoats and natty black derbies tilted sportily.

Lockjaw's orb was flashing about to locate Carol.

He said impatiently, "Well, where's Carol?"

Bessie knocked on Mama's door.

I heard Mama say feebly, "Cum en."

Bessie opened the door, and Lockjaw strode in wearing a no-
nonsense look on his lopsided face with Red on his heels. I went
down the hall into the bathroom and stuck an ear against the wall.

I heard Mama blurt out rapidly, "Mistah Hudson, thet
deceivin' heifer uv mine don fell en the kitchen an' drapped uh fo
munt white varmint an' mighty near give me uh stroke. Natchully
she layin' up weak an' sick an' cain't go tu no pahty wif yu. Mabbe
yu ken take Bessie stead uv Carol. Thet Bessie is sho bootiful when
she's fixed up."

There was a long tortured silence.

Then Mama pleaded, "Please, Mistah Hudson an' Mistah Red,
don' look at me lak thet. Ah sweah thet heifer drapped uh varmint.

Them bloody clothes she wuz wearin' is soaking en th' bathtub. Please, Mistah Hudson, sen' Mistah Red tu see Ah ain't lyin'."

I heard Lockjaw tell Red to look in the tub and tell Bessie he wanted to see her. I ran into the kitchen. In a minute or so I heard Red and Bessie go into Mama's bedroom. I went back to the bathroom.

Red said, "That john looks like a slaughterhouse."

Lockjaw said, "Bessie, how would you like to get dressed up in a grand worth of glad rags and go to a fancy blowout with me?"

Bessie said, "Wheah's them glad rags?"

Mama said, "They's en mah closet."

I heard Bessie's epic feet going across the floor and the closet door open.

Lockjaw said, "Bessie, you better try the shoes on first."

After several long moments Lockjaw said, "Hell! Your dogs are too big. Bessie, you're out of luck. The stores are closed, and your big bare dogs wouldn't match the costume. Red bundle that stuff up and let's get outta here."

I heard their steps going toward the bedroom door and then stop.

Lockjaw said, "Mrs. Tilson, I'm coming by tomorrow with a croaker, and he better tell me Carol's had a miscarriage. If she ain't . . ."

The front door slamming behind them sounded like a pistol shot. I went down the hall to look in on Carol and bumped into Bessie and Mama coming out of her bedroom to do the same thing. Carol's bright eyes focused on Mama who fidgeted and leaned over to touch her. Carol moved away, and her great hazel eyes flooded tears.

And then I felt Mama quiver beside me, shaken by Carol's gently whispered question, "Mama, why yu kilt mah baby?"

Mama croaked from a choking throat, "Shet up, heifer! Yu lyin' an' th' truf ain't en yu. Ah ain't kilt yo' baby. Ah wuz chestizin' yu 'bout thet nasty peckahwood fuckah an' yu fell. He tu blame fuh biggin' yu. Heifer, Ah want yu tu stop bad moufin' me 'bout that peckahwood bastid varmint, yu heah me!"

Carol just lay there staring up accusingly at Mama.

Mama shouted, "Yu tryin' tu bus mah haht opun wif them evul eyes uv your'n, ain't yu? But th' Lawd knows Ah ain't kilt thet varmint."

Mama turned and saw Bessie's hostile eyes. She fled down the hall to her bedroom. I told Carol I'd search the garbage bin again for her baby come daylight. She smiled, nodded her head and closed her eyes.

Bessie got the bedding that Papa had used from the hall closet and made my bed on the sofa. I lay there exhausted, and my kid's brain tried to make the insane pieces of the night's horror puzzle produce a sane picture. At some agony-racked moment, I fell into deathlike sleep.

I awoke chilled in the dreary gloom of a headstone grey dawn. I got up and lit the small gas heater across the room. Then I remembered my promise to Carol to find her baby in the garbage bin.

I dressed in a hurry and went quietly past Mama's door on the balls of my feet. I was at the back door when I decided to look in on Carol before I searched the garbage bin.

I tiptoed into the bedroom. A long lump that was Bessie rose and fell in deep sleep at the foot of the bed. Carol was uncovered lying on her back. I leaned over to pull the covers over her.

I saw something tiny that glowed starkly white between her breasts. I leaned closer. I went woozy at the sight of it. It was the head of her dead baby resting on her chest. The rest of him was wrapped in Carol's yellow silk Sunday handkerchief.

I sat on the side of the bed to give my legs a chance to strengthen. I felt a wetness on my thigh. I looked down and saw a slender dark rivulet had stained my pants. And the raw stench of blood made me suddenly nauseous.

I looked closely at Carol's face, and my heart jumped rhythm. It was ghostly pale and waxen. I stared at her chest. It was still. I touched her arm with a shaky hand. It was stiff and cold and clammy.

I heard a mad creature gibbering inside my head, and then he screeched me into darkness absolute. I was on the floor when I opened my eyes. Bessie was weeping and pressing a cold towel against my face.

Mama was sitting on the side of the bed holding Carol's corpse in her arms and shrieking at the top of her voice, "Mama's po' li'l baby gurl. Ah luv yu. Ah luv yu. Fuhgive me. Please fuhgive me. Mama's po' li'l baby gurl."

I stood up and looked on the bed for the baby. It was lying on the dresser still wrapped in the yellow silk shroud. The place where Carol had lain was a dark mass of half-congealed blood. The strenuous search in the garbage bin for her baby must have hemorrhaged her, and while she lay asleep she bled to death.

Bessie tenderly took the tiny body from the dresser top and led me to the living-room sofa. Bessie and I stopped weeping after a while and sat in a grief-stricken stupor. The strange thing was, Mama stayed in there shrieking and begging Carol's corpse to forgive her.

Lockjaw and Red came at ten A.M. with a short black M.D. to cross-check Mama's story about Carol's miscarriage. The three of them brushed by us and rushed down the hall.

Bessie and I followed them to the bedroom. Mama was still clutching Carol tightly, and Carol's face appeared to be sleeping as it rested on Mama's shoulder facing us.

The doc was a take-charge guy.

He stepped forward and placed a hand on Mama's shoulder and said, "Now, Madame, please let the patient relax so I can get on with my business here. I am desperately pressed for time this morning."

Mama turned wild, tear-reddened eyes up at him as the doctor put a hand to Carol's waist to support her change to the examining position. He jerked his hand back and looked confused.

He spun around and said, "Mr. Hudson, the patient is deceased. I suggest you call the attending physician or the police."

He started to leave.

Lockjaw, without taking his eye off Carol, blocked his way and said, "You're gonna be the attending croaker that signs the death certificate. The butchering peckerwoods in the coroner's morgue ain't gonna chop up that beautiful girl even though she never gave me a smile."

Mama placed Carol back in bed.

Lockjaw stood there gazing down at Carol, and then, without taking his eye away, he said, "Red, get across the hall to Five Lick Willie's phone and call Crockett the undertaker. Tell him where she is and tell him I want her handled like she's British royalty, like a princess. You know, mahogany casket and all the rest of it. You hear that, Red? The goddamn best and nothing less for her. Close your stupid mouth, Red, and move."

He stood there like a man in a trance. Mama sat there on the side of the bed thanking him over and over like a litany for guaranteeing a high-class funeral for Carol.

But Lockjaw's face didn't register that he heard her at all. Finally, he cleared his throat and turned away swiftly and went away through the front door. But not before I had seen a tear glisten as it rolled down the monster's scarred cheek.

Junior came home from Ida's place about fifteen minutes after Lockjaw left. He really took Carol's death hard. He rolled on the floor and wailed like a baby until the undertaker came at noon.

I guess Junior felt guilty because he wasn't at home when we all needed a man in the house so badly. And maybe, just maybe, he remembered that he had done his part to drive Papa away.

Railhead drove Bessie and me to the Southside to tell Papa about Carol. Fortunately, when we got there, Papa was taking a bath. Soldier convinced us it would kill Papa to learn about Carol because of the still shaky stage of his illness.

Papa really looked disappointed not to see Carol. We told him Carol had eloped with her guy and we hadn't heard from her.

When we got home the flat was crammed with Hattie Greene and her children and some people from Mama's church come to pray. Bessie and I kept the secret of what had really happened to Carol to ourselves, even from Junior.

Carol's funeral was held at Mama's church, and old-timers said it had more flowers and was the biggest and richest ever held in that church.

Lockjaw didn't come to the funeral. And neither did Frederick. I found four postal cards and two letters from him among Carol's things. But all had been sent from different towns in Minnesota, and none had a return address.

I notified the cafe where Carol had worked that she had died. I was sure that I would hear from Frederick when he got back to town and found out about Carol.

Carol's family sat on the first bench near the casket and viewed her remains first after the services. I can't forget how torn down and lonely I felt inside as I stood and looked down at her lovely face for the last time. Her tiny baby was nestled on her shoulder.

I fought hard to control myself, but I couldn't help remembering the night I lay in her arms and she rhapsodized her dreams in that breathless voice of hers. And how could I not remember how pretty and pure she looked that last day in her white uniform and her shy warm smile? And how could I forget the rapture in her eyes when she fell in love and became a woman?

At graveside, the grain in the mahogany casket stood out richly beneath the brilliant April sun. I felt a new pang of sorrow for Carol who could never again walk in her favorite kind of day.

Mama wept wildly as the casket was lowered into the grave. Jonnie Mae Hudson, Lockjaw's sister, and Junior were on each side of her giving her support and speaking to her comfortingly.

Suddenly, Mama uttered a guttural cry of anguish and jerked her arms free and hurled herself with arms outstretched toward the yawning grave. Several men, including the minister, flung themselves on her at the very rim and pulled her back.

She struggled and fought them like a crazy woman and screamed, "Bury me wif mah baby gurl. Ah don want tu stay up heah. Git yo hans offen me an' bury me wif mah baby."

Jonnie Mae and several of the church's sisters saw Mama home and put her to bed. Junior took Ida home where he practically lived. Jonnie Mae, Hattie Greene and Bessie fixed food for the hungry sisters. Everybody had gone by five P.M.

I lay down on the sofa, but my whirling brain wouldn't let me nap. At eight P.M. Mama got up and went to the kitchen. I heard her washing dishes.

I went to the kitchen and started drying them. I was drying a steak knife when I got the terrible urge for the first time to kill Mama. I stood there staring at the pulse in her throat and feeling a strange kind of scary ecstasy thinking about plunging the knife to its hilt to start the scarlet spurting.

I stood there ecstatic and terrified. My hands trembled so violently I locked them together and hid them behind me. I could see clear as real Mama thrashing to death on the kitchen floor like a chicken with its head hatcheted off.

I dropped the knife and ran to the bathroom. I locked myself in.

I was leaning against the face bowl sweating and panting when Mama knocked and said, "Sweet Pea, yu awright?"

I fought for breath and managed to mumble, "Yes, Mama, dear, I'm awright."

10

THE WIZARD OF WOO

Two days after Carol's funeral I made my bed on the sofa. Sleeping in the bed where Carol had died gave my mind wrenching nightmares. Bessie and Junior were in the streets, and Mama was asleep. I was falling asleep when I heard knocking on the door.

I looked out the window to see if a police car or Lockjaw's limousine was out front. I went and put an eye to a thin crack in the doorjamb.

It was Frederick. I held my breath and heard Mama snoring. I eased the door open and stepped outside into the hall. Frederick's round face was drawn. His merry blue eyes were sad, and his pug nose was red like he had been weeping.

He said in a breaking voice, "I got in an hour ago. The chef at the cafe told me. Where is she?"

I said, "Oh, Frederick! She was buried with the baby two days ago in Rosehill Cemetery."

He stood silently with a piteous look on his face. I didn't tell him about Mama's bestial part in the miscarriage. I did try, in a kid's clumsy way to comfort him.

Just before he left he said bitterly, "Why did God take her? She was the loveliest, sweetest girl I ever met and will ever know."

Then his cherub face softened, and he had a dreamy look in his eyes.

He almost whispered, "Sweet Pea, it was magical with Carol. I never felt dwarfish and pudgy and comical looking like I know I am. Girls of my own race in subtle ways never let me forget it. But Carol, bless her angel heart in heaven, made me feel six feet tall, handsome and loved."

He turned and walked dejectedly away. I went to the window and watched his old Model A career madly and disappear into the lonely April midnight.

With Carol gone, 1939 was a lonely year for me. Junior was seldom home. Bessie was openly hostile toward Mama and in defiance, ran the streets with Sally, and with Railhead when he could catch up with her.

I had no close buddies at school because I didn't take to sports. But otherwise, I wasn't doing badly in school. I had been advanced to the fifth grade, which was only one grade behind for an eleven year old.

Connie, the landlady, had a stroke that paralyzed the whole right side of her body. She was a no-good woman, but she looked so pitiful with a crutch and dragging her leg that I couldn't help feeling sorry for her. And her only relative, her son, never came to visit her any more, not even to get money.

I couldn't visit Papa and Soldier as often as I wanted to because Papa would quiz me dizzy about Carol and where she was and why she didn't write him. I'd get nervous and have a helluva headache after all the fast lies I'd have to tell him.

Lockjaw and Red dropped in several times for short visits. I didn't hear Lockjaw mention the money Mama owed him. In fact, he almost always brought a slab of corned beef or some other delicacy. I guess he had one soft spot in his ruthless heart, and that for Carol's Mama.

Mr. Cox, Railhead's papa, dropped dead while shining a

customer's shoes in the Loop barbershop where he had worked for twenty years. A pal of Mr. Cox told Railhead that his papa's boss had to canvas the black shoe shiners and porters in the neighborhood of the barbershop to find out "what the hell is Bill's last name so I can send some funeral flowers?"

It was strange and awfully cold-blooded that after twenty long years, Mr. Cox, like multitudes of other black men and women, wasn't really a human being to his white boss, but only a shadowy flunkey with a mop and toilet brush and shine rag who answered to the name of Bill.

On a blustery Saturday night at the end of the first week in December Mama had unexpected visitors drop in. They were Marva Pike, the curvy coffee-cream-shaded secretary-treasurer of Mama's church, and the secretary's mother, Sister Pike and stentorian-voiced Reverend Owens who was the assistant pastor and heir apparent to the pulpit of the slick extortionist with the debauched yellow pimp face.

Sister Pike cleared her throat noisily and said, "Sister Tilson, the Lord has sent us on a sad but necessary mission."

Then Sister Pike rolled and lowered her cow eyes apologetically and said, "Sister Tilson, all the members of our church know of your high regard and . . . uh . . . affection for our beloved pastor. My heart is heavily burdened to have to tell you that Reverend Owens and myself are starting a movement to drive Reverend Rexford from the pulpit of The Church Of Divine Holiness.

"And we know you will help us after you find out that Reverend Rexford is nothing but a thieving no-good nigger that has been using church money for diamonds and furs and a Northside love nest to fornicate with his white slut sweetheart."

Sister Pike heaved her monumental chest to catch her breath and nodded to Reverend Owens who shook his head sadly and said, "Sister Tilson, Sister Pike has spoken the gospel truth.

"When I found out the truth about our pastor, I went out into the open country and threw myself on my knees. There, under God's heaven, I wept and prayed for righteous guidance because I love Reverend Rexford like a brother of blood, and I had a confused and troubled mind.

"Sister Tilson, the earth shook beneath me when I heard the Lord denounce the pastor. We must drive him from the pulpit of our precious church."

Mama sat motionless through the whole thing. Reverend Owen's rundown on how he had unearthed the scandalous truth about Reverend Rexford lasted for half an hour.

The fateful details of the good reverend's detective work were that a black city garbage man who was a tenant in a house the reverend owned was transferred to the plush near Northside of Chicago to pick up garbage.

His first Monday on the new route he spotted a gleaming black Cadillac limousine that seemed familiar. It was parked in the driveway of an attractive bungalow.

It worried him, and since he was a devout elder of The Church of Devine Holiness, his eyes were drawn to the license plate number of his pastor's black limousine parked in front of church the next Sunday.

The next morning as his truck approached the suspect bungalow, his weathered eye saw Reverend Rexford in the doorway. He was kissing good-bye a pulchritudinous young platinum blond white woman who probably seemed to coruscate like an unattainable jewel in the morning sun.

His garbage man's brain maybe turned moss green with envy as he watched the wizard of woo get into the limousine and gun away.

While dumping the bungalow's garbage into his truck, Elder Elijah watched as a shabby black woman with a work-hacked face and fluid-puffed ankles hobbled down the street and went in the back door of the bungalow.

He glanced at the name plate on the pole mailbox near the

sidewalk and saw that the silky haired wizard was shacking for real under a Mr. and Mrs. moniker of Filipino derivation. Elijah feverishly picked up his route in half the time and sped to Reverend Owens with the electrifying news.

Late that afternoon Reverend Owens was waiting in his car down the block when the bone-tired cleaning woman finished her labors at the bungalow. He gallantly gave her a lift all the way to the Southside and picked her clean of information. And got her another job paying more.

The wizard had indeed set up the blonde in the bungalow, and her closet was crammed with expensive finery the dazzled pastor had suckered for. And he was being cuckolded at least twice a week by a penniless young white guy who sang in the dives along North Clark Street, when he got a chance.

After Reverend Owens had given his outraged account of the pastor's costly dalliance with taboo white pussy he passed the ball of condemnation to sloe-eyed Marva Pike with an elaborate bow and jerk of shoulder that looked suspiciously choreographed.

With tortured eyes and in a voice that staggered the piercing rim of hysteria she told how she had aided and abetted the pastor in his embezzlement of fifteen thousand dollars of church money.

She had done it, she said in lofty language, because, "The pastor made me his abject slave and avid fellatrix through his marvelous mastery of the art of cunnilingus and his peerless skill with his confection penis. But now I want him to suffer for cheating on me."

Mama decoded it slowly because her face turned charcoal gray. Marva's mama frowned disapproval of her candor. Reverend Owen's face had a look of painful disgust, like perhaps he had found a used menstrual pad in his plate of hog balls.

Mama seemed more than eager to see the pastor destroyed. She agreed to boycott church services the next day. The plan was to zing the pastor at a special meeting in midweek to be arranged by Reverend Owens who would convince the pastor to face and strangle the vague and wild rumors that he had been keeping a white harlot with church funds.

Reverend Owens was naturally going to conceal from the pastor the fact that hanging witnesses and evidence had been gathered until the terrible session of truth. Marva, the main witness, was to continue with the pastor in a manner not to alert him to the solid threat to his ministry.

Just before the trio left to recruit other church members to the cause, Reverend Owens's face became solemn and he boomed, "Sisters, don't this mess make you sick? When I was a boy, the majority of black preachers were dedicated good men that everybody, especially young men, looked up to and respected.

"A mule kicked my papa's brains out when I was twelve years old. Sure, I missed him because I loved and honored him. But my hurt was healed and my need for a strong man in my life was filled by the pastor of our church.

"Prisons and gutters across America are crawling with black men. Many of them could have been saved for a better way back in their boyhood. But too many pulpits in our black churches are filled with flamboyant crooks and racketeers, many, of whom, are also drunks and sex maniacs that corrupt and prey on attractive young women of their congregations. They betray religion, our race, and our young people. Reverend Rexford must go!"

Late Sunday night one of the pastor's flunkeys brought a sealed letter to the door. Mama slammed the door in his face. Sister Pike came by Monday night to tell Mama that the special meeting was to be held on Thursday evening at eight P.M.

Junior had promised Mama that he would go with her. But at eight P.M. she was still waiting for him to come home. She took me with her, and the pastor hadn't arrived when we got to the church at eight thirty.

The front rows of pews were crowded with about sixty grim-faced sisters and brothers who had begun to shift about impatiently. We squeezed into a center front pew that was in a direct line with the pulpit.

In about fifteen minutes the pastor and a dozen lackeys and deacons came through a rear doorway behind the pulpit. The pastor had a beatific smile lighting his corrupt face, and he oozed oily charm as he approached the pulpit. And then the light went out in his face as he saw that no one was standing except his henchmen to honor his entrance.

He gazed blandly at the hostile faces before him and leaned forward with insolent grace. His long fingers were tented innocently beneath his chin like a pickpocket lulling a sucker. His brooding black eyes were devious pools of cunning.

Then suddenly he threw back his head and snapped it forward close to the microphone and screeched, "Satan!"

The sound tortured the nerve ends unbearably like the prongs of a fork scraping the bottom of a tin pan.

And then he screeched it three times in rapid succession before he shouted, "He's here tonight. Children, my heart is aching with sorrow and love for you because I am looking at the mean expressions on your faces. But I am going to forgive you because I know that Satan sent you here tonight to do his work."

Then the crafty little charlatan vibrated the church with fake evangelical fury when he shouted, "God! God the Father is here tonight standing beside his humble servant knowing that I'm pure in heart and deed.

"What was that you said, God? Hallelujah! Amen! Bless your precious name. But please, God, don't punish the sheep for the poisonous lies of the wolf that brought them here tonight with evil minds.

"God, you are reading my secret heart, and you see that I lead a life of strictest celibacy, and I, as a black man, aware of the white man's crimes against my poor people, would rather be dead than have sexual interest in his women.

"But, God, you taught me to love and to help everybody

regardless of race and color. And it was you, Lord, who directed me to go everywhere I was needed. You sent me to the Northside to lay my healing hands on a poor white spinster sick in mind and body. And some black lying snake in this church is trying to show my good works as evil. And about the church's money, you know how I sacrifice many of my comforts to save church money. I would never steal the church's money for—"

The pastor cut off his defensive ranting with a gasp, and his jaw hung loosely as he stared toward the rear of the church like a condemned man seeing the electric chair of his first and last name.

Everyone turned to follow his stricken stare and saw Sister Pike enter with the church bookkeeper and treasurer, Marva in tow and a tired-faced black woman who had been the maid in the pastor's love nest, hobble ahead of them down an aisle toward the front of the church.

They sat in a front pew and Marva gave the pastor a withering look as she tightly clutched several green fiber-bound ledger-type books in her lap. The pastor watched with shocked awe as the Reverend Owens rose from his seat behind the pulpit and went to sit beside Sister Pike.

Brother Elijah, the garbage man, popped up brave and tall from his seat as if on cue and said loudly, "Reverend Rexford, I ain't got the slew of brains and book learnin' you has, but my eyes is good as your'n or anybody's. And you been lyin' up there 'cause I saw you ticklin' tongues and swappin' spit with a young pretty white lady on my route."

The pastor's lips quivered, and his yellow face seemed to change to an unhealthy aqua hue. Several of his hooligans rose threateningly from their seats flanking the pulpit. The pastor commanded them back to their seats with an airy slash of his palm.

He curled his mouth contemptuously and said sweetly, "Dear Brother Elijah, that rot gut gin he guzzles has him seeing what is not."

Then his voice came sibilantly through the microphone, "Sit down, you drunk lying feckless bumpkin."

Brother Elijah mumbled and sat down.

A frail-looking jet-black woman waved work-battered hands as she stood and said in a whiney voice, "Oh, Reverend Rexford! We loved you with all our hearts, and could forgive you for anything but messing with a white woman. I thought you had some sense."

Tears started brimming in her eyes, and she sat down abruptly.

A husky black sister stood and said angrily, "I ain't got no education neither and doesn't know what that name is you called Brother Elijah. But I hope you know what I mean when I call you a heartless bastid to throw away my sweat and blood money on your white whore. Long time ago I sent a nigger to the graveyard for fooling with my money like that. I should—"

Reverend Owens jumped to his feet and said quickly, "Brothers and Sisters, we didn't assemble here tonight for bloodshed. We are here to determine the truth or falsity of the rumors concerning our pastor and certain church funds. Now I think Sister Marva Pike, our secretary-treasurer, wants to cast a little light on the situation."

The pastor's reaction was instant, extreme and shocking.

He screamed, "Reverend Owens, you goddamn Judas! You can't hurt me. God sent me like Jesus to endure the abuse and vilification of my enemies."

Mama startled me when she leaped to her feet and shouted, "Niggah, yu shet thet blasphemin', lyin', suckin' mouf uh yose. Jesus hepped po' peeples. He nevah stole frum 'em. Yu uh dirty low-down niggah thet's goin' tu th' basement uh hell."

The pastor's hooligans were halfway to Mama when the mob in the pews stood and glared at them. They halted and looked up inquiringly at the pastor.

He shook his head and said loudly, "I am bringing this meeting to an end."

A burly sister shouted, "This is our church, and we want some satisfaction about our money. Who do you think you are? We want to hear what Sister Marva has to say."

The pastor grinned fiendishly and screamed, "You damn idiot! This is *my* church. Mine! Mine! Understand? I am the king here, the boss of my church. Whatever I do in or out of my church is my personal business. Now, I declare this meeting at an end!"

The pastor turned away to leave.

The ex-murderess sprang forward shouting, "You shit-colored sonuvabitch, you ain't gonna' misuse me like this. And the rest of the sisters and brothers slaving in the paddies' filth ain't going to let you get away with throwing their money away on your white bitch. We gonna' whup the pee outta' you and fire you."

The pastor walled fear-wild eyes back at the mob surging toward him. He galloped through the rear door behind the pulpit with his spooked hooligans trampling his heels.

The mob followed through hallways and the church kitchen in profane pursuit. But when Mama and I reached the backyard, the pastor's limousine was torpedoing away and several of the mob were struggling up from the alley floor.

I looked up at Mama, and the round bright moon shone full on her face. I will never forget her face that night. It seemed so strangely evil and witchlike. And as we walked home I had the overpowering feeling that Mama wasn't ever going back to church.

Just as had been planned, Reverend Rexford was driven from his pulpit and Reverend Owens became the new pastor of The Church Of Divine Holiness. And just as I had felt that night when the sinful slicker took flight, Mama never went back to that church or any other.

But on several late, dark nights, I heard Mama up and about. She would go out the front door almost without a sound. I'd go to the front window and watch her go into the mysterious blackness of Prophet Twelve Powers's house.

11

BESSIE'S RED SATIN DRESS

Around the middle of June in 1940, Sally Greene left home and became one of Grampy Dick's whores. I heard Junior mention to Bessie several times that he had seen Sally and Grampy together.

Bessie had Railhead's nose wide open and quivering for her. When he wasn't out front in the street overhauling the motor on his Buick, he stayed underfoot in our flat night and day to be near her.

His presence kept her from flirting freely and joy riding with the slick guys in the sharp cars. Bessie treated Railhead like a mangy dog.

He'd blow up and stalk away vowing never to look at Bessie again. But he was so weak for her, he couldn't stay away for a full day. He'd come back sniffing after her with a terrible pleading look in his eyes. I felt so sorry for him. I really did.

One afternoon in June, a day or so after school had let out for the summer and about a week after Silly left home, I saw Bessie leap up from the sofa and run excitedly out the front door.

I looked out the front window and saw her get into Grampy Dick's blue LaSalle. Railhead stood comically in the middle of the street smeared with auto grease and watched open mouthed as Sally roared the LaSalle away.

Railhead stopped working on his Buick when the sun started to fade and hung around our flat waiting for Bessie to come home.

Mama got in around eight thirty P.M., and Bessie was still out. Railhead was so upset he finked to Mama that Bessie had left with Sally in Grampy Dick's LaSalle.

Junior paced the floor and raved about what he would do to the pimp he caught his sister with. Mama was grim faced when Railhead and Junior left at eleven and Bessie still hadn't come in.

I went to the bedroom around twelve, where I had started to sleep again because the nightmares about Carol had stopped. I could hear Mama moving restlessly about in her bedroom.

Junior came in, and I heard him tell Mama that he and Railhead had searched on foot for Bessie or Grampy's LaSalle, but had seen neither. I heard Junior go down the hall to the living room to bed down on the sofa for a rare night at home.

I was jarred awake, close to daybreak, by Bessie reeling drunkenly against the bed near my head. Through sleep-clogged eyes I saw Mama standing grimly in the doorway watching Bessie struggling out of her clothes.

Bessie took a radiant red satin dress to the closet and put it on a hanger with loving care. Mama was still motionless in the doorway with a hand hidden behind her back.

Bessie turned and walked toward the bed. And then Bessie's cloudy eyes focused on Mama, and she angrily flung her bra toward the top of a chest of drawers beside the doorway.

The bra whipped across Mama's face as Bessie mumbled something that sounded like, "Goddamn spy."

Mama just stood there swelling up and breathing fast.

Junior peered nervously over Mama's head and said, "Bessie, don' yu be cussin' Mama . . ."

Bessie sat down heavily on the side of the bed and started to undo the fasteners on her garter belt from her stocking tops.

Mama lunged furiously and seized a fistful of Bessie's long hair as she gripped a sturdy wooden leg from a broken table. She jerked Bessie's head back toward her spine. There was a cracking sound as Bessie's throat formed a curve.

Bessie's mouth and eyes popped wide open, and she groaned gutturally like perhaps a deaf mute in agony. Mama literally thrust her contorted face against Bessie's face.

Mama showered spittle when she screamed, "Yu evah cuss me agin, yu stinky-butt whore, an' Ah'm goin' to bus yo' brains out. Yu heah me, heifer?"

Junior put his hand on Mama's shoulder and said, "Hell, Mama, come tu yosef. Yu gonna break Bessie's neck."

Mama flung Bessie away, and she fell across my feet nodding her head and sobbing.

Mama stood glaring down at her and said, "An wheah yu git thet dress? Yu ben turnin' yo' ass up tu mens fuh money?"

Bessie lay there shaking her head and staring at Mama with utter hatred.

Mama raised the club and shouted, "Heifer, yu goin' tu tell me wheath thet dress come frum?"

Bessie sat up and said softly, "Grampy Dick th' pimp bought it fo' me 'cause he loves me. Ah tole him Ah wuz wishin' fo' uh red satin dress almos' since Ah wuz born an' he bought it fo' me."

Mama wheeled and stomped to the closet and snatched the shimmery dress from its hanger. Bessie cried out and flew at Mama with her long fingers slashing the air like spastic claws. Junior moved swiftly and bearhugged her from behind.

Mama said, "Don' hol her. Ah need tu beat thet whorishness outta her."

Mama started ripping the dress to pieces. Bessie struggled so desperately that Junior had to put a full nelson on her to keep her from breaking away.

Mama looked down at the pile of torn fabric and said to no one in particular, "Ah'm jes' uh po' black widow woman tryin' tu hol mah famli tugethah an' mah gurls ain't wearin' nuthin' uh nasty pimp bought."

Junior released Bessie and stood between her and Mama. Bessie guffawed bitterly and said, "Mama, yu sho uh black widow, uh black widow spidah. Yu say you gurls? Yu forgit Carol's dead? An', Mama, how ken yu forgit yu killed her an the baby? Mama, Ah'm gonna hate yu fo' Carol an' fo' mah dress 'til Ah die."

Junior turned gray with shock and leaned against the edge of the open closet door for support.

Mama's stricken eyes locked on Junior's face as she blurted, "Thet lyin' heifer. She jes' evul 'bout thet dress. Don' lissen tu thet lie 'bout yo' mama."

Bessie said quietly, "Carol tol' me 'bout yu beatin' on her belly an' Sweet Pea seen yu do it. Ah ain't lyin', Junior. Mama got uh evul haht an' thet's why we ain't got Papa and Carol enymo."

Bessie burst into tears and hurled herself across the bed. Junior shifted his eyes from Mama's face and studied my face for a long moment. I couldn't block the tears, and Junior knew that Mama was guilty. He snatched the table leg from Mama's hand and turned toward the doorway. Mama grabbed his arm, and tears flooded his eyes as he violently pulled himself free.

Mama followed him down the hall pleading, "Honey Pie, don' treat me lak uh dog. Don' bus' mah haht opun. Lemme tel yu sumpthin'. Cum heah an' lemme tel yu sumpthin', Honey Pie."

Junior went out the front door and slammed it in Mama's face.

Mama got dressed to go to work. She came into the bedroom and kissed me on the forehead. She moved toward Bessie sitting on the foot of the bed. Bessie leaped to her feet and fled around the end of the bed into a corner.

She crouched there breathing heavily and with her eyes blazing hatred like a wounded jungle cat at bay. Mama halted, and they were tense statues staring into each other's face for what seemed like forever.

Finally, Mama heaved a sigh and turned and left the flat for work. In less than an hour after Mama left, Bessie had dressed in a red cotton dress and packed some of her things in a shopping bag. I cried and told her I was afraid for her and begged her not to leave.

She hugged me close to her and said, "Sweet Pea, Ah luv yu, an' Ah'm goin' tu miss yu, dahlin'. But Ah cain't stan' Mama no mo'.

"Don' be scahed fo' me 'cuz Grampy gonna look out fo' me, an' he tol me some day he goin' tu set me up en mah own sportin' house, an' Ah'm gonna have twenty gurls takin' mah orders. He said Ah'm gonna be the fanciest, richest black madame en th' wurl. An' Ah'm gonna have uh dozun red satin dresses en different styles."

She kissed me good-bye and was gone. I ran to the front window and watched her wiggle wickedly through the golden innocence of the June morning and disappear.

I didn't eat or take off my pajamas for the rest of the day. I was so worried and lonely I stayed at the front window until Mama came at eight P.M. I was hoping to see Junior and even Bessie coming home. But it didn't happen.

Mama and I scarcely ate or slept for three days after Junior and Bessie left. I had never before seen her face so drawn and her walk so leaden. And I wasn't looking like a model in a health magazine either.

Railhead popped in often to ask if we had heard anything from Bessie. He swore to Mama that he didn't know where Junior was, and then lied and said he didn't have the slightest idea where Ida, Junior's girlfriend, lived.

Railhead vowed that when he got his Buick running, he would find Bessie and bring her home forcibly if he had to.

Around noon of the fourth day of his absence, Junior came home. Mama had stayed home from work and was in her bedroom with the door closed.

I was in my bedroom lying across the bed. Junior spoke to me and started packing a woman's bright green suitcase with his things from the closet and drawers.

There was the stink of bootleg whiskey about him, and his clothes looked bedraggled like he had slept in them. He was hollow eyed and jerkily nervous, like he had been on a long drunk.

I started to tell him about Bessie. But he told me he had found out from Railhead. He heard Mama open her door, and his befuddled look showed he was surprised she was home and that he had really wanted to avoid her when getting his clothes. Mama came into the room and stood beside him.

He kept his eyes averted as he packed hurriedly and said, "How yu, Mama?"

Mama said, "Ah ain't ben no gud since yu lef en uh huff. Honey Pie, Ah'm goin' tu lay down an' die if them clothes uv your'n go frum th' flat. Yu ain't nevah goin' tu have no gud luck an' see yo' Mama livin' again, an' yu be tu blame."

Junior's hands trembled and froze in the action of shutting the packed suitcase.

He sank down weakly on the side of the bed and whined, "Mama, yu oughta stop talkin' thet junky jive. Whut Ah don? Po' Carol en her grave an' Bessie whorin' en them streets. Ah'm feelin' so sad an' sorry fo' them lak Ah ken lay down an' die. Mama, don' yu feel sorry 'bout them gone frum th' flat? Yu ain't spectin' tu lay down an' die 'bout them, huh?"

Mama's face was covered with such fury that Junior cringed away and flinched when she leaned close to him and said harshly, "Shet up yu stooped-piss britches, 'cose mah haht is achin' fo' mah gurls an' fo' Papa thet yu druv uhway thet night."

Mama sat on the side of the bed between us and said passionately, "Ah'm goin' tu tel yu uh sekrit 'bout mah life thet Ah ain't nevah tole yu, an' 'ceptin' Cousin Bunny, ain't nobody knowed it. An' mebbe yu bouf ken be uh li'l sad fo' yo' po' wukhoss mama thet luvs yu an' mabbe yu ken luv me mo' an' won't nevah turn yu back on me."

Junior and I sat stunned on the edge of the bed as Mama rose and walked past us several times with a strange faraway look on her face.

Then finally as she continued to walk slowly to and fro she said in a choked voice, "Ah wuz eight en Georgia, an' Ah seen mah sleepin' papa kilt by uh white man wif uh mask an' uh bonin' knife he lef en Papa's throat.

"Mama wuz layin' side uv Papa screamin', but thet butchah didn't harm uh hair uv her'n. He run frum th' cabin entu th' moonlight an' Ah seen frum his built an' the ways he moved thet it wuz Mistah Dawkins, th' ownah uv th' sawmill thet Papa wuked at.

"Ah tole Mama it wuz Mistah Dawkins, an' she whupped me an' tole me Ah wuz mistaken, thet she knowed it wuz uh stranguh.

"Some white men frum th' mill put Papa en th' groun en th' woods behin' th' cabin lak uh dead dog th' nex' day. Mama was shaped bettah then eny woman Ah evah seen, an' all th' mens, white an' black, wuz sniffin' her trail 'til we moved en wif Mistah Dawkins.

"We wuz s'posed tu be sumpthin' lak housekeepahs, onliest thing Mama wuz en his bed lak his wife an' Ah did th' scrubbin' an' cleanin' while Mama didn't do nuthin' 'cept res' an' dres'.

"Mama died when Ah wuz ten. Mistah Dawkins put me en his bed an' used me lak uh woman 'til Ah run uhway two years latah wif uh ole scuffin' niggah tu Baton Rouge, Louisiana.

"Th' law throwed him en jail an' me en ten fostah homes 'fore Ah wuz foteen, slavin' fo' po' white trash, an' starvin' 'til Ah wuz nuthin' but uh skelefin."

Junior and I started bawling.

Junior jumped up and threw his arms around Mama and wailed, "Mama! Please! Don' tel' no mo'."

Mama slipped out from under his arms and pushed him firmly back to the side of the bed and continued. "Th' las' famli Ah wuz wif wuz th' crooless. Thet wuz jes' befo' Ah gut uhway tu New Orleans an' met up wif mah play Cousin Bunny, an' she taken me tu Vicksburg, Mississippi, wheah Ah fust seen yo' Papa preachin' on thet cornah.

"Gittin' back tu thet las' famli, them white devuls used tu beat me an' lock me en uh pitch-black root cellah. But uh sweet ole black woman always come tu me wif uh bright candle an' kind wurds tu keep me frum bein' scahed an' lonely.

"Thet same ole woman ain't nevah deserted me aftah all these years. She still come now wif her candle when evah Ah'm lonely an' got uh troubled soul.

"Now lissen hard 'cuz Ah'm g'ttin' tu uh mattuh fo' th' las' time an' Ah ain't talkin' 'bout it no mo'. Ah hates white folks worsen they hates mercy and jestus fo' black peepuls.

"Ah whupped Carol fo' lettin' uh peckahwood big her. But Ah luv her en her grave, an' Ah so wuzn't aimin' tu hurt mah angel gurl bad. But Ah ain't sayin' Ah wouldn't whup her agin if she cum frum th' grave an' let thet peckahwood big her again."

Mama stopped pacing and looked sternly at Junior's face for a long moment, and then she riveted her eyes to the suitcase on the bed.

Junior said quickly, "Mama, dahlin', Ah ain't goin' no place. But whut yu gonna do 'bout Bessie?"

Mama turned toward the door and said over her shoulder, "Bessie bad lak mah Mama. Ain't nuthin' Ah ken do 'cept hope she cum tu hersef befo' sumpthin' turrabul happun tu her en them streets."

Railhead and Junior worked feverishly on the Buick in the daytime, and at night they went on foot and searched likely sections of the vast Westside fruitlessly for a glimpse of Bessie, Sally or Grampy Dick.

Two weeks after Bessie left home, a master mechanic from down the block stopped and saw the shambles of the Buick's disassembled engine and took pity on the bumbling neophytes.

He took some vital moving parts of the Buick's engine and machine tooled them in his garage shop to proper precision. In a day and a half, the Buick's engine was running like a fine Swiss timepiece.

Around seven P.M. on the day the Buick was repaired, Railhead came to our flat to get Junior for an all-out search for Bessie.

His eyes were bloodred like he had been smoking reefers, and he brought a half-gallon jug of port wine with him. He and Junior talked heatedly about dirty low-life pimps and Bessie.

They guzzled the jug dry and flashed their weapons. Railhead had a butcher knife and a snub-nosed .38 pistol stuck in his waistband hidden by a seersucker jacket. Junior had a switchblade knife and a blackjack.

When they got ready to leave, I asked if I could go along. They both hollered no. I begged and cried, and finally they told me I could. But they warned me that if I got underfoot and did or said anything stupid they would put me on a streetcar for home.

I wrote Mama a short note telling her I had gone with Junior and Railhead to bring Bessie home. I put it on her bed and raced to the Buick where Railhead was already under the wheel revving the motor. Junior was on the front seat beside him sucking noisily on a long fat reefer.

As Railhead rocketed the Buick down the street, he said, "Jack, I'm gonna' make The Pink Angel on Roosevelt Road. If we run into that pimp sonuvabitch, let me put my foot in his ass first.

"Jack, you better hold my heater. If I lay eyes on that bastard that stole Bessie from me, I might play the murder game. I'll keep the blade. Maybe he's got a shiv and enough heart to fight back, and I can chop his pretty face up."

Railhead gave his pistol to Junior who shoved it into his own waistband. I started to wonder if it had been a good idea to come along.

Railhead got a parking place in front of The Pink Angel. A pale pinkish neon sign atop its weather-mauled facade blacked out and burst on in frenzied sequence.

It bounced greasy light off the lacquered noggins of two cruel-faced black guys decked out in psychedelic slax suits who got out of a lavender Caddie convertible in front of us. They strutted across the sidewalk and into the sinister murk of the bar.

A rusty tin angel hanging askew above the doorway seemed to gaze down in awe at the blood-and-puke-stained sidewalk.

We sat in the Buick for an hour and watched pimps and whores, dope peddlers and square john suckers parade in and out of The Pink Angel.

Several of the pimps I had seen before, hanging around Madison Street and cruising by our apartment building. I saw a skinny, fair-complexioned guy with a wolfish face coming from across the street toward us.

I was trying to think where I had seen him before, when Junior pointed and said excitedly, "Rail, Ah seen thet stud wif Grampy uh hundurd times."

Railhead turned his head and looked at the dapper skeleton nimbly jaywalking through the stream of traffic.

Railhead hammered the heel of his palms against the steering wheel and said joyfully, "I'm hip to the stud! He's Kankakee, an H-connection. Gimme back my heater. I'm gonna' make him tell me where to find Grampy."

Kankakee was maybe twelve feet from the Buick when Railhead stuck his head out and shouted, "Howya doin', Kankakee? Come here a second."

Kankakee frowned and stiffened and walked hesitantly to the side of the Buick. He ignored Railhead's extended hand and stooped down and quickly swept his crafty gray eyes over the interior of the car. He then scrutinized Railhead's up-turned face.

His long keen face creased to a sneer as he backed away and said, "Later, pally. I don't know you."

Railhead quickly blurted, "Goddamn, Jack, I'm Rajah's brother. Remember? I was with him a couple of times when he usta cop stuff at your pad on Cottage Grove."

Kankakee backed away another foot and said, "Maybe I do remember you. So what, pally? I'm not dealing a speck any more, and I ain't hip to no sources whatsoever."

Railhead half opened the car door. He had a wide smile on his face.

He said, "Kankakee, don't be leery. I ain't a hype. I don't wanta' cop no stuff. I want you to hip me where to find a stud we both know. I gotta' find Grampy Dick tonight. Where is he, Kankakee?"

Kankakee's lupine mouth curled in grotesque contempt that Railhead was stupid enough to violate him with the question. Kankakee removed his snow-white Panama hat and looked inside it mockingly as if searching for Grampy. Then he peeped in his shirt pocket and patted the pockets of his sky blue gabardine suit.

He hunched his shoulders and said, "Pally, you stumped me."

He walked away toward the front of the Buick. Railhead grabbed the .38 from Junior, leaped to the street and Junior jumped to the sidewalk.

Kankakee spun around and froze at the sight of Railhead racing toward him and pointing the snub-nosed .38 at him. Railhead rammed the muzzle against Kankakee's chest as Junior stood grimly behind him with the blackjack in his fist.

They roughly prodded Kankakee into the Buick on the front seat between them. Junior patted and searched him from shoe to coat collar.

I was drawn into a palpitating knot in a corner on the backseat. Junior rested his left arm on the back of the front seat as he pressed the blade of his switchblade knife against the side of Kankakee's throat. Railhead tore the Buick from the curb and drove in silence to a dark side street and parked.

Railhead said coldly, "Motherfucker, where is Grampy Dick working his girls? Where's his pad?"

Kankakee said shakily, "Pally, I swear to Christ I don't know where he's cribbing. I ain't seen him in a month. I got a wire off the vine his whores are humping somewhere on the Southside. How about cutting me loose, pally?"

Railhead leaned forward and looked at Junior as he removed the ignition key and jerked his head toward the street.

Railhead opened the door and said, "Nigger, you get cut loose when we find Grampy."

He and Junior went to the front of the Buick and looked through the windshield at Kankakee while they held a lively discussion. Finally, Railhead came and opened the car door on the driver's side.

He pointed his pistol at Kankakee's head and said, "Where is Grampy?"

Sweat rolled down the side of Kankakee's face.

He squeaked, "Pally, I hipped you to all I know. Gimme a break."

Railhead waggled the pistol and said stonily, "Come outta' the car, cunt. I'm gonna' make you find him."

Kankakee slid gingerly out of the car and stood facing Railhead with his back turned to Junior who was leaning against the front fender.

Railhead smiled oddly and said, "Cunt, you sure look like a peckerwood standing there. I'll bet your mammy is a white bitch. She's gonna' read the paper about your dead ass if I don't find Grampy Dick over there tonight."

Railhead kicked Kankakee in the belly. And on the violent cue, Junior leaped forward and smashed the blackjack down on Kankakee's head and shoulders.

His Panama hat sailed into the air, and he wobbled like a slowing top and fell on his back. Railhead and Junior grabbed under his armpits and lifted him to his feet.

They walked him between them to the rear of the Buick. Through the rear window I watched Railhead support Kankakee while Junior snatched off Kankakee's necktie and tied his hands behind him. Then Junior gagged him with a handkerchief and opened the car trunk.

I heard a bumping sound in the trunk just behind the rear seat, and then the slamming of the trunk lid. Railhead and Junior got in

the car and ignored me as they lit reefers and smoked in silence. I
had a funny floaty feeling from the acrid smoke hanging inside the
car. Railhead started the motor and pulled away.

Junior said, "Rail, we gotta' find Bessie an' git off thet Southside
fas'. Them studs whut runs them gamblin' jints we heisted is achin'
tu fuck us up lak they did Rajah."

Railhead said, "We ain't gonna' be over there that long. That
dope-dealing bastard back there knows every whore, street and pimp
hangout on the Southside. He's gonna' beg to help us when we let
him outta that funky trunk."

I was like in a nightmare that I wished would end and I would
find myself back at the flat. We passed police cars several times on
the way to the Southside. Each time I broke into a cold sweat.

I was certain the police would notice the hard mean look on the
faces of Railhead and Junior and stop us. And when they found the
weapons and Kankakee bound in the trunk, I knew they would beat
us to death. The whole experience in that Buick from beginning to
its horrible ending was the most harrowing and unforgettable of all
my life's cruel happenings combined.

Railhead pulled into an alley at Wentworth and Twenty-ninth
on the Southside. He and Junior went to the trunk and brought
Kankakee to sit shaken and rumpled between them. Railhead and
Junior just sat there glaring at him. Kankakee massaged the back of
his neck, and then jiggled his head as if to shake it clearly.

He croaked, "Maybe his girls are humping on 'Four Trey.'"

Railhead cruised up and down Forty-third Street from South
Parkway to State Street for over an hour. We saw pimps and whores
galore, but we didn't spot Grampy, Bessie or Sally. Railhead began
cursing and threatening Kankakee.

We were passing Spiro's poolroom under the El tracks for the
tenth time when Kankakee said, "Pally, pull over in front of the
poolroom and hit your horn."

Railhead did. A slender black guy lounging near the poolroom doorway and chomping on a hot tamale came across the sidewalk to the car. He bent over and peered into the Buick.

Kankakee leaned across Junior and said, "How ya doing, Willy?"

Willy's face showed instant and dramatic suffering.

He moaned, "Kee, I ain't got no bitch, no wheels, and no scratch. I ain't forgot that I'm kin to you for a fin. I'm gonna' mash it on you next time you show."

Kankakee said, "Pally, forget the fin. Where in the hell is Grampy Dick and his girls?"

Willy said, "Ain't you heard? Grampy's on his ass. He got trimmed in a blackjack game by a mob of slick niggers from New York. They swindled him for his bankroll, jewelry and wheels. He blew whoreless. All them whores got in the wind when they got hip how he chumped off. He hangs out on 'Five One' greasy as Porky Pig."

Railhead stuck his mouth close to Kankakee's ear and whispered.

Kankakee said, "Willy, you hip to where them two latest and youngest packages he copped before he blew whoreless are humping?"

Willy said, "Yeah, I'm hip. I dug them freak bitches on 'Trey One' humping their asses off for the paddy pimp Toronto Tony. Oh yeah, that paddy shot at Grampy night before last and run him off 'Trey One.'"

Junior stiffened. Then he pushed his head and shoulders out of the car and jabbed his switchblade toward Willy's throat.

Junior snarled, "Git outta' mah face, niggah, crackin' 'bout mah sistah 'fo Ah stick mah shank en you goozul pipe."

Willy threw his hands up and scuttled backward as Railhead jerked the Buick from the curb. Railhead put Kankakee out of the car at South Parkway and drove toward Thirty-first Street like a madman.

Railhead shook his head and said over and over, "A lousy peckerwood pimping on my woman, ain't that a sonuvabitch?"

Junior's hand trembled violently as he pulled heavily on a fat reefer. Thirty-first Street was uproarious from Prairie Avenue to State Street. Railhead cruised slowly past myriad drunks, whores, hustlers and suckers laughing and cursing and clogging the sidewalks.

Several times Railhead and Junior went into noisy bars and searched for Bessie. Around three A.M. they bought a fifth of gin and parked on Thirty-first Street near Indiana Avenue.

They had emptied the bottle and Railhead was about to U-turn back toward State Street when Junior pointed and hollered, "Ain't thet Sally?"

Railhead eased the Buick toward the intersection. It was Sally! She was twisting her big rear end and hanging on the arm of a paunchy middle-aged white guy in work clothes.

They crossed Indiana Avenue and walked down Thirty-first Street toward Prairie Avenue. Railhead followed a half block behind them until they went into a basement apartment beneath a dilapidated house on Prairie Avenue near Thirty-second Street.

He parked three doors away and said, "Jack, we'll cool it. She's gonna' turn that old bastard in a flash and hit these streets."

They sat fidgeting and cursing as time passed and Sally didn't show. They were talking about interrupting Sally's business when the white guy came out and walked past us.

A couple of minutes later Sally came down the sidewalk toward us. Railhead and Junior got out and stood on the sidewalk beside the Buick. When Sally was almost abreast of them Railhead stepped to the middle of the sidewalk and blocked her way.

She halted and backed up. Her thickly made-up face was a hateful mask in the dim glow of the street lamp. Her eyes glittered strangely as she quickly shifted her eyes from Railhead to Junior.

She smiled crookedly and said, "Well, I'll be damned. It's Junior Tilson and Railhead Cox. You studs want to do some business?"

Railhead said sneeringly, "Do business with a 'come dump' for peckerwoods? My name is Charles. I don't let no funky bitches call me Railhead. Where's Bessie?"

Sally backed away another half step. Junior moved quickly to her side.

She looked up at his hard face and said shakily, "You niggers better stop fucking over me and split back to the Westside. My old man greases the heat down here, and I don't have to take no shit."

Railhead grinned and moved close to her.

He said harshly, "You silly bitch. I'm gonna' cave your face in. Where's Bessie?"

Sally backed against Junior and said shrilly, "Ain't this a bitch? How am I supposed to know where some whore is. Chicago is a—"

Railhead's fist made a crunching sound when he punched her in the eye. She fell to the sidewalk on her knees. She moaned and pressed her hands against her face. Railhead stooped over and grabbed a fist full of her hair.

He jerked her head back and said, "I'm gonna' do something bad to you. Where's Bessie?"

Sally said, "She got a bad break last night."

Junior said, "She en jail?"

Sally waggled her head no.

Railhead said, "You just ain't gonna' tell us where Bessie is."

He slipped the butcher knife from his waistband and pressed the blade against her throat.

He looked at Junior and said, "Jack, this bitch ain't gonna' hip us where Bessie is. I'm gonna' put her light out."

Sally yelped, "I'll hip you! I'll show you where she is."

Railhead and Junior picked her up and hurled her onto the front seat. They got in.

Sally said, "Turn right at the corner."

Railhead roared the Buick away and said, "What the hell did that peckerwood you hump for do to her?"

Sally blurted hysterically, "Tony didn't do it! A paddy trick did it. I warned her about him. I told her he didn't look right. But she wouldn't listen. She thought I was jiving her because I was afraid she'd make more money for Tony than me last night. The fool thought Tony would cut all his girls loose and marry her. She was my best friend, but after she fell in love she . . ."

Railhead said, "Shut up! Where now?" as he turned off Prairie into Thirty-second Street.

Sally pointed and mumbled, "Go down that alley over there."

Junior seized her and shook her violently.

He screamed, "Whut happuned tu mah sistah?"

Sally gasped. "The trick was a maniac . . . He killed Bessie."

Junior slumped back on the seat as Railhead turned into the alley. I was numb with shock. It seemed that the Buick had crawled through the narrow filthy tunnel for hours before Sally said, "There it is! She's in that burned building."

Railhead drove another fifty feet and stopped beside the fire-blackened shell of a garage. Junior got out and stood at the side of the car. Sally started bawling.

Railhead took a flashlight from the glove compartment and got out of the car. He stood at the open door for a moment, and watched Sally cry. Then he reached inside and grabbed her wrist. He pulled her out of the car and pushed her around the front of the Buick.

I got out and followed them into the burned out garage. Railhead's flashlight played across the gutted skeleton of an old car.

Sally said weakly, "She's under there."

Railhead and Junior got on their knees and peered beneath the hulk. They pulled out a dark shapeless thing. The flashlight shone on the bloodstained gray of the army blanket shroud.

My legs started to give way. I sat on the wreck's running board. Junior knelt beside her. His face looked older than Mama's and his hands shook so terribly the blanket flapped eerily as he struggled to unwrap her.

Railhead said hoarsely, "Helly! Stop assing around, Jack."

He reached and snatched the blanket from Junior's hands and

bared the butchered horror to the waist. Her bucked eyes were frozen in hideous terror as they stared up at Junior.

The fiend had hacked off her nose to the whitish bone of the bridge, and her lips had been raggedly slashed away to give the awful visage a grisly bloodstained grin. Where her breasts had thrust, there were blackened stumps.

I closed my eyes tightly, but I couldn't shut out the heartbreaking sight. I wanted to run. But all I could do was sit on the running board rocking and crying. Then like in a dream, I followed as Railhead and Junior carried her down the alley and put her in the car trunk.

As Railhead drove down the alley, he said, "Who dumped her up here?"

Sally said, "Tony had to move her out of the joint so I could work. He just stashed her until he could figure out all the angles."

Railhead said coldly, "You a dirty nigger bitch to let that peckerwood throw Bessie away like a dead dog."

Junior muttered, "One peckuhwood kilt her, an' anuthah one throwed her en th' alley."

Railhead stopped the car and cut the lights. I saw headlights moving on Thirty-third Street a hundred yards away. Railhead turned on the seat so his back was against the door as he faced Sally. His arm came up, and his pistol was pointed at the side of Sally's head.

He said, "Bitch, look at this."

She turned her head and squinted her left eye that Railhead had lumped nearly shut.

He shoved the pistol's muzzle against her forehead and said, "I'm gonna' pull this trigger if you try to play any stuff on me. Where is your old man?"

Sally said, "I don't know. Honest, I don't!"

Railhead said, "He's gonna' cop your scratch. Where? When?"

Sally didn't answer. The pistol made a clicking sound like the cylinder was in motion.

Sally blurted, "He picks me up at the joint after the bars close. What are you going to do?"

Railhead ignored her and drove in silence to Prairie Avenue. He parked several doors from the basement apartment. The street was still except for an occasional passing car and a few drunks staggering from Thirty-first Street.

It was scary the pitiful way Sally begged Railhead and Junior not to hurt Tony and the rigid way they sat like under a hellish spell until daybreak.

A white Caddie convertible with the top down swept by and double-parked in front of the basement joint. It was Tony. He glanced toward the basement and hit three short blasts on the Caddie's horn. Then he leaned back and lit a cigarette.

Junior croaked, "Whut we gonna do, Rail?"

Railhead said, "He's gotta' heater. We gonna' tee roll him. Take your kicks off and come behind the bastard while I'm talking shit to him."

Junior took off his shoes and eased from the car. He crept on hands and knees to the side of a car parked just ahead of the Buick and crouched tensely on the curb. Railhead leaned forward and looked intently into Sally's face. She opened her mouth to say something.

He tapped the barrel of the pistol against her cheekbone and said, "Chump bitch, you don't wanta die for the peckerwood."

She shook her head.

He said, "Climb across me and stand by the door. Call that motherfucker down here and cut me into him as a vine connection. You get slick out there or try to split and I'll put another hole in your ass."

Sally climbed out and stood facing Tony's Caddie.

She shouted, "Daddy! Here I am, back here."

Tony looked back, and the Caddie came roaring toward us in reverse. It screeched to a stop abreast of the Buick. Junior darted out of sight toward the front of the car ahead. Tony, hatless and immaculate in a cream-colored suit, leaned across the seat and flung open the car door.

Sally said, "Daddy, this Westside stud wants to rap to you about copping some vines."

A look of annoyance creased Tony's handsome face.

He said, "Forget it, baby. Get in the car."

Sally turned away and looked at Railhead. Railhead stuck his head out with a big grin on his face and said, "Man, I'm hip you pretty and pimping a zillion. But helly, you don't have to go ninety on ugly-ass Railhead. I been knowing Sally and Bessie way before they was whores. I got Hickey Freemans your size in that trunk that you ain't gonna believe at a double dime."

Tony smiled thinly and slid across the seat to the street. He took a cigarette from a gold lighter case and stepped to the Buick's front door that Railhead had half opened. He lit the cigarette and held out the case to Railhead. Railhead shook his head and started out of the car.

Sally screamed, "Look out, Daddy! He's got a gun!"

Tony backpedaled and pawed desperately at his breast pocket. Railhead was aiming his pistol at Tony's chest when Tony's leg shot out and kicked the pistol from Railhead's hand.

I heard it clatter beneath the car. Junior was a blur as he streaked toward Tony's back who had finally freed a small black automatic.

Sally screamed, "Behind you!" just as Junior brutally smashed the blackjack down on the top of Tony's head and pinned his arms to his sides in a bear hug.

The automatic bounced to the pavement. Railhead got the butcher knife off the Buick's front seat. He grinned at Sally cringing against the side of the Caddie.

He pranced over and stared at Tony struggling feebly in Junior's bear hug. Then in a sudden terrible backhand he stabbed the heavy blade in and jerked it across Tony's belly.

Tony belched a gout of blood over Junior's hands, locked across his chest. Junior dropped his arms away and walked dazedly toward a wide-eyed knot of black people in pajamas and robes huddled on the sidewalk.

Tony stood reeling and looking down at his ripped belly. His entrails were oozing from the long slash in his trousers front like curly red eels from a ragged fishnet. He had a puzzled look on his chalk white face like perhaps he wasn't convinced they were his own guts. He shuddered and scooped his palms underneath the glistening nest. He was trying to stuff it back inside himself when he collapsed and fell flat on his back.

I got out of the car and went to Junior on the sidewalk. Sally was kneeling beside Tony and weeping. Railhead leaned on the Buick's front fender and stared stonily at her. There was the sorrowful cry of sirens, and then seemingly suddenly the police descended.

Junior left the sidewalk and walked toward two black cops in uniform who were looking at Tony and shaking their heads.

Junior held out his bloody hands pleadingly as he whined, "Ah ain't knowed he wuz out tu sho nuff kill th' peckahwood."

Railhead, handcuffed and in the grip of two towering white cops, snarled, "Dummy up, cunt! It was self-defense."

I slipped through the crowd and caught a jitney cab at Thirty-first Street and Indiana Avenue to Forty-seventh Street. I made it to Papa's rooming house where I was hysterical and thoughtlessly blurted out everything about Bessie and Junior.

I knew I had made a mistake when I saw how grey Papa's face got and how he shook like he had palsy. Soldier gave me and Papa a sedative and put us to bed. Then he went to contact Mama and to help her with the tragedies of Bessie and Junior.

Bessie's funeral was held in the chapel at the funeral home, and it cost Mama less than two hundred dollars with most of it on credit. Mama cried, but she didn't lose control like she had at Carol's funeral.

Papa collapsed at the chapel and couldn't go to the cemetery. Soldier composed and delivered the eulogy. I cried harder after he'd said the beautifully poignant things about Bessie than I did at the grave.

Soldier looked like a magnificent Indian chief as he stood at the lectern and said, "Bessie Tilson, she was in her early pretty teens the first time I saw her. She was a good girl, fresh from a Mississippi plantation.

"Old big evil Chicago had excited her though. I remember the wild music in the little girl laughter. And now that she's no longer pretty and lies here dead, I can remember a sad thing about her in life.

"I remember that no matter how gay and happy she seemed to be, there was always a shadow—a little girl lost look in her eyes.

"She was starved for love and affection like everyone must be who has been denied Mama's bosom. She sought them in the jungle and found death.

"Perhaps like the multitude of trapped black females she drank to push back the awful walls of despair and loneliness. I know that whenever I hear a young girl's bubbly laughter, I'll remember Bessie and that little girl lost look in her eyes.

"She's gone and left the flashy dresses and men she loved so much. She's escaped the torment of that dark world where innocence is reviled and evil applauded.

"Perhaps her mischievous spirit is somewhere way out there in the blue of heaven watching us saying good-bye to her here and laughing with that long-ago music in her voice and with a little girl 'found' look in her eyes."

12

A DOLL FELLA FOR DORCAS

I visited Papa at least three times a week after Bessie's funeral. He had started to cheat on his strict no-sweets, low-fat diet, and he looked drawn and weak.

Soldier told me Papa was even drinking wine again and often had to be reminded to take his insulin shots. Soldier told me that somebody at Bessie's funeral had inadvertently let Papa know about Carol while extending sympathy.

Railhead and Junior went to trial for first-degree murder in Criminal Court, several weeks before Christmas in 1940. Their lawyers from the public defender's office advised them to plead guilty and avoid the electric chair.

The black lawyer for Junior explained to Mama that with a hostile witness like Sally for the prosecution it was foolhardy to buck the white folks.

They took the lawyers' advice and each drew sentences of 99 years in Joliet Penitentiary. Grief-stricken Ida Jackson, Junior's girlfriend, was drunk and called the prosecutor a dirty motherfucker in court. She got thirty days.

I was in a Criminal Court's corridor with Mama after the

sentencing. She was really in a bad way, what with Bessie's death, the tension of Junior's trial and then the shock of the sentence. Mama was wailing and clutching at Junior's lawyer. She just couldn't understand why Junior got such a stiff sentence since he had no prior record and Tony had been a pimp.

Finally, the harassed lawyer jerked himself free and said angrily, "Damn it, Mrs. Tilson. You should be bright enough to know why he got the book thrown at him. He helped to kill a white man in Chicago. He's lucky he didn't get the chair."

The chain of violence and tragedy that had claimed three of the Tilsons locked around Papa less than a week after the New Year of 1941 came in.

Papa had crawled behind a pile of junk furniture in a storage room in the basement of his rooming house and died of diabetic coma. He was found with an almost empty quart bottle of cheap muscatel wine.

Soldier was convinced Papa had hidden himself away from the possibility of taking or being given his lifesaving insulin shots.

Soldier notified Papa's father who had disowned Papa when he married Mama. The old man sent money to a Southside mortuary to prepare the body and ship it down South.

For weeks I moved about like a sleepwalker. I avoided Mama as much as I could. It was sickening the way she hugged me and sweet-talked me and tried to alibi away the evil things I had seen her do.

The sharp hurt in what had happened to the twins, Junior and Papa dulled as the year 1941 staggered by.

I took an interest in school and the library I had never had before. Most of the time I could keep sad things off my mind and not be lonely. But between midnight and dawn, I often awoke screaming out of nightmares about Carol's baby and Bessie's butchered body.

A few days before the attack at Pearl Harbor, Connie, our land-lady suffered her second stroke. Hattie Greene was dressing Mama's hair for a visit to Junior. She was telling her about how Connie was lying helpless in her house down the street.

Hattie said, "Sedalia, I knocked and knocked on her front door to pay my rent early yesterday morning. I went to the back door and saw her through the glass lying on the kitchen floor in all her clothes.

"Her funny eyes were wide open looking at me, but I thought she was dead because she wasn't moving her body at all. I was turning away when I saw the dirty bitch move her eyes. I realized she was paralyzed.

"A few minutes ago I went and peeped at her, and she ain't moved a peg. She abused and robbed black people all her life. She'll be dead and stinking before I help her."

Mama and Hattie recounted Connie's bad deeds and laughed about her plight until I got a headache and went to bed. I lay there long after Mama had gone to bed. I tossed about, alternately worried and angry. I worried about Connie lying crippled and all alone in the darkness.

I got angry with myself for worrying about her when I knew so well how crooked and rotten she was. But what could I do to help her? She was probably locked in. And even if I got in some way, I couldn't lift her or anything.

My kid's mind kept busy. I thought, *It's no use. Mama and everybody in the block hate her. If I help her, they'll hate me too.*

Finally, I argued myself out of bed and into my clothes. I eased out the back door with the intention of calling a hospital or the police about Connie.

I realized when I reached the deserted street that it was close to two A.M. and I couldn't wake up anybody to make a phone call for Connie, and I didn't have a nickel to use a pay phone blocks away.

I walked by Connie's dark house several times before I got the courage to go down the walk to the rear of the house. I went across the screened sun porch to the kitchen door. I peered through the door glass. In the dimness I saw a dark form that could have been Connie sprawled on the bright-colored linoleum. My hand trembled as I twisted the doorknob. The door was open.

I stepped inside, and the stink of feces bombed my nose. I stood at the door and tried to see a light switch. Then I noticed a tall refrigerator near the form on the floor. I went gingerly to it and swung open the door.

Light leaped and spotlighted Connie's hard pale face. Her round bird-of-prey eyes seemed to glow with vivid blue light as they stared up into mine unblinkingly. She was drooling from the corner of her tiny mean mouth.

I looked at her cruel face and remembered Woodrow Spears, the little black guy she had cheated, and how she'd called Carl, the cop, and his buddy to cave in Woodrow's skull.

I scowled and started to step around her to leave. I stopped cold. She was rolling and crossing her eyes frantically. It was strange and weird to see the sweat pop out on her face as she desperately manipulated her eyes to plead for my help.

I went through a doorway into the dining room. I flipped a wall light switch and looked about for a phone. I walked into the living room and turned on a table lamp. There was a phone on a table at the end of a sofa.

I sat down and thumbed through a memo book. I saw the office and home phone numbers for a Doctor Holzman. I woke him at home and told him about Connie.

He asked who I was and would I stay until he came. I told him the back door was unlocked and hung up. I took a hassock to the kitchen and propped up Connie's head and shoulders. She sipped a little water through a glass iced tea straw.

Before I left, I said, "Your doctor is coming. Please, please, don't tell anybody it was me that helped you."

I got back into the flat and out of my clothes without waking Mama. I stood outside her bedroom and listened to her snoring. I thought about how much she hated white people and especially

Connie and how she'd get so furious she'd have to massage her chest if she had known I'd called Connie's doctor.

Then I got the realization that for the first time in my life I had been brave enough to defy her and had gotten away with it. I was dizzy with the thrill of it, and I felt like I was going to burst in exhilaration.

I went to the front window and watched for Connie's doctor. True to the extinct wonder of the good old days, he was there inside of twenty minutes. And within another twenty minutes Connie was being trundled into an ambulance. She passed away a week later and the whole block was ecstatic.

The hoopla and hysteria of the Second World War seemed to compress time. I was sixteen years old and graduated from McKinley High School in 1944. I liked casual clothes and dressed up salads. Girls were wild about me, but I never met one that really moved me.

I dropped them quickly and rushed desperately to a new one hoping to discover a steady sweetheart. Almost all of my sexual contacts with girls were fiascos. I either failed to get hard or I couldn't stay hard long enough to ejaculate.

I loved to get ravishing in drag and pick up studs on those rare occasions when I got high on gin. Guys really turned me on. I thrilled to the drunken core when they sodomized me and I could suck them off.

This recklessly freakish creature that surfaced I named Sally in contemptible memory of the "come dump" that had led big dumb Bessie to ruin.

Mama and I got along fine, that is, as long as I didn't let it slip that I had a mind of my own and that I wasn't preciously cuddlesome and adorable Sweet Pea.

Back in 1942, Prophet Twelve Powers caught a term in the federal penitentiary at Leavenworth, Kansas, for using the mail to defraud.

Mama proved right away that the midnight trysts in the lair of the sorcerer had been made with much more than sensual intent. He left her with a practicing knowledge of his craft and a bountiful stock of oils, candles, incense, dream books and, of course, enemy destruct powder.

Mama was, naturally, happy to quit slaving for the hated white folks who often forgot her name and addressed her "hey, girl."

As Madame Miracle she was respected by her many clients who sought her good-luck products and counsel. After I finished high school, I worked full time with Mama. I answered the phone and received her clients from twelve noon to eight P.M. five days a week.

Mama was deadly serious in the role. She stopped using makeup altogether, and wore only loose-fitting long black robes. She wore her hair straight back and pulled into a neat bun at the back of the head.

I helped her as much as I could with grammar and reading. She helped herself until daybreak on countless occasions. She lost nearly all of her draggy Southern accent, and seldom made a glaring grammatical error in conversation.

She had enough money saved in 1944 to put down a sizable sum toward the purchase of the building where we lived.

Hattie Greene, Railhead's mother and the rest of the longtime tenants had moved away. Mama had a public image of dignity and wisdom. On the surface she seemed self-confident, free of inner turmoil, even happy.

But many late nights I heard her pacing the flat for hours from living room to kitchen. I guess terrible guilt about Papa, the twins and Junior was festering inside her.

Just to escape the possessive pressure of Mama's presence I went to a birthday party around the middle of May in 1945. I had turned seventeen on April 5 of the year.

The celebration was on the Southside at Fifty-sixth Street and South Parkway Boulevard. Ray, the guest of honor, was a horny young guy who had been in my gym class in school. Several times he accidentally pressed himself against me in the shower.

Ray's folks had gone to Wisconsin for the weekend, and there were a dozen teenage girls and guys smoking pot and drinking wine when I got to the party around two P.M.

I didn't go for the pot. I nipped a little wine.

The wine was cheap. The apartment was hot and funky. And the guys and girls had evenly paired off with each other. Ray was stoned slobbery and sure he was for me.

I slipped away to the street. I went down the Boulevard to Fifty-fifth Street. I went into a drugstore on Fifty-fifth Street and Prairie Avenue. I sat on a stool at the fountain and sipped an icy glass of lemonade.

A moment later a powerfully built regal-looking girl with velvety, ebony skin and a shining cloud of blue black hair swirling about her shoulders, floated in and sat on the stool next to me.

She ordered a Coke. She was pure class in a rich black silk dress and short white gloves on hands shaped startlingly liked Carol's. She was the most elegant girl I'd ever been so close to.

I felt untidy and sweaty in my limp clothes. Several times I stole quick glances at her in the mirror behind the counter. I almost fainted because each time her big black luminous eyes seemed to be staring hypnotically into mine.

She fascinated me and I wanted to get acquainted, but I couldn't think of one thing to say.

A husky old black guy about forty, in sharp clothes, peered through the window. He came in and walked past. He came back and leaned over to whisper something to the girl.

She jerked her head away and ignored him. He turned and glared at me. I stood up and glared at him and went to the jukebox at the end of the counter. I punched Billy Eckstein's "Cottage For Sale" and went toward my stool.

I stopped cold. The dapper nuisance was sitting sideways on my stool flapping his mouth to the girl who was still ignoring him.

And I saw a pulpy growth behind an ear—a prizefighter's

cauliflower! I stood angry and frustrated. I thought, *I'm quick and strong, but what can I do with even an old prizefighter? Maybe I'll just walk out and forget the whole thing.*

Billy Eckstein started singing, and the girl turned her head and smiled at me. I walked slowly past several people eating at the counter. I was looking for a knife or an equalizer of some kind for the nuisance on my stool.

I had to show that classy girl I had some kind of manhood. The waitress stooped down behind the counter for something.

I scooped a red pepper shaker off the counter and screwed the top off. I palmed the shaker and walked up to the pug. I stood beside him. He glanced at me and went on with his monologue.

I said, "I want my stool."

He sighed wearily and said, "G'wan shitass, before I put some knots on your bead."

He put a knobby hand on the girl's arm, and she pulled away. She looked up at me and started to get up. I was excited and scared.

I said loudly, "Leave her alone. Get off my stool."

He stood up grinning and looking down the counter like he had forgotten about me. I jumped back when his grin faded and I saw his jacket twitch at the bicep.

I felt a zephyr as the roundhouse went by. He was off balance with his head down when almost in one motion I hurled the contents of the shaker up into his face and kicked him between the legs.

He fell to the floor rolling and howling and alternately clutching at his crotch and eyes. The waitress screamed and rushed toward the phone booth.

My legs almost gave way as I went out the door behind the chic Amazon. I saw her big shapely legs flashing down Fifty-fifth Street toward a red car parked at the curb. I started toward her but changed my mind and went up Prairie Avenue with the intention of catching an El train at Fifty-eighth Street.

I was at Fifty-sixth Street when the Amazon pulled up in a '41 maroon Mercury sedan and pushed open the passenger door. I got in.

She pulled down Prairie Avenue and said, "I'm Dorcas Reed. You were wonderful. Who are you?"

I just sat there and stared at her. I was thunderstruck. The voice! Her voice, like her hands, was so much like Carol's.

She snapped her fingers playfully before my eyes and said, "Wake up, pretty. I like you. Who are you?"

I mumbled, "Swee . . I mean Otis, Otis Tilson. Your voice reminded me of someone."

She laughed and said, "Uh-oh! That's my luck. I run myself ragged to save you from the cops, and your heart is bleeding for someone else."

I noticed she was passing Fifty-eighth Street, but I had lost interest in the El station.

I said, "I'm not in misery. You reminded me of my sister. She's dead."

She said softly, "I am so sorry."

She reached Sixtieth Street and turned left toward South Parkway.

She said, "I thought you were behind me when I went to the car. I was really upset when I didn't see you, and I thought I wasn't going to be given a chance to help you after what you did."

I said, "I'm sorry that crazy guy forced me to do what I did. But I'm glad you came looking for me."

She crossed the boulevard and parked inside cool Washington Park. She closed her eyes and rested the back of her head on the top of the seat.

She said dreamily, "I have loved this park since I was a toddler. Mother was alive then and brought me here to escape the tumult and ugliness of the Southside.

"I am sure thousands of black kids would never see a flower in bloom or see a robin if there were no Washington Park."

I scrutinized every plane in her magnificently strong face. And I gazed at the long shapely, almost boyish leanness of her thighs against the dress silk. I had never before been so excited by a girl . . . or a boy.

I slid across the seat toward her. She smiled and kept her eyes closed. I gently caressed her temple and throat with my fingertips.

She crooned, "Ooeee, pretty fella. You have a touch. But then I'll bet your steady little sweetie thinks so too."

I whispered in her ear, "I don't have one. But I bet you have a steady guy."

She opened her eyes and said, "I have been engaged to a fella since I was ten years old. He's in the army overseas."

My heart fell.

I said, "So you're the one in misery?"

She said, "I am not. I miss him and worry about him because we've been such dear friends and he's in a combat zone. I might even love him in a mild low-voltage way."

She paused, frowned thoughtfully, then smiled wickedly and said, "But a girl like me wants to feel carnal about her fella."

She shivered in mock ecstasy and said, "You get what I mean?"

I nodded.

Then she said, "Our families always have been extremely close for as long as I can remember. It has always been unthinkable to them that Ralph and I would marry anyone except each other. Dad idolizes Ralph."

I said, "What is Ralph like? How does he look?"

She opened her bag and took out a billfold. She handed me a color snapshot. The guy was gorgeous! He was stripped to brief swim trunks and had apparently just emerged from the sun-dappled water behind him.

He was more than six feet of sleek muscled café-au-lait toned, beautiful brute. Suddenly I felt so scrawny and weak, and the photograph shook in my hand as I dropped it in her lap

I looked away at a gang of kids having a water fight and said, "He's a big handsome guy. He's got fabulous muscles and everything."

She said, "I can't imagine any girl with my handicaps who wouldn't be frothing at the mouth with anxiety to marry him."

I turned toward her and said, "What handicaps? I think you're beautiful!"

She moved her serious face close and looked at me intently.

I gazed into her enormous black liquid eyes and said, "You're beautiful, Dorcas. I wish I had met you a long time ago."

She threw an arm around my shoulder and drew me close. I lay my head on the plush hot pillow of her bosom.

Her voice broke with emotion as she crooned huskily, "You are the tenderest, sweetest, prettiest doll fella alive."

We talked and clung to each other until hoodlum night black-jacked day away. I remember that she wanted to drive me home. But I refused because I was afraid for her to pass through the treacherous Westside alone on her way back home.

She took me to the Fifty-eighth Street El station and stood on the platform with me until my train came. The scent of her Channel No. 5 lingered on my clothes and skin. My brain spun on a wild, fragrant, merry-go-round all the way home.

The moment I put my foot in the flat Mama led me into the living room that was done up in sparkling white and gold to impress her clients.

Mama had a palm pressed over her heart. She caught her breath and said, "Some girl—or woman—named Dorcas Reed called a minute ago for you, and I almost had a heart attack. She sounded like Carol. Where did you meet her?"

I lied, "At the party, Mama. At the party."

Mama rolled her eyes at me and said, "Sweet Pea, don't you dare be impatient with me. I've been on this tricky earth much longer than you, and I'm going to protect you. How old is she?"

I struggled to keep my irritation from showing.

I said, "She's nineteen and statuesque."

Mama frowned and said, "She's what?"

I said, "She's tall like Bessie was except her feet are small and her hands are delicately tapered and shaped like Carol's were. And Mama, her face is fiercely beautiful. Her nostrils flare, and her eyes glow like she could murder someone—or make love to him. The strange thing about her is that she thinks she's ugly."

Mama said, "She's probably right about that. Sweet Pea, that girl is older and more experienced than you are. How does she live? Is she kept by a jealous man that would put you in the grave?"

I laughed and said, "Mama, she's a big shot. At least her father is. He owns a funeral home on upper State Street, and she helps him with everything from embalming to conducting a funeral. Mama, she's smart and classy."

Mama rose abruptly from the white satin sofa and stood for a moment with her eyes closed as she pressed her palms against her temples like she was treating a bad headache. Then she opened her eyes and stared at me with an expression of extreme commiseration on her face.

She said softly, "Sweet Pea, don't you get your heart broken. A slum fellow like you don't have a chance with a girl like that. Her father will see to it. If anyone despises poor niggers more than the dirty white folks, it's so-called high class niggers like him. Sweet Pea, please promise Mama you will forget her so they can't hurt you."

I said passionately, "Mama, I read that a young guy my age should be in training to become a man. Mama, stop putting pressure on me and protecting me.

"Mama, I wish I had gotten a bloody nose or a bust in the mouth at least once when I was a kid. Give me a break, Mama, and a little air.

"Listen to me, Mama, and if you love me, please understand what I'm trying to say. Mama, help me! I'm hurting and I'm scared. I'm running as fast as I can. But Mama, I can't escape because something like a bitch dog is hot inside me, filthy, freakish and itching for guys.

"Mama, sometimes I get so scared and my chest fills and hurts until I feel like I'm going to explode. I went to that party today to get away from you and your pressure and protection.

"My other reason was I had a queer passion for the guy who gave the party. Mama, I'm sitting here hurting because I know that if he had played me right and not gotten stupid drunk, he could have used me like a whore.

"Mama, don't tell me to leave Dorcas alone. She's the only girl I ever met that could be important to me. I need her, Mama! If it doesn't work out maybe it will be like a bust in the mouth I've needed to prove to myself I can take it like a man."

Mama said, "You hurt me, Sweet Pea, when you said you left me to get away from me and that you needed her . . . a stranger. But Sweet Pea, I forgive you because I love you.

"Sweet Pea, love, honor and appreciate your mama and make me happy like a man would and you will never be a man lover. I won't tell you to drop that girl anymore. But it can't work with her, Honey Pie. You'll find out, middle-class niggers are snakes."

Mama kissed me on the forehead and went to bed. I sat looking out the front window and thinking about Dorcas and her father and what she had said about Ralph.

Then I remembered a word unfamiliar to me that she had used to describe how she desired to feel toward her man. I got a dictionary and because I only knew the word phonetically it took a while to locate "carnal."

I read the lengthy definition and sank back weakly on the sofa. I thought, *Dorcas is fuckish as hell. She wants to fuck me! But I didn't even get a little hard when we were together.*

I spent all that time with a big beautiful sexy female, and I never had a thought that she might have had something marvelous between her legs.

Maybe I have already changed into a goddamn cock-sucking faggot. Then I thought, *Perhaps I was bombed numb in my crotch by the first sight of her in the drugstore. I guess I had the kind of awed adoration for her that an old rich kook has for a precious one-of-a-kind work of art.*

I'll be all right. I'm out of the trance now. I don't have any reason to doubt myself. She called me. She's crazy about my face.

I wish I could screw my head onto a body like that gorgeous sonuv-abitch Ralph has. He's probably fucked Dorcas a thousand times since they were kids.

I wonder why she lost that carnal feeling for him? And if she never had it, was it because his dick was too big or too small or he stank or picked his nose?

Then she could be lying about the way she feels about him to string stray guys like me along while she's waiting for Ralph to come back.

I know one thing for sure, if I can't get hard for her, then I can't get hard for girls, period. I'll be in terrible trouble, because I feel my chest aching just thinking that I might fail.

Suppose she's got an odd cunt, and her main thrill spot is not on top, but six inches deeper than my tiny dick can reach. I wish there was no sex pressure with her. I could just gaze at her and caress her and worship her forever.

But, I'll be great with her in bed. I'm certain I will. A real tiger, that's what I'll be. Too bad I've got that bitch Sally still inside me to make things tricky. Maybe I better stall off sex with Dorcas as long as I can.

The phone jangled me out of my reverie. It was Dorcas, and she called to make sure I was home safely and hadn't forgotten that Saturday night coming was ours together. And hadn't I told her I was twenty years old? After I hung up, I wondered if Mama had told Dorcas that I was only seventeen.

I thought our Saturday night would never come. But it did, and I went to the Southside early to visit Soldier before my date with Dorcas.

He still lived in the same rooming house where Papa had died. Soldier was jolly and looked much thinner, but well.

I was surprised when he told me he had been out of Veteran's Hospital less than a week where he had gone with severe stomach problems. He told me that Lockjaw Hudson and Cuckoo Red had been killed the week before in an auto accident while vacationing in Mexico.

Dorcas picked me up at the El station on Forty-seventh Street. I gave her a bunch of "glads" I picked up from a sidewalk vendor. It thrilled and excited Dorcas, like I had given her a fistful of diamonds.

We saw a stage show at the Regal Theatre, and then we went to the lakefront and parked. We sat there talking softly and watching magical stars flaming and floating in the blue blackness of Lake Michigan.

Then she started kissing me. She got hot as hell. She moaned and thrashed her thighs. She squeezed my hand. She suddenly pulled my hand between her thighs and pressed it against her cunt.

Panic and shock jerked me rigid! She wasn't wearing panties! She had creamed herself wet and slimy, and my middle finger was in "it."

I roughly snatched my hand away. The pulsation of her "thing" and "its" heavy bush of hair had had the instant effect on me that a furry animal with a wildly beating heart and wet mouth was going to bite off my finger.

Naturally in the next instant I knew this was not true. But it was too late. I had reacted negatively and violently to her body.

A headshrinker told me in later years another reason that I almost jumped out of my skin like a bumptious ass was that my finicky mind hadn't put together the delicate combination of loss of fear of failure, and of my pedestal reverence for her, and, of course, any sensual message from the brain to erect.

Dorcas looked hurt and befuddled as she drove silently away from the lakefront. I suggested food. She looked dazedly at me and nodded her head.

We went to a Chinese restaurant on Sixty-third Street. She only picked at her food. She looked out the window at the parade of giggly young couples going into a transient hotel across the street.

She said, "Sweetheart, where are we going when we leave here?"

I said too quickly, "To the El station at Cottage Grove. Mama has a touch of flu. Baby, why did you ask?"

She sighed and looked right into my eyes for a helluva long sweaty moment.

Then she said, "Darling, I am going to ask a terribly personal question. I hope in my confusion that I will not be impertinent."

She paused and tenderly cradled my hands in hers. She caressed the knuckles with her lips, and then held my hands against her cheek. My heart mauled my chest when she beamed the trillion-watt soul power of her eyes into mine.

She almost whispered, "Pretty fella, why did you recoil from that part of me which is the why and how of love and life and should surely be your most natural destination?"

I gently escaped my hands to my lap so she couldn't feel the tremors and the sudden wetness in the palms. I was beginning to feel slightly hostile because she was shooting me through hot grease.

I was surprised to hear my voice lie so clearly and smoothly, "Baby, I didn't recoil from 'it.' I admire your class, and you carry yourself like a lady. You dress like one with gloves and all. I was shocked and acted like a bumpkin when I found out that you had no panties on, and you put my hand on 'it' so suddenly."

Her eyes were getting cold, and I was desperate to think of something she'd buy.

I said, "OH! I think I know why I snatched my hand away."

She didn't say anything. She nodded.

"Baby, dear, maybe in my subconscious I was afraid to play with it or anything because I knew I couldn't stop until I had gone all the way right there in the car where a cop might show at any minute. What do you think, baby?"

She sat there staring at me and crawling her thumbs rapidly across her red lacquered fingernails.

Finally she said, "Otis, I think you ought to tell me the truth."

I held my breath. Did she suspect that in a way I was a cunt myself?

I said, "Dorcas, if there is something I haven't told you about out there at the lake, it's hidden from me. Let's be sweet and forget about it."

She went on like she hadn't heard me. "I know my body is too long and top heavy. I might even be too black. My nose is too wide and flat, and my mouth is too wide, and my lips are too thick.

"Now you be sweet and agree with me. Tell the truth and admit you never thought I was even attractive, much less beautiful. Say it!

"I am no fool. I know when a woman that a man thinks is beautiful opens and offers herself as I did to you, he takes her on the spot or the goddamn dog foams at the mouth until he can get her to a bed, any bed. Let's get the hell out of here. I've got a headache."

She drove me to the El station in silence. I got out and stood beside the car on the driver's side.

She looked up at me and said softly, "I'm sorry I lost my temper. You know this is the second time we have seen each other. I wonder if the second meeting that a man and woman have isn't really more crucial and important than the first and the last, and I wonder how often is it that the second is the last?"

She shot the Mercury away. I stood and watched it disappear down Sixty-third Street. Then I went up on the lonely El platform.

I felt like bawling when I looked down on the street. I saw lucky guys with their girls coming out of the joints hugging and kissing and going to a bed somewhere.

CHAPTER SLUM

13

THE MAGNIFICENT HARD-ON

I was disconsolate and preoccupied for a week with the fear that I had lost Dorcas. In Mama's presence, of course, I smiled and pretended that all was running smoothly with Dorcas. I didn't want her to have the satisfaction in knowing her dire prediction might be coming true.

Several times I started to call Dorcas at the funeral home where she and her father lived in an apartment on the second floor.

But because she had told me that she hadn't yet told her father about me because of his fondness for Ralph, her soldier suitor, I didn't risk calling and having her father answer the phone. And she told me her father had once practiced law, and I wasn't exactly aching to be quizzed by a pro about Dorcas and me.

By Saturday afternoon tension had pumped my chest tight with aching pressure, and freak Sally was prodding me to go in the street and get high.

Then like always when I got looped on gin, I'd go to Marion's pad on Lake Street and doll up like a sexy bitch and find some guy to break off with.

Marion was a red-haired, green-eyed white queen about twenty-five whom I had first seen in the cafe on Madison Street where Carol had worked.

Marion dressed exclusively in drag and fabulous wigs and only her close friends knew that he wasn't a woman. He held a highly responsible position at Spiegel's mail-order house and wrote salable risqué stories and articles for magazines.

He preferred to be called Lucy, and he called me Tilly. I didn't object when I was guzzling gin and wiggling my round ass in drag borrowed from Lucy.

I had decided to get out of the flat just for a bit of fresh air (a casual capitulation to Sally) when the phone rang. Life was instantly beautiful again. It was Dorcas! She had missed me and wanted to see me. Should she pick me up? No, I told her. I'll be at the Forty-seventh Street El station at eight P.M.

I left home right away so I could have time to visit with Soldier. He was in the community kitchen of his rooming house drinking whiskey with a pretty, high yellow woman in her early thirties. I was happy to see him clowning and cracking jokes like the jolly Soldier of old.

I went walking on Forty-seventh Street toward Cottage Grove Avenue killing time until eight P.M.

At Evans Avenue, I think, I heard a wild chorus of ribald laugher and saw a small group of black men and women on the sidewalk ahead. They had their backs to me and apparently were enjoying immensely the funny antics of a drunk or perhaps, I thought, old man Casey, a colorful black trainer of chickens who performed hilariously comical routines with his feathered protégées on South-side streets.

I reached the excitement and peered through an opening in the spectators. It wasn't funny. It was a death struggle.

A short, muscular young guy wearing a soldier's dress khakis was sitting astride the belly of a middle-aged, dark brown-skinned man dressed in the uniform of the Chicago Police Department.

A glistening red rill on his close-cropped skull leaked blood down the side of the young guy's maniacal face. His powerful hands gripped the ends of the cop's necktie and steadily tightened the noose until the cop's protruding eyeballs oscillated madly and his purple tongue lapped his chin.

A man in the crowd shouted, "Croak him, buddy! Send that dirty motherfucker to the cemetery!"

I plucked at the sleeve of an old guy on a cane in front of me and said excitedly, "Mister! He's going to kill him! Why don't they stop him?"

He turned his seamed face toward me and said, "Son, that nigger gittin' kilt is Beeman. He busted black folks' heads and shot for nuthin' but heads and guts for years.

"He slipped up behind that soldier and busted his head for talking to a woman he's sweet on. Ain't nobody gonna stop Beeman from gittin' kilt, jes' like that Indian Joe up on Fifty-first Street.

"I don't feel nuthin' for Beeman, and other dirty treacherous niggers with badges killin' and cripplin' they own kind for the white man."

I had to turn away because Beeman was unconscious on the sidewalk, and the GI was stomping Beeman's face into a mushy scarlet mask. And the joyful squeals of the women and the vulgar applause in the men's laughter rode eerily on the balmy May air as I fled the carnage.

I reached the El station twenty minutes late for my date with Dorcas. I saw the Mercury parked a few yards away. I went and found it unlocked. I got in and waited.

In less than five minutes I saw Dorcas leave the drugstore on the corner at Prairie Avenue and Forty-seventh Street.

I saw her lurch when she stepped off the curb. She stopped and looked down at the back of her foot or leg. I got out and went to her. She wasn't hurt, but she had broken off the high heel of her shoe.

She limped on one tiptoe to the car. She decided to go home and change her shoes. I volunteered to have coffee or something on Forty-seventh Street until she got back. She insisted that I go along.

She parked on State Street almost a half block from the funeral home. Shortly after, a tall, brown-skinned guy in a blue business suit came down the sidewalk with a short black guy from the direction of the funeral home behind me.

They stopped beside the car parked in front of the Mercury. They had an animated chat, and then they shook hands. The short guy got in the car and pulled away.

The tall guy started up the sidewalk toward me. I had switched my attention to an unlucky guy across the street fixing a flat tire whose jack buckled, dropping the rear of his car with a resounding whoomph.

So I was startled to hear a loud, officious voice blast my ear from the sidewalk side, "Well, who are you?"

I turned and looked full into the arrogant face of the tall guy bending over glaring at me through the open window frame.

I said snappishly, "Why?"

He sucked his front teeth noisily.

He swept his sleepy maroon eyes up and down State Street and said ponderously, "Because I am the . . . legally . . . registered owner of the vehicle in which you sit."

Suddenly I knew who the pompous bastard was and why his eyes had swept State Street. He was Dorcas's ex-mouthpiece father, and he was cop happy. And he was getting thrills shooting me through hot grease.

I said, "My name is Otis, and I'm waiting for Dorcas, Mr. Reed."

He snickered and said, "I would prefer your last name for the purpose of the moment. You do have one?"

He was rattling me. As a result, inadvertently, I kissed his black, lousy, middle-class ass.

I replied too quickly and too respectfully, "Yes, sir! It's Tilson, Mr. Reed."

He screwed his face into puzzled agony and said archly, "We are not acquainted with any Tilsons. Where did you meet Miss Reed?"

I said with a mocking, sadiddy, middle crust nigger accent, "I met Dorcas . . . I saw Dorcas for the first time in the dining area of an apothecary on Garfield Boulevard."

He sputtered, "You mean . . . are you implying she let you pick her up? And how do you justify your insolent persistence in referring to Miss Reed by her first name?"

I said nastily, "I'm telling you that I let Dorcas pick me up. I guess Dorcas introduced herself by her first name because she is not a phony and she was grateful.

"A pugilist waxed carnal insisted that Dorcas let him do an indecent act. I kicked him between the legs and took flight. Dorcas picked me up in this car, and we got acquainted. She's the sweetest and most beautiful girl I ever met."

His eyes narrowed, and he looked cunning. I turned my head and looked out the rear window to see if Dorcas might be coming down the sidewalk to pull me out of the hot grease.

He said, "Miss Reed has to mind things until I get back. We have time to understand each other. Do you know about Ralph Duncan and his family?"

I was getting angry.

I said, "Dorcas told me about them."

He snickered again and said, "He's going to be my son-in-law soon."

I said, "I doubt it. Dorcas may disappoint you. She confides in me. I don't think he's that important to her any more."

He sucked his front teeth hard and said, "Goddamnit! Don't you talk to me that way. What would a jitterbug know about my personal life?

"Ralph and his family are important to me, and what is important to me is important to my daughter. His father's insurance firm handled four million dollars in new policies last year. What the hell did your old man turn over last year?"

I said, "Nothing; he's dead."

He said, "Before what did he do?"

I started to lie and say that Papa had been an engineer or a doctor, but I thought, *Dorcas is real, and she's in my corner. I'm not going to do a dance for this phony pot of shit.* I got out of his car and stood on the sidewalk.

I said boldly, "We chopped and picked cotton in Mississippi, and he shoveled snow and did porter work up North. Why?"

He cut an eye up the sidewalk toward his funeral home. I looked and saw Dorcas coming down the sidewalk toward us.

He turned and smiled toothsomely in her direction, and then from the side of his mouth he hissed venomously, "Stay away from my daughter. I don't want her associating with low-life cotton-picking niggers from Mississippi."

I remembered what Mama had said about him. And I realized that he wanted Dorcas to think all was well between us. I saw the opportunity to blast his ass off with impunity. But just in case he blew his cool, I moved out of range so he couldn't punch me in the mouth or something.

Then I smiled sweetly at Dorcas twenty feet away and stage whispered, "Kiss my cotton-picking ass, Snake. You phony nigger motherfucker, I'm going to marry her."

I was still smiling when Dorcas reached us. The nigger aristocrat had turned gray and sucked his front teeth desperately. Dorcas was heavenly in a fresh diaphanous pink dress with pink satin pumps. I couldn't resist visualizing myself in a similar costume.

Dorcas beamed up into his tense face and said, "Cecil, don't look so annoyed. You should know I didn't simply walk out and leave things. Lee came back from the coroner's office and took me off the hook. I see you two have met."

I said, "Yes, Dorcas, and he's a great guy."

Cecil constructed a grotesque smile and mumbled something that sounded like . . . "nice young fellow."

He extended a sinewy hand, and in the distracting presence of Dorcas I thoughtlessly held out my hand. His paw seized it in a lightning quick pincer and crushed tears to my eyes.

In the glow of the street lamp I saw the muscles in his heavy wrist cording. He was saying nice things about me and grinning at Dorcas behind me as he went on torturing me.

My left hand was buried in my trouser pocket frantically trying to open the needlepoint blade of an inch-long miniature knife. Cecil was putting so much pressure on my hand I was getting faint.

Finally the midget blade opened. I brought it out in my palm. Cecil said hello to an elderly lady who passed us and stopped to chat with Dorcas. I aimed the little razor-sharp stiletto at a fat, pulsing artery in the fleshy web between his thumb and index finger and viciously plunged it in.

He stiffened and freed my aching hand. He held his wounded hand stiffly at his side and stole a surreptitious glance at the dark dots speckling the sidewalk.

He looked down at me with insensate hatred and rammed his stabbed hand into his trouser pocket. He abruptly stepped past us and almost bowled over the elderly lady hobbling down the sidewalk in his frantic wake as he pumped his long legs urgently toward the funeral home.

Dorcas turned and watched him with a puzzled look on her face and shook her head. We got in the car and pulled away. Cecil's nerve-mangling handshake had lasted only a few seconds. But my hand was hurting and throbbing like he had tortured me for hours.

She frowned and said, "Cecil acted so peculiarly. Surprisingly, he seemed to approve of you. So it wasn't that. I don't understand him tonight."

I said, "Baby, he probably remembered something that had to be done right away. A big shot guy like him is bound to have sudden emergencies in his life. I wouldn't worry about it, darling."

She gave me a searching look, but she didn't say anything. We went to the Music Box on Sixty-third Street and had several bottles of beer. Then we went for a ride all the way to the Thirties.

My heart leaped when she drove down Thirty-first Street and passed the corner at Indiana Avenue. I remembered that night Railhead and Junior spotted Sally and stalked her and forced her to show us Bessie's butchered corpse.

Near South Parkway we passed a storefront Holiness Church. A portly black woman was going inside. We got a brief glimpse of frantic pandemonium and heard the raw rhythm of ecstatic feet and tambourines.

Dorcas pulled to the curb and said, "Let's go in for a few minutes."

We went into the oven heat and sat on metal chairs in rear. The long room was packed with swaying, sweating, shouting enemies of Satan.

A dozen black women grimacing in orgiastic bliss danced voluptuously in the funky aisle. They cast torrid eyes up at a gigantic picture of a lustful, blue-eyed, golden-haired Christ hung high on the wall behind the shrewd-faced woman minister standing calmly in her battered pulpit and gazing blandly down on the licentious presence of the Holy Ghost and The Fire.

As we walked to the car I thought, *I wonder how many fanatically religious black women like those back there close their eyes in sex with their black husbands and sweethearts and imagine that their adored, dazzling, white Christ has made an especial divine visitation so their Jim-Crowed black cunts can host his pristine, pink prick.*

While driving up South Parkway Boulevard, Dorcas said, "I suggested that we go in that church. Frankly, I went out of curiosity and perhaps callously to be entertained.

"I am not especially religious. I'm afraid that I didn't give your feelings a thought when I dragged you in there like we were going to a circus. You might have deep feelings about religion. I hope you weren't offended."

I laughed and said, "I believed in all that jazz, and it was important to me when I was a little kid down on the plantation and my Papa preached from-the-heart gospel.

"Papa was like a saint all his life. I can't think of one hateful thing he ever did. But, baby, devout Papa didn't have God in his corner. Before Papa crawled away to die, my heart would break listening to him praying for a job—just for a chance to feed and shelter his family so he could hold onto his manhood and self-respect.

"Then I saw that corrupt pastor of Mama's church living in the lap of luxury. I could never understand why God failed Papa, who loved him, and rewarded the crook.

"Then I realized that sweet, good people like my sister Carol were punished too. When I went to grammar school, I used to pass a house where an old, old man sat on the front porch in nice weather.

"Many times I saw an old woman fussing around him to make him comfortable. One day I heard older kids say that the old man had killed the old woman who was his daughter and the only friend he had in the world. Then he killed himself.

"He had done a terrible thing like that without any reason except that he was past a hundred years old and had become senile and lost his judgment.

"I remember how I first started wondering if God was like the old man. Maybe he had just grown so old he didn't realize he was doing horrible things to good people who loved him. Maybe God had had his awful lucid moment and was overcome with guilt at the infinite carnage and heartbreak he had wrought even among innocent children, like the old man who destroyed himself. Dorcas, I decided that whatever the case, I'd better not get too involved with him."

Dorcas looked at me oddly, and then changed to a pleasantly light topic.

Dorcas and I saw each other at least once a week and often twice a week during the summer of 1945. We hadn't sexed, but we were close and devoted to each other.

Many times when we met I sensed that Dorcas was burning for

sex with me, but somehow, I managed to avoid sexing her without coming to crisis.

I had to know that the psychological moment was perfect for me before I attempted to make love to her because I couldn't afford to fail.

It was good for both of us that we used up a lot of potentially erotic energy swimming in Lake Michigan and playing tennis in Washington Park.

Dorcas's father apparently never mentioned to her that our first and only meeting had had slightly savage aspects. To avoid another meeting with him, I explained to Dorcas that despite the fact that Cecil and I had rather good thoughts about each other, I wanted to stay away from the funeral home. I knew how fond he was of Ralph Cecil, and I didn't want to make things awkward for Cecil.

In the last part of August, Dorcas picked me up at the El station, and she was wearing the sexy pink dress and satin shoes she had worn months before and that I loved to see her in.

We went to the Play House on South Parkway Boulevard and drank draught beer and danced to jukebox music.

We were catching our breath in a booth when Dorcas looked serious and said, "Ralph called from overseas the day before yesterday. He is going to be mustered out of service next month.

"It was heartbreaking the way he poured himself out to me, and like our parents, he is certain we will marry when he comes home. I am not the least bit certain about that. But I couldn't hurt him. I didn't try to dissuade him from his thinking. Perhaps I should have. I just don't know. I am so confused. He loves me . . . It wouldn't be a bad life with him at all. Let's forget it for now and drink lots more beer and dance the soles off our shoes."

I danced and laughed and drank mechanically. Dorcas went to the restroom and left me alone in the booth.

I thought, *Gorgeous Ralph is coming home with all those sleek muscles and a marriage license in one hand and an honest to Pete stiff dick in the other hand.*

She's carnal, and I'm the screwed up bastard that touched her cunt and flirted with a straitjacket. But she's forgiven me because she's acting fuckish tonight. And she's never been sexier. She's got a hot, juicy one all right.

Goddamnit! I'm getting hard! It's bigger and longer than I remember. I am hard! I got quite a tool. I got that feeling! I'll make her holler. Tonight I'm going to turn tiger and kill the freak, Sally. I have to hurry and get Dorcas in a bed while I'm hard and feeling powerful like this.

Dorcas came back to the booth and held out her arms to dance.

I got up and said, "Baby, I feel carnal. Let's get in the wind."

Her face lit up, and she went quickly toward the door. We went out South Parkway Boulevard to the Park Vernon Hotel at Sixtieth Street and Vernon Avenue. It overlooked the section of Washington Park where we had parked for hours that first day we met.

I felt wonderful. But I took no chances. I kept my right hand busy in my pocket stroking my tool to keep its readiness.

Dorcas's eyes shone brightly and looked larger and prettier than ever as we went to our third-floor room. We reached our room. I unlocked the door and moved slightly aside so Dorcas could go in first.

But she hesitated at the threshold, smiling slyly down at me, for one hellish, destructive fragment of a pounding, torturous instant!

I felt my power draining from me and my precious, my magnificent hard-on, collapsing against my trembling fingertips. She tossed her head and her hips and went into the room. I stood in the hall staring at her back and feeling hatred for her shaking me for what I was positive she had been thinking at that awful moment of hesitation.

My head was roaring with thought. She started to ask me to carry her across that threshold in a playful way, perhaps like Ralph, the muscle buff, had done the trillion times he has fucked her.

I looked so goddamn puny and inadequate standing here, she didn't have the heart to ask the impossible of me. Then the perverse bitch gave me that shitty smile when she toyed with the idea that maybe she should carry *me* across the threshold.

I'm her little private freak show. Contempt is where her kicks are at. She's getting revenge for that night at the lake.

Dorcas went hurriedly into the bathroom without noticing that I hadn't followed her into the room . . . I went in and sat on a chair near the window. She came out in panties and bra and walked to the closet and hung the diaphanous pink dress on a hanger. She came to me and turned her back.

She said, "Undo my bra, Love."

I did. She slipped off the pink bra and panties and put them on the dresser top. She posed before me in all her voluptuous blue black splendor.

Her thick bush had the luxuriant sheen of crow feathers, and a heart-shaped hairy carpet led to the rim of her belly button.

I turned my eyes downward from the imperious invitation of her jutting velvet tits with nipples deliciously deformed to the size and color of black cherries.

She dropped to her knees in front of me, and I shut my eyes against the vision of the strong, shapely curves in the long, power- ful thighs. The sheer physical majesty and epic sexuality of her was terrorizing away my self-confidence and blowing all the fuses in my crotch.

She kissed my closed eyelids tenderly and slipped off my loafers.

She crooned, "Doll, fella, let's shower and do something naughty."

I opened my eyes and gazed at her stupidly. Beer, frustration, the impact of her nude dimensions, ambivalence and her sweetly adroit handling of me had me in a kind of giddy trance.

I remembered I was supposed to be angry with her. I knew it was something terrible she had done to me because I felt like bursting into tears as my mind tensed in its struggle to remember her crime. I made a solemn vow to remember as I followed her into the shower.

The needles of the prickly water gave me a warm glow, and

I felt an encouraging, flickering pull in my balls when Dorcas soaped my crotch.

I lay in bed beside her switch-sucking and brutally gnawing the erected black cherries, and rapidly stiff fingering into the melon red slash in her fat, jet bush. She was writhing sensuously, and her guttural groaning was laced with a sharp whining high note of joyful pain.

I raised my eyes and looked up at her contorted face.

I thought, *She's savagely beautiful, like an African warrior in his death throes. And a tiger is going to conquer her—ME!*

And with that solitary, magical thought, I felt myself erecting gloriously—HARD!

I uttered an ecstatic sob as I moved to mount her. I was going to spear into and master her crimson cunt and discover my eternal manhood in its pungent fire.

I was raising myself on an elbow and swinging a leg across to top her when she squeezed my spear and suddenly rolled over on me—pressing her palms down on my chest and pinning my shoulders to the bed like a vanquished wrestler.

She mounted me in a squatting position over my crotch and guided my quickly fading shaft into her. We stared into each other's eyes as she frantically tried to stuff the shriveled limpness inside her.

She said helplessly, "Did I do something wrong?"

I was drained of imagination, hope and reason. I was a pathetic dwarf trapped beneath a clumsy colossus with my manhood imprisoned forever in the unreachable depths of her unconquerable bloodred cunt.

Humiliation was strangling me, and rage was poisoning me.

I said harshly, "Stop pulling on my thing. It won't get hard any more. I feel terrible."

She flinched and said, "Don't get panicky and nasty. And please don't feel terrible. I'll make it hard again."

I said, "I had a wonderful hard-on, and you killed it. I'll never forgive you for that."

She laughed nervously and said mockingly, "Sweetheart, don't be that square. Your little 'pee-pee' will get hard at least once more before you die."

I blurted out, "Not for you it won't. You're rough and clumsy like a man. I don't have any feeling for you. You're burly. Maybe it would have been proper to carry me across the threshold when you got the idea."

She squeezed her face between her palms and shuddered from the raw shock of my stupidity. She stared at me with big stricken eyes. She moved her lips, but she didn't speak. She kept looking at me and cocking her head from one side to the other like an inquisitive puppy trying to solve the riddle of a strange object.

I said, "You're mashing the shit out of me."

She rolled off me and stood at the side of the bed looking down at me piteously.

She shook her head and almost whispered, "Otis, you were only seventeen like your mother told me. Poor little fella. You need to grow up. I thought I loved you, but I am through with you forever. I was foolish to call you after that experience at the lake. You're not well. Get help, Otis. You're in trouble."

She turned and gathered up her clothes and went to the bathroom.

I lay there hearing the mild roar of the shower. I felt a pang of remorse for my rage. I remembered how lovingly she had bathed me.

She came out of the bathroom fully dressed and with a serene face. She went straight to the door without so much as a glance in my direction. She opened the door. She paused and looked back at me.

She said in a soft voice, "Otis, do you have carfare to get home?"

I snapped, "Don't worry about me. I'll get home."

She stood there idly twisting the doorknob, scrutinizing me with misty intense eyes like she was going on a long lonesome journey and was engraving my image on her brain to cherish along the way.

The love in her eyes pierced my soul and made me ashamed of my cruelty. I lowered my eyes so she couldn't see my misery.

There was utter silence. I heard her draw a deep breath and exhale. I looked up.

She smiled wryly and said softly, "Bye now, Doll Fella. And the very best of luck always."

I mumbled, "Good-bye, Dorcas. The same for you."

The door shut, and she was gone.

I lay there numbly, staring stupidly at the ceiling. Then it hit me. My precious, irreplaceable Dorcas was gone. I leaped from the bed, raced to the window and jerked it up. I stuck my head out and looked down on Sixtieth Street. The red Mercury was already pulling away toward South Parkway.

I shouted, "Dorcas! Dorcas, come back!"

But the raucous wind muffled the sound of my voice, and the red Mercury disappeared.

Pitifully, inanely, I lay my head on the sill and to the blank horror of the lonely street blubbered, "Dorcas, Baby, forgive me. How could you expect a little cotton-picking nigger from Mississippi to learn right away how to treat a classy lady who wears gloves even in the summer time? You're perfect, tender, beautiful, and I love you. I love you. Come back. I need you, Dorcas. Come back and save me."

14

MADAME MIRACLE'S
STINKING LITTLE FAGGOT

In a haze of grief, I dressed and left the hotel. I walked several miles through the chill late-August night before taking a streetcar home.

Two days later I had Lucy call the funeral home for Dorcas. An employee told Lucy that Dorcas was out of town indefinitely. I figured that she had gone to one of the coasts to get away from me and to wait for Ralph to be mustered out of the service.

I missed Dorcas as much as I had Carol. My days were spent jumping hopefully to answer the door and telephone. But it was never a telegram or a call from Dorcas. My sleep was riddled with nightmares.

Mama saw that I was distraught and drinking quite heavily, and she knew it was because of Dorcas. I never told her the real reason Dorcas ended our affair. I lied and said Dorcas's father had broken us up.

I had struggled successfully against going wild and picking up some guy to use me like a woman. I guess I had that strength because all hope wasn't dead that Dorcas would get in touch with me and give me another chance.

I was reading a black paper in early October when I saw what I had dreaded. It was the inevitable photograph. Ralph Duncan was guiding Dorcas's hand as she cut into the wedding cake. The accompanying story said they were to honeymoon in the Bahamas, after which the groom was to take an executive position in a new branch of the elder Duncan's insurance firm in the East.

Fifteen minutes later I was walking out of the flat. I had one purpose: get a gut full of gin, fast.

I drank in a skid row bar on Madison Street where the price and the quality of the poison was rock bottom. I had drunk the sharp edges off Dorcas's marriage and had lit a cigar when I noticed the clock on the wall read seven P.M.

I called Lucy and told her I was coming over to get glamorous. At nine P.M. I walked in and sat at the bar of Tony Carlo's Music Box, on the Southside at Sixty-third Street and South Parkway Boulevard.

I checked my makeup in the compact mirror. My small sexy mouth was moist and red with lipstick, and my tip-tilted nose and slightly almond-shaped hazel eyes gave my satiny yellow face a pixie-like cuteness.

I was resplendent in a fitted sky blue Lillie Anne woolen suit trimmed lavishly in white fox, a blue velvet purse and shoes and sheer indigo-shaded hose. A white pillbox hat sparkled atop the silky shoulder-length auburn wig. And, of course, I wore chic, short white gloves on my delicate hands.

An expensively dressed middle-aged guy left his stool at the end of the bar and came quickly to stand beside me. He sported fiery diamonds and flashed an obese bankroll when he peeled off a fifty to pay the bartender for my Tom Collins and his double Scotch. I fumbled in my purse.

I smiled demurely and said, "Thank you."

He stuffed his bale of money into his inside coat pocket and poked out his skinny chest.

He said thickly, "Miss Pretty, I ain't done nothing for you yet. You heard of me? I'm Cadillac Thompson. Who are you?"

I said, "Tilli Jones."

He dumped the double shot past the gaudy dazzle of his gold teeth.

He nodded toward his change from the fifty on the bar and put his hand on my knee and said, "Pick it up. It's yours."

I shook my head. "Why? For what?" I asked.

He said, "I don't blow no time courting and jiving and bullshitting even a beautiful young bitch like you. Pick it up, girl, and go get in that black Cadillac up the street. I'm gonna' take you to the Southway Hotel. I know a tender young bitch like you ain't never had her cunt and her asshole sucked at the same time. Don't worry, I'm gonna' sweeten that chump change with a C note, and this!"

He popped open his cavernous mouth and lashed out the longest, widest, reddest tongue I'd ever seen—except on a cow.

I was about to tell him I was married and couldn't play, when the elderly yellow-skinned bartender, while frantically wiping the bar in front of us, said from the corner of his mouth, "Goddamnit, Cadillac, raise. You gonna' get this young lady slaughtered. Charlotte is in the joint watching you freaking off!"

Cadillac jumped like he had been shot and scurried away to the john in the rear of the joint. The bartender started to say something to me, but some guy banging his glass against the log pulled him away.

I sat trembling on the stool as I tried to spot homicidal Charlotte in the mirror behind the bar. I saw a tall, muscular woman with a tense black face striding angrily from the front of the joint straight toward me.

She stopped and stood behind me. I watched in the mirror as she sneeringly looked me over. Then she moved to the bar beside me and started picking up Cadillac's change from the fifty-dollar bill.

She said in a venomous voice without looking at me, "You motherfucking shit-colored bitch. You know who I am?"

I said, "No, lady . . . I don't."

I spun my legs to get off the stool on the other side. My back was turned to her. A sudden pressure in my side cut off my breath. I looked down over my shoulder. Charlotte was pressing an ice pick against my side.

I looked into her wild eyes and said pleadingly, "I haven't done anything. Please . . . Don't do it!"

She laughed and pushed harder. I saw the bartender coming toward us.

She shoved her face close to mine and gritted, "You been fucking my man a long time, haven't you, whore?"

I gasped, "Lady, I'm a stranger. I never saw him before tonight."

She said, "You lying, half-white bitch. I think I'll waste you on GP."

I was at the point of blurting out that I was in drag and could prove I was the possessor of a penis when the bartender leaned across the bar and shouted, "Jesus Christ, Charlotte, are you out of your mind? This young lady is nothing to Cadillac. He cut into her and went into his routine. Look at her. Why the hell would she want Cadillac? Besides, she just got in town and she's a friend of mine. Now lay off."

She frowned and looked rapidly from him to me. She slipped the ice pick up her coat sleeve, threw her head back and laughed loudly and long.

She wiped tears from her eyes with her sleeve and said, "Honey, I was just jiving. I wasn't going to do you no harm. You sure looked comical, girl. Mr. Henderson, give her a drink on me."

I said quickly, "No, thank you, Mrs. Cadillac . . . I mean . . . Thompson."

I went to the ladies' john. I came out and as I passed the men's john, I saw Cadillac peeping out through the narrowly cracked door.

He stage whispered, "She still out there?"

I ignored him and stopped at the bar when I noticed Charlotte had gone. I gave Mister Henderson a five-dollar bill and a big warm kiss. He insisted that I have a drink on him. I gulped down a double gin and went to the street.

I started down the sidewalk toward the corner. I stopped and cut across the street. Charlotte had a rapidly growing audience watching her perform against a black Cadillac. She had flattened all four tires, and apparently had sprung the lock on the Cadillac's gaping trunk lid.

She had taken off her topcoat and smashed out every one of the Caddie's windows and started to demolish the form and shape of the battered car with Herculean swings of a heavy bumper jack.

Wary of her spotting me and switching targets, I skulked through the El platform shadows to the safety of a jitney cab going north on South Parkway Boulevard. I got off at Fifth-fifth Street and went into the Hurricane Lounge.

I sat at the bar drinking Tom Collins and thrilling to my toes at the way young guys kept pestering me and whispering lewd some-things in my ear.

But none of them really appealed to me enough so I could reveal my secret and risk instant and loud-mouthed exposure in the bar. And on the other hand, a young guy could be dangerous when put in a sexual cross like taking a pretty girl to a room and discovering he had been tricked by a stud.

Coming back from the ladies' restroom, I passed a booth and thought the back of a brown-skinned guy's head was familiar. But I was too looped to remember to look at his face when I sat at the bar.

I was making eyes at a handsome black guy in his thirties down the bar when somebody bit the side of my neck. I turned angrily like a lady to tongue-lash the culprit. I smiled instead.

It was cute brown-skin Ray whose party I had gone to the day I met Dorcas. And he wasn't slobbery drunk like then, just high.

The bartender brought my change from a ten-dollar bill. I opened my purse and pushed the bills into a coin purse bulging with close to a hundred dollars in tens and twenties. I noticed that Ray's eyes lingered inside my purse, but I was high and glad to see him, so I promptly forgot about it.

He looked me up and down and said breathlessly, "Damn! I

didn't know you went all out like this. You look like a sure enough pretty bitch. Shit, you look like an ice-cream cone to me. You dig?

"I've been dreaming about that dime-sized round eye since I first dug your fabulous yellow butt in the shower at school. You hip to it? Now take this key to the blue convertible Chevy out front and wait for me."

I nodded my head toward the rough-looking black girl watching him from the booth where he had been sitting.

I said, "Ray, I already had a helluva close call tonight. I'm not going to let you get my throat cut."

He pressed the key into my hand and laughed.

He said, "She's just a nice girl I picked up an hour ago. I can cut her loose without a hassle."

I took the key and waited impatiently for almost half an hour, but at midnight we were checking into a Westside hotel, near home.

I had decided to do it that way because I knew how infrequently streetcars and El trains ran from the Southside in the wee hours.

We got naked and kissed and petted while we drank the fifth of gin we brought with us. He insisted that I wear the wig and hose.

I had paid for the room and the gin. But I didn't feel like I had been conned or anything, because Ray was a boss freak, and so sweet. We swapped out on everything—even-steven.

He took as good as he gave. He sodomized me, and he loved it when I sodomized him. He frenched me like I had never been before. In the heat of his frantic passion he told me at least a hundred times how beautiful I was and how much he loved me and needed me.

After it was over, I lay in delicious exhaustion, too spent to move. My rectum tingled, and I felt tiny temblors of sensation shake me like the nerve quakes in a woman at orgasm.

I watched Ray's handsome face frowning in the dresser mirror as he repeatedly bungled the tying of the Windsor knot in his blue silk tie.

I thought, *He loves me, and this has been the most complete and beautiful sex I've ever had with anyone. From this moment on, I am going to be happy because I'm through with girls and the heartbreak behind them.*

I'm beautiful in drag. I'll stay in it for Ray until I die, and we could even get married and no one would know I wasn't a woman. Lucy fools everybody, even experts, and I'm prettier and look more like a woman than she does.

I should have known my luck had to change. OH! How perfect after we are married to adopt a baby, and then move far away and new friends would really think I had given birth to Ray's baby. This is happiness. This is love. I feel so good. I want to scream!

I said, "Darling, why not forget that silly knot and take your clothes off and stay. We're paid up until noon."

He darted a peculiar, devious look at me through the mirror that made me uneasy. But he flashed his lopsided, little boy smile and I was happy again—sure that I had been mistaken.

He said, "Baby, I have to split. It's three thirty in the A.M. There's something I gotta do for my old man early this morning."

I said, "All right, Honey. Come over here. I think I've got enough strength to make a Windsor."

He came over, and I sat on the side of the bed. He tongue kissed me and knelt on the carpet between my legs. He embraced my waist and caressed my spine with his strong fingers while I put the knot in his tie. I was dizzy with happiness.

I said tremulously, "I hope it's like this with us forever. Don't you?"

He stood up suddenly and grinned down at me.

He said, "Me and you, Baby."

He went to the closet and got his pearl gabardine topcoat. He threw it across his shoulders cape-style and stroked his hand across his hair as he peered into the mirror.

My heart jumped rhythm because I was certain I had caught that devious, darting look again.

He said, "Baby, you got a brush?"

I said, "Sure, Honey. There's a small one in my purse right there on the dresser."

He opened the purse and spent a helluva long time rummaging about in it. It puzzled me because the purse only contained a compact, cosmetics and comb and brush.

It didn't even contain the bulgy coin purse with the hundred or so dollars in it. I had removed it and tucked it in one of my shoes under the bed when I undressed. I knew we were going to be drinking and sexing. I had been afraid that Ray and I would fall asleep afterward and some slick maid or desk clerk would pass key in and clean us out.

I felt like I was going to suffocate when he pulled out the brush and stood there with a tense face, slapping the back of the brush into his palm, staring at me through the mirror with cold eyes.

I said, "Ray, what's wrong? Please, Honey, don't look at me like that."

He turned and faced me and managed a monstrous grin that ripped at my insides.

He cleared his throat and rasped, "Baby Sweet, you got some bread?"

I lay back weakly on the pillow and said "A little. Why?"

He came and sat on the side of the bed. He lit a cigarette and puffed the tip to a vivid red. He blew a cloud of smoke into my face.

He said, "Baby, stop shucking me. You had a nice piece of bread in the Hurricane."

I said, "Ray, please don't spoil things. Let me keep this good feeling I got. Don't say anything else about money. I'm your girl. I'm in your corner."

I swung my arm over the edge of the bed and plucked the change purse from my shoe. I opened it and peeled off a twenty-dollar bill. I smiled and held it out to him.

He curled his lip and said coldly, "Nigger, come off of that girl shit. You ain't no bitch. You're a queer stud. Get hip to yourself. Jack, you got to lay two bills on me. I fucked up some bread that belonged to a terrible stud. I'm in bad trouble. Now unass the two bills."

My head felt like he had split it open with a white-hot axe.

I said harshly, "Ray, you're full of shit. You're not smart enough to jive me out of a nickel. And I'm prettier and look more like a girl than that ugly, black whore you were with in the Hurricane."

His face suddenly became so ugly and twisted with rage it frightened me. He moved his right hand upward and tricked my eyes to follow, as he adjusted his coat on his shoulders. I didn't see his left hand push the glowing end of his cigarette into my navel.

I was wounded, hurt beyond instant pain. I actually felt frigid— so cold I shivered and my teeth chattered. Then the icy fuse detonated a searing powder keg of pain and blasted agony to a trillion tortured nerve ends.

I clutched my belly and leaped from the bed. I ran to the bathroom and drew a washbowl full of cold water. I stood there sloshing water against my belly. I remembered my money. I held a wet towel against me and went to stand near the dresser where Ray was counting my money.

I said, "Why did you do that?"

He said without looking at me, "Freak, you called my wife a bad name."

I said, "You're not going out of here with my money."

I looked about for a weapon of some kind to put me on par with his brawny six feet. There was nothing. He folded the bills and put them in his trouser pocket.

He grinned down at me and said, "My wife knows I hustle queers, but I had a bitch of a time convincing her to let me run the game on you. In fact, your bread I'm taking her is the only thing that will convince her that you really are a stinking faggot."

I laughed contemptuously and said, "I bet you don't tell that funny-looking black bitch about how I fucked you in the ass, and how you sucked the stinking faggot's prick and asshole."

I saw his right hand make a fist so I shot out my bare foot at his crotch. He grabbed my leg and upended me. He grabbed the other leg and dangled me in the air.

He started kicking me between the shoulder blades, and then his foot bombed the back of my neck and I swung into blackness absolute on a screaming rope of pain.

I came to dreamily and heard the tinkle of water. I smiled and thought, *Ray is taking a leak.*

I attempted to raise myself on an elbow. Racing pain from my head to ankles jolted me wide awake. I burst into tears because I realized that Ray had continued to kick me even after I blacked out.

And my luck had gotten worse. There was somebody for everybody the old saw went. But for a stinking faggot like me there would never be anybody who really cared. Until I died or some fruit hustler killed me there would be only beatings, heartbreak and tears.

I lay there on the carpet thinking about shoving the dresser under the ceiling light fixture and wondering if it could support my weight . . . long enough to . . .

I just didn't have the energy to do away with myself. I dressed without sponging off or combing out the snarls in the wig. It was a little after five A.M. when I dragged myself to the street.

Dawn hadn't broken, so I decided to risk slipping into the flat in drag instead of changing into my clothes at Lucy's as I usually did.

Luckily there was no one on the street when I walked down the block where we lived. I went into our building and worked the key noiselessly into the lock on the flat's door. I turned the key slowly and carefully pushed open the door.

I stuck my head inside listening for sounds of Mama moving about. All was quiet. I stepped inside and took off the high heels. I crept down the hall in my stocking feet and went past Mama's closed bedroom door to my dark bedroom. I had removed the suit jacket when the bright ceiling light flashed on and Mama was standing in the doorway looking horrified, angry and disgusted.

She whispered sibilantly as if afraid to be overheard, "Sweet Pea, how could you do this to your mama? Anybody see you like this that knows us?"

I sat on the side of the bed and said, "Madame Miracle, none of your suckers or tenants saw me."

I took off the white peau de soie blouse.

Mama said, "Where have you been all night?"

I looked at her wearily. I stood and stepped out of the skirt. I removed the half slip and padded bra and turned slowly to model the black and blue bruises covering my back and thighs.

Mama gasped, "Sweet Pea! You've been beaten!"

I felt suddenly woozy. I lay down on the bed.

I grinned feebly and said, "Not beaten—kicked and stomped."

Mama was holding both hands against her chest over her heart. She leaned over and looked intently at the runny blister on my blackened navel.

Mama sighed and left the room. She came back with a tube of Unguentine and alcohol and cotton.

While putting the salve on my navel she said, "Who did this?"

I said, "It doesn't matter, Mama. I'm lucky he didn't murder me."

She turned me on my side and dabbed at my back with an icy wad of alcohol-soaked cotton.

She said, "You could get killed next time. Come to your senses and stop wearing women's clothes like some nasty freak. I didn't raise you like that. I've always been a good mother. How could you bust my . . . do me like this after all I've done for you?"

I thought about the night she and Junior drove Papa away, and how cruel she had been to Carol and Bessie. I remembered like it all had happened yesterday. I moved across the bed away from her hands.

I stared into her eyes and said, "Mama, you're wrong. I'm not like a nasty freak. I am a nasty freak who loves drag and guys. And I'm not stopping until I pick up some guy like the one that butchered Bessie, and he'll do me a favor and chop me into little pieces."

She jerked herself erect and folded her arms across her chest and stared down at me with a poker face.

She said solemnly, "Sweet Pea, I love you, and I am going to do what is best for you. I can't let you disgrace me and destroy the great confidence that many troubled souls have in Madame Miracle's power to help them. I am going to save you and my image. I am not going to let you put me back to cleaning filth for the dirty white folks. I am going to put you in a sanitarium until you can think right."

I said coldly, "Why does Madame Miracle have to send the only kid she's got left to the nuthouse for help? Mama, do me a favor and don't be a good mother like you said you've always been, and don't love me because I remember you loved Carol and we know why she's in the cemetery.

"And Mama, did your love make Bessie hate your guts and make her leave home and whore? Papa was driven away from home and crawled into a hole like a dog to die. Junior is rotting in prison for 99 years. Why, Mama? Why?

"I dare you to put me in the nuthouse. You do and I'll write a note or scratch one on a wall before I kill myself telling your suckers and the world all about wonderful Madame Miracle and how, with her great wisdom and love, she helped her children and their Papa into the grave."

She stood there evil eyeing me with a knitted brow for a long moment. Then she turned and walked toward the bedroom door. She paused at the threshold and looked back over her shoulder at me.

She shook her head and said pityingly, "Mama's mixed-up little man and his wild imagination."

I hollered at her retreating back, "I'm the phony Madame Miracle's stinking little faggot!"

15

THE FREAKISH FIFTIES

After the Second World War ended in 1945, the years of my life seemed to slip away almost imperceptibly and surprisingly painlessly (except on one horribly exclusive occasion) until 1959.

These illusions were due, perhaps, to the desperate gaiety I found in my butterfly affairs with an endless variety of guys and in my endless, numbing drinking.

Pain! Gibbering, excruciating, heart-busting, everlasting, exclusive pain crashed through my numb haze in 1956 on April 6 at two forty-five P.M. at the Obee Funeral Home on the Southside.

The heavyset, handsome proprietor was sunning himself outside the doorway. A young guy I'd been drinking and sexing nonstop with for two days pulled to the curb in front of the establishment. I was in flashy drag and half drunk.

I walked up to the proprietor and said, "Am I too early for Mr. Edward Cato's funeral?"

He said softly, "Miss, I'm sorry, but you're very late. Mr. Cato was buried yesterday afternoon in Rose Hill Cemetery."

I said, "Isn't today the fifth of April?"

He said, "No, Miss, today is April 6."

Soldier was buried. Dear, beautiful, warm, kind, loyal, unforgettable Soldier was buried, and I had had a dick up my ass and missed his funeral.

I started ripping off my dress and the long red wig. An openmouthed crowd quickly gathered. I flung myself into the gutter and smashed my head against the curb.

I screamed over and over at the top of my voice, "He was the best friend I ever had, and I'm the filthy, stinking, drunken tramp, cock-sucking, asshole-licking, lousy faggot bastard that missed my best friend's funeral. Somebody kill me. Please. Won't one of you kill me? Kill me somebody. Please! Please! Kill me! Kill me! Please!"

My young stud finally got me into his car and away as the police roared to the scene. It was weeks before I got myself together and took a drink.

Three months after Soldier's death from heart failure, I went out to the cemetery and spent all day at the graves of Soldier, Carol and Bessie. Typically, he was helping a guy push his stalled car to a garage when he suffered the fatal attack.

Except for faint lavender circles beneath my slightly less bright hazel eyes, and, of course, the permanent loss of the marvelous vitality and compulsion of the young to leap up into the heavens and rearrange the stars, I hadn't become altogether ugly and broken down at the age of thirty-one.

Mama, on the other hand, by 1959 had aged visibly—much more than her fifty-four years. Her once erect carriage had developed a subtle stoop. And prematurely, her sexy chest and rear end, like her face, had lost its soft roundness and become loose and gaunt, like the withered angular frame of an old woman.

She also became a victim of what she believed to be severe heart trouble and a mysterious but enervating malady affecting her legs.

Doctor Sykes, a competent Westside M.D. and psychiatrist, was Mama's physician in 1957 when the dramatic symptoms of her two complaints surfaced.

He was terminated because Mama said, "I know I got serious things wrong with me, and all that yellow fake does is ask me a thousand embarrassing questions about my mama and papa, and you and Carol, and the other kids and Frank."

Doctor Sykes told me confidentially that Mama's periodic heart trouble and the extreme weakness and threatened collapse of her legs did not have organic cause, but that symptoms she demonstrated gratified unconscious needs and desires.

He also told me that for her, the complaints had become real and could affect her like real organic disorders. He suggested that perhaps Mama suffered terrible pangs of guilt for past deeds, and great anxiety that I would turn my back on her and leave her.

The symptoms, in effect, shouted for her, "Sweet Pea, see how sick and afflicted I am! I am being punished for my past wrongdoing. You can't leave me now. If you do, I'll die of a heart attack, or perhaps I'll become helpless, unable to walk. Then I will be on your conscience."

On another occasion, Doctor Sykes gave me his "pedestal reverence" theory as one possible reason, among many, including my fear of failure to perform successfully, why I hadn't been able to have successful sexual intercourse with Dorcas years before.

Doctor Sykes may or may not have been correct about me and Dorcas, but he was right on target about Mama, because she almost always suffered her symptoms when we quarreled and I threatened to leave, or when she suspected that I might leave her forever.

Mama went to a general practitioner who treated her neurosis with saccharine mumbo jumbo and pills galore.

The demand for Mama's "instant success oil" and "enemy destruct powder" and her counseling hocus-pocus fell sharply after the war ended.

Over the years Mama had hired several different lawyers to get Junior free on at least parole. But it seemed impossible. He and Railhead were classified as incorrigible.

Mama visited Junior every month except when he was in solitary, which was quite often. I went with her often during his first years in Joliet. But somehow I got the feeling he would be happier to visit with just Mama. So I wrote him twice a month and put money orders inside my letters for things he might need.

Mama had saved plenty from the big buck boom and sucker explosion years of the war. And she owned the apartment building where we lived.

A friend of Lucy's taught me exotic dancing, and in 1947, I started dancing in small cabarets around the Chicago area that featured female impersonators.

By 1957, exotic dancing had lost, for me, its allure and reasonable income, and its frenetic gyrations had put the torch to my stamina. Lucy encouraged me to work in Spiegel's mailing department—as a female employee, naturally.

I never wore women's clothes in Mama's presence, and unlike I did as a teenager, I didn't now hurt or bait Mama with hateful and accusative references to the twins, Junior, and Papa.

But I could, and did quite often, become hostile toward her and would storm out of the flat when the pressure of her cunning attempts to dominate me became unbearable.

I had been her prisoner since my aware late teens, straining and thrashing to escape the strangling web of her cloying possessiveness and iron determination to hold me by any means.

Lucy, the homosexual, was my only close friend, and through her, I met many other homosexuals and discovered there is among them practically none of the racial bigotry and hatred found in the so-called straight world of the heterosexuals.

On Christmas Eve in 1959, Lucy and I went to a big bash thrown by Stel, an affluent white lesbian and retired Eastern madam, who lived in a fourteen-room house on Warren Boulevard, which was a Mecca for not only a select group of gay people on the Westside, but for many from all sections of Chicago.

All of the nonsexual action was in the spacious basement bistro, which was furnished to resemble the commercial type right down to flashing and rippling neon beer and whiskey signs.

Lucy was mixing business with pleasure. She had been commissioned by a risqué magazine the week before to write anonymous and earthy profiles on diverse gay types.

She sat strategically on a long black vinyl sofa near the door of the barroom away from the hubbub at the bar and tables. And, too, in that spot, she could see all likely subjects for her article, coming and going.

Lucy was well known and liked by everyone. I wasn't surprised, while getting half stinko at the bar, to notice Lucy was having good luck.

In fact, she and her tape recorder were almost hidden by a half-crocked group seated on the sofa and on chairs in a rough circle around where Lucy was seated on the end of the sofa.

They were gesticulating in what looked like a round-robin discussion. It looked interesting, and I had met them all, so I sauntered over and squeezed in beside Lucy on the sofa.

A tall black guy named Art, with a potbelly and graying hair, had a hurt look on his puffy face.

He was saying, "Goddamnit, Lucy, Mother Thomas and me didn't bust up 'cause he caught me eating a broad up. The reason we busted up happened at Mother's birthday party.

"A young fine freak queen kept rubbing his tender round ass against my jones. Shit, I was dumb, drunk and aching to do my thing to that cute freak.

"I took him in one of the johns and was piling this foot of pure hot joy into him when I remembered the big mirror was two-way. Mother was watching, and so were twenty other people.

"He almost had a nervous breakdown and heckled me night and day about how rotten I was to play him cheap before his friends. I woke up one early bright morning with Mother's tongue in my mouth. She was in drag and slobbery drunk. Her mouth stank like a sewer. I got wide awake and saw that Mother had freaked off with some dirty bastard. Mother's face and lips was crusted with shit.

"I got a golf club and beat his nasty white ass upstairs and down. He peed like a puppy all over the mansion. I did a year in the slammer. Now, Lucy, that's how I busted up with Mother Thomas."

Lucy turned to an old white queen named Larry, with wispy white hair and a sad face, dressed in a shabby business suit.

Lucy said, "Larry, how is your love life?"

The old man swallowed and looked at Lucy with filmy blue eyes.

He cackled bitterly and said, "It's a damn sight worse than it was when I had money and was younger and had a big house like this one."

He paused and closed his eyes rapturously.

He said dreamily, "Then I had more than my share of lovely ladies with nice stiff cocks. But now that I'm broke and old as weather, I'm not complaining. I still get beautiful laddies to haul my ashes when my old balls get heavy."

We all laughed.

Lucy said, "Larry, I don't suppose you would care to say what your secret is?"

The old queen daintily wet his lips with an acrobatic tongue and said, "It's all quite simple. I live over a bar in the tenderloin, and there are never enough cunts hanging around to go around at closing time.

"I sit on my downstairs stoop and case the luscious things when they hit the sidewalk, all hot to pop off from the teasing cunts. And sometimes a laddie will need a bed for the night or a meal.

"I tell you I get some living jewels to grace my humble bed. Every old lonely bitch like me should find himself some room over a bar in the tenderloin."

Lucy put a fresh reel of tape in the small recorder in her lap.

Princess, a tiny, black middle-aged queen, sat beside me dressed in a gold leather dress and boots and a platinum wig that framed his hard face.

Lucy said, "What's happening with you, Princess?"

He answered in a shrill falsetto, "Everything, Lucy! And it's all groovy. I don't sell reefer and whore anymore. I'm a respectable bitch. I own two restaurants and property in Evanston."

Lucy said, "Did that Southside hassle iron out with those black studs that were salty because you took Reggie, that cute white stud, in out of the cold and bought him a Cadillac? Remember they were bad-mouthing you, saying you had paddy fever?"

Princess exploded. "I don't give a motherfuck what the goddamn nigger studs said about me. I don't have white fever. Color don't mean shit to me. A stud can be yellow, orange, pin-striped, or black, just so he can con me that I'm happy.

"And Reggie did that for more than a year. I have had more than a hundred white and black studs in the last twenty years. They have busted my head, shot me, stabbed me and swindled me out of my bread.

"Sure I'm a cocksucker and a low-life freak. But I'm a human being, and I need more than my asshole punched. I need affection and companionship. Reggie was a lying, double-crossing, cunt-loving Judas, but he kept my head fucked up with his sweet bullshit. He really had me feeling like an honest to God cunt, and my stupid feet never touched earth for that year he conned me. All the other conniving bastards ripped me off for every red cent and split within a month."

Lucy said, "Princess, I guess after Reggie, you'll just go for one-night stands? After all, you can't expect to equal Reggie's youth and looks, much less top him."

Princess sighed and said, "Lucy, I wish I could be satisfied, hitting and running. But I'm a crazy bitch that has to shack with a stud to be content, even though I know the sonuvabitch sure as hell is going to rob me, try to kill me or cripple me and split with a cunt.

"I'm a queer, and for queers, there is no tomorrow, just today. Just when we are certain we have caught the brass ring of happiness, we discover some slick double-crossing stud has dipped it in shit.

"Lucy, I got afraid and stopped looking a long time ago for the end of the gay rainbow because I know what is really waiting there for us—a pot of lonely death."

The Princess killed my spirits so I went back to the bar to get respirited. In an hour or so Lucy joined me. We were juicing and chattering drunkenly when apparently, magically, from the jungles of Africa, materialized a chieftain, no doubt of the proud, statuesque and beautiful Watusi tribe, wearing a lumber jacket and horribly rough trousers.

He stood between Lucy and me, and I wondered why Lucy introduced him by the Anglo name of Mike Bowers, instead of by some poetic tribal name.

I was so excited I almost tinkled on myself when he caressed my thigh. I mumbled something and went to the john to tinkle and freshen my makeup. I stood in the john palpitating and visualizing his finely chiseled jet-black face and the remarkably large dark eyes so romantic and tragic and wise, as if they had witnessed and shared all the love, sex, tragedy and heartbreak of the world through all time.

And those eyes I was sure had looked into my freak soul and become soft with a tender promise. I was sunk, hooked, and everything was happening in an enchanted fog.

I was floating when I left Stel's with him and got into his ancient Ford and went to his bleak room in a transient hotel on Madison Street. But he and his kitten—gentle lovemaking—made me oblivious to everything but the wonder of his presence.

Mike told me he was almost penniless and without wardrobe because he had recently finished his second term in the federal prison at Atlanta, Georgia, for narcotics trafficking.

He also told me he never knew his father, and his mother was killed in a fight when he was thirteen. He had made it on his own since then and served three prison terms in his twenty-three years.

I had close to three thousand dollars in a savings account. About two weeks after I met him I had withdrawn fifteen hundred dollars and bought him sparkling new clothes, rented a nicely furnished three-room apartment just three blocks from Mama's building, and he was able to trade in the rattletrap Ford on a used but extremely clean '55 Chevy.

I still worked at Spiegel's and moved my wardrobe of women's clothes from Lucy's place to Mike's, where I spent most of my time.

Mama met Mike and didn't get any attacks, and she didn't seem to mind that I slept with Mike and that I spent only brief moments with her. I guess she felt there was no reason for panic and jealousy over a man. She must have known I was too starry-eyed to suspect that a love affair between two men is a doomed proposition.

Mike demanded that I stay in drag and wig when in his presence. I was really happy for the first time in my life, cooking and making a home for Mike.

He seemed happy and content too . . . until the spring of 1960. Then he got restless and began tending bar on weekends on Madison Street. I'd wait in the apartment for him to get off because he worked in a straight bar, and I was well known on Madison Street.

I didn't want to embarrass him by hanging around on his job. The time until he got home didn't seem so long after we got a telephone. We talked to each other several times a night.

Then in June Mike started working six nights a week in the bar, and he started coming home later and later. He treated me indifferently and punched the hell out of me when I asked questions.

I borrowed Lucy's car one Saturday night near the end of June. I parked half a block from the bar where Mike worked, a few minutes before closing time.

Mike came out of the bar with a pretty light complexioned girl about nineteen and pulled away in the Chevy.

I felt so old, and I was so hurt because she was so much like me physically—except she was radiantly young—and the possessor of a precious, fuckable cunt to offer Mike.

I trailed them to a hotel on Roosevelt Road and watched them go to the desk and register. I went to the apartment and changed into male clothes. I sat at the window with a fifth of gin getting drunk and waiting for Mike.

At daybreak, he parked haphazardly in front of our building with the rear end of the Chevy poked toward the middle of the street.

He got out and walked unsteadily around to the passenger side of the front seat and jerked open the door. He bent over and stuck his head into the car. He checked the floor, the seat and dumped a dashboard ash tray into the street

Then he stooped and scrutinized his face in the rearview front fender mirror. He dabbed furiously at his mouth and cheeks with his handkerchief.

Finally he managed to lock the car. He came into the apartment and didn't see me at the window. He looked in the bathroom, kitchen and bedroom. He came into the living room and grunted when he saw me. He collapsed on the sofa with his long legs stretched out under the coffee table and beyond.

He cut a bloodshot eye at me and said, "Why the hell are you up and in stud clothes this early in the morning?"

I said bitterly, "I'm on my way to suck a yellow cunt. I'm curious about its apparently irresistible taste and allure for stupid young studs. And I suppose you stayed out until this early in the morning to admire the glory of the sunrise?"

His jaw muscles rolled, and he yanked his legs from beneath the table and leaned toward me at the end of the sofa.

He said sternly, "Grandma, I'm gonna give you a fat mouth if you don't stop signifying and talking shit to me."

I stood up and picked up a pointed, dagger-type letter opener from an end table.

I said, "You touch me and I'll send you to your dead mammy. I'm sick of you tramp niggers using me. I took the wrinkles out of your starving gut, put some decent clothes on your black lousy ass and rescued you from that disaster you were riding in. Some chippie has let you stick your head up her sour ass, and now I'm old, gray-ass Grandma!"

He had his head between his palms staring down at the floor. I was standing six feet away on the end of a red rectangular accent rug.

Suddenly he exploded in a blur of motion, and I flew into the air and crashed the side of my head against the edge of the end table. He had violently jerked the other end of the carpet from beneath me.

I lay half-stunned and watched helplessly as Mike loomed above me snarling in anger. He straddled me and battered my face and chest with his iron fists until I passed out.

I came to in a tub of warm water, and Mike was tenderly bathing me. I couldn't see because my eyes were swollen shut. He toweled me dry and carried me to bed. He cradled me in his arms and cried and begged me to forgive him.

Then because I was his hopeless slave and sucker, I lay there blind, bruised and battered and let him sodomize me until my rectum was raw and quivering.

And despite all the agony and the pain, I watched him sleeping and hated myself because I loved him. I lay thinking about the pretty young girl and crying, but remembering and still thrilling to the maddening sensation of his plunging organ burying itself in the freakish depth of me.

Mama was sympathetic to me, but she didn't condemn Mike or advise me to leave him, I guess she was hoping I'd get so much abuse that eventually I'd come home and never leave her side again.

Mike agreed to quit tending bar if I would finance him in the soft narcotics racket—that is, he would sell reefers and pills like bennies, yellows and reds instead of heroin and cocaine and other hard narcotics.

I withdrew my remaining fifteen hundred dollars and he got his stock. He had made wide contact for customers while working at the bar and the phone rang constantly.

About a month after he started dealing, a customer called and wanted a half pound of pot delivered to his pad. Mike was expecting an important call from his connection and might need the new '60 Caddie we owned.

I called a cab to make the delivery. The customer lived in an apartment building on Douglas Boulevard on the Westside.

I was ringing the customer's bell in the foyer of the building when two city narcotics detectives rushed in and took me to an unmarked car and searched me and found the pot pinned to the crotch of my trousers.

I was booked for possession, and bail was set at ten thousand dollars. I was afraid to call Mike for fear the police would monitor the call and trace our address where I knew Mike had pills and pot stashed.

I called Mama, and that night, a bondsman came, and I was released. I went directly to the apartment to see Mike and get a thousand dollars to repay Mama for paying the bondsman's ten percent fee for posting my ten thousand-dollar bond.

I didn't see the white Caddie out front. I unlocked the apartment door and turned on the lights. I went into the bedroom. All the dresser drawers were on the floor and bed—empty!

I looked in the closet—bare! I rushed feverishly about the apartment looking for a note explaining and telling me he'd contact me later. But there was nothing. Mike had taken all my lovely drag and accessories.

I stood in the bedroom stunned. Suddenly, I heard someone in the living room. I went to the bedroom doorway expecting to see Mike. Instead, I saw the two detectives that had arrested me.

They had followed me and come through the front door that I had left open. They searched the apartment and found ten rolled reefers held together with a rubber band in the toe of an old pair of shoes Mike had left.

The cops wouldn't believe that I didn't know where Mike was. They were very angry with me after the manager of the building told them the apartment was in my name. They arrested me again and booked me for possession.

Mama came to see me the next day and told me she thought it best that she only spend additional money on a lawyer to defend me.

Two days later, I was transferred to County Jail and placed on a hold-over tier while awaiting trial. My tier held about twenty-five accused armed bandits, pimps, murderers, strong-arm robbers and assorted practitioners of mayhem and cutthroatery.

We lived in two parallel rows of barred single cells, which, in the morning, were automatically unlocked by a screw from a control box within a barred cubicle at the front of the dayroom where the inmates ate and spent the long day until bedtime.

The only time that guards came into the dayroom and the cells was during shakedowns. Every tier had an inmate barn boss who had been chosen by the jail officials to keep order and cleanliness. And the barn boss distributed the food that arrived in tin plates on a dumbwaiter from the kitchen.

The barn boss was naturally the most jailwise, vicious, cunning, brutal inmate available to the jail officials.

Our barn boss was a massive hulk of cruelty accused of smashing out a pal's brains with a brick over a twenty-five-cent debt.

The tier was a seething pit of violence and sex. There were several bloody fights in the dayroom and in the toilet off the dayroom almost every day.

And on general cleanup day when the cells were opened for scrubbing, new young inmates were taken in the cells and forced to take every sexual abuse in the book.

At night after lights-out, the male inmates in the cells across the courtyard would light matches to show their erected dicks and balls to the screaming female inmates on the tier above my tier.

The female inmates would do likewise to show their cunts in bold relief to the profane males across the way, cheering the bitches on as they jacked off their stiff cocks in the yellow glow of the matches.

Often, apparently, females sharing a cell would really play dog for the guys across the way, because excited shouts rode the night air like, "Sit in her face, baby! Bite that bitch's tiddie off. Fuck that long cunt whore, you big dick bitch."

It was perhaps the horny sights and hot sounds of this nightly bacchanalia that kept the caged hoodlums on our tier inflamed and edgy and eager to assault and rape one another.

At thirty-three I was fairly safe from wholesale rape. That is, unless I tipped my secret or somebody came in from the street that knew me and told that I was an experienced "round eye." If this happened, then, I would be a target for violent mass rape just like a tender youngster.

After witnessing a week of violence and brutal rape, I was terrified and so nervous and ill with a pounding headache that I, unfortunately, put in for sick call with the hope I could be transferred to the hospital until my trial.

A guard took several of us to sick call, including the straw boss. We were put into a large cell with milling inmates from other tiers on sick call.

I was sitting on a wooden bench beside the straw boss when a paunchy, bald guy with a vaguely familiar voice stopped in front of me and said, "Hello, Baby Sweets."

I stared up at the guy's seamed face and tried to place him.

He said, "How can you forget me, Sweet Butt? Show me your belly button."

In that instant, I remembered him. It was Ray! He had ground his cigarette into my navel sixteen years before.

I said, "Hello, Ray," and went to the other end of the cell.

My knees shook when I glanced back toward the bench. Ray was sitting next to the straw boss saying something to him, and the straw boss was winking at me.

I saw the doctor and tried desperately to convince him I was ill enough for the infirmary, but he only gave me a pill and sent me back to the tier.

I went to a corner of the dayroom and had chills one moment and hot flashes the next when I saw the straw boss grinning and talking to the barn boss. Then they both stared at me.

I didn't sleep that night because I knew the next day was general cleanup day, and I was certain to be beaten or raped or both.

Morning came and after a breakfast I didn't touch the barn boss issued cleaning materials. I looked around the dayroom and didn't see anybody paying me any attention, so I went to my cell with soap and a rag to clean the bars.

Ten minutes later I had my back to the cell door rinsing out the rag in my face bowl. I felt a presence and whirled around. The giant frame of the barn boss filled the cell doorway. He was breathing fast and heavily, and his cruel black face was tense with excitement. The front of his trousers poked out like a midget tent.

He waved his ham hock hands through the air and croaked, "Now, Lil Bit, I ain't gonna' kick ya ass or nuthin', so don't go gittin' scared. They say ya ken sure nuff suck a dick, and ya asshole ain't no bigger'n a dime. Git them pants down. We gonna' have a light party."

I backed away and said, "That guy lied on me. I'm not funny. Please leave me alone."

He put his hand in his back pocket, and I thought for a moment he was going to draw a knife. But he brought out a snuffbox and opened it. It was packed with Vaseline.

He walked toward me and said hoarsely, "Git them pants down, nigger. I'm gonna grease ya and fuck ya this mornin'."

I shouted, "I can't do anything with you. I don't have any feeling for you. Go away! Keep your—"

He grabbed me by the throat and strangled me into silence. He kept putting on the pressure until I was almost out.

He stuck his wild face close to mine and whispered, "Mother-fucker, I'm gittin' my nuts off, or I'm killin' ya."

He slightly loosened his hands around my throat.

I choked out, "Please don't kill me! I'll do what you want."

He made me bend over wide legged and support myself with my hands against the face bowl. While he was sodomizing me I saw the shadows of several others lurking outside my cell.

No sooner had the barn boss withdrawn from me than the straw boss pushed into me, and when I protested and tried to straighten up to eject his penis, he punched me in the kidneys and spine.

Fifteen of them were in line and had it timed so that when one of them pulled out of me, the next in line was there to ram into me before I could even catch my breath, much less straighten up.

Several of them had monstrous dicks, and the pain was horrible, but I couldn't scream for help. I was afraid they would kill me.

When it was over I crumpled to the cell floor moaning and feebly dabbing a cold wet rag against my torn, bloody rectum. I went to sick call the next day and was given three stitches. I told the doctor what had happened, but he just shook his head.

A week later I went to trial, represented by a lawyer Mama paid for, and received one year in the House of Correction. I guess I was lucky. I might have gotten time in the state prison or county jail.

16

ENCORE, DOLL FELLA

I served out my sentence in the laundry at the House, and the time passed quickly and without unusual events. Faithful Lucy and Mama wrote often and sent weekly money orders.

I was released in 1961 and naturally went to Mama. I went back to Spiegel's to work, and Lucy was still my best friend.

The experiences with Mike and the jail sentence had calmed me considerably. I still drank and dolled up in drag occasionally and picked up some guy for a hot moment, but I didn't go hog wild anymore, and I didn't get serious about any guy.

I dated several young female employees at Spiegel's, but nothing really came of it. I guess I was slowing down at thirty-four, because most of my free time was spent visiting Lucy and at home with Mama—until I had to flee her pressure.

Mama's heart and legs seldom gave her trouble now. I guess that was true because I wasn't doing anything or involved with anyone that threatened her possessive position.

Mama's profession was on the wane, but she wasn't weeping. She was well fixed.

I have often wondered about and puzzled over why and how the six years between 1961 and 1967 evaporated as if some kindly sorcerer had cast a spell and bewitched my brain to convince me those dull dreary years never existed.

In February of 1967, I was on a streetcar going south on Cottage Grove Avenue. An old Plymouth I owned was in the shop, and I was eager to buy some wild sport shirts at a shop on Sixty-third Street and Cottage Grove Avenue.

At Fifty-first Street, I noticed a new, blue Buick staying abreast of the streetcar, and the driver, whom I couldn't see, was steadily blowing his horn.

I didn't know anybody who owned a blue Buick, so I went back to my newspaper. Several blocks farther south, the streetcar stopped for a traffic signal, and I heard the horn of the Buick blowing even more insistently beside the streetcar.

I looked down at the street, and I thought my eyes had gone haywire. A tall, powerfully built woman with an African warrior face had stepped out of the blue Buick and was pressing the horn with one hand and gesticulating wildly that I get off the streetcar.

It was Dorcas! The light turned green, and the streetcar rattled forward. I sat there staring down at the Buick doggedly keeping abreast of the streetcar.

I half rose to go and stand at the exit door so I could get off at the next stop and let Dorcas pick me up. But I sank back into the seat when I remembered the pure agony when I lost her.

I was frozen in my seat when the car reached the Fifty-eighth Street stop. And the persistent blue Buick wouldn't go away with its tantalizing horn.

At the Sixty-first Street stop, I tore myself loose from the seat and rushed to the street. Dorcas pulled to the curb, and I walked a palpitative thousand miles to the Buick.

I stuck my head in the window and said, "Hello, Mrs. Duncan."

She frowned and said, "Hi, Doll Fella. I am no longer Mrs. Duncan. Please get in."

I got in, and after two minutes in each other's presence we knew there was still magically sweet voltage between us.

And after we lunched, we went to Washington Park and parked in the same spot we had that first day we met. Just like then, we sat there excited and thrilled to find each other until darkness fell.

I had forgotten the jazzy sport shirts in the hypnosis of joy. And on the El train going to the Westside, I was deliciously aware of a posthypnotic suggestion that I had promised to come and stay at the funeral home with Dorcas. Her father had passed two weeks before, and she was lonely and needed my help with the business.

I broke the news to Mama, and she had the first trouble with her heart and legs that she had suffered in years.

I wasn't able to leave immediately as I had planned. It took a couple of days of Mama's doctor's placebos and soothing reassurances from me before I could move to the funeral home.

Dorcas and I slept in separate bedrooms, and she made no sexual demands. I sexed her on occasion, but always I had to visualize a homosexual experience from the past to perform successfully.

I kept Mama placated by frequent visits and even more telephone calls. I learned a great deal about the mortuary business and lost my squeamishness of the dead.

Time passed rapidly in the hectic business environment of the mortuary, and for a year I had not dated a guy.

I visited Mama in April of 1968, and she shot me through hot emotional grease about Dorcas and just unhinged me and destroyed my fine balance.

I left Mama and hit the sauce and wound up brutalized by a fruit hustler call Big Lovell. I was sick with shame and left Dorcas because I didn't want to hurt her further.

The black rebellion exploded in riot and flames on the Westside. I went back to Mama until order was restored and danger no longer threatened her.

She didn't know that I was determined to escape the neurotic web she had spun around me through all the long years. A week after the black rebellion ended, I sat down beside Mama on the front-room sofa.

I said, "Mama, I'm going to get myself a place to stay now that I know you will be all right."

She looked puzzled and said, "Sweet Pea, why do you need a place to stay when you have a home right here with me?"

I said calmly, "Mama, one of the thousand strangling reasons is that you just called me Sweet Pea for the trillionth time. Mama, don't press me and make me say things to hurt you.

"Just realize that with all of your good intentions, you're doing to me what no human being should be allowed to do to another human being.

"Mama, I'm intelligent and reasonably healthy. I should have amounted to something besides an aging cocksucker if you hadn't killed and smothered every instinct and striving of manhood you ever saw in me. Mama, I'm leaving in the morning. I have to know what life is like without you."

She started weeping and had a heart seizure. She couldn't breathe, and her legs gave way. I gave her a sedative and put her to bed.

That night I packed my things to really go into the world on my own. I didn't sleep much that night. I was past forty, but Mama had so damaged me I, perhaps, had the trepidation of an adolescent thrown out to face the unknown horrors of the world for the first time.

I dressed early the next morning and took coffee and toast to Mama in bed. She smiled wanly. I went to the bedroom and got my suitcase.

I went into her bedroom and kissed her cheek and said, "Goodbye, Mama, I'll call you and write you."

I turned and walked toward the front door. I had my hand on the knob when I heard Mama cry out, "Sweet Pea!" and then a crash.

I spun and saw Mama lying apparently unconscious with a long scarlet gash on her forehead. I called Doctor Sykes, and because he was fond of me, he came and treated the head wound and conducted tests on Mama's legs.

He took me aside and told me she couldn't walk. She had what he called functional paralysis. I stayed with her for a while until she got a nurse and wheelchair.

Then early one May morning, I went into her bedroom and sat on the side of the bed. The nurse hadn't come. She started crying.

I said, "Mama, I'm all packed and ready to go, and nothing is going to stop me this time."

She blubbered, "You mean you would leave me when I'm like this?"

I stood up and said, "Mama, if I don't leave I know I'll do something terrible in this flat. You have money to take care of yourself and to pay for help."

I leaned over to kiss her good-bye. I had my lips pressed against her cheek when I heard the faintest, most dulcet metallic scrape and caught the most infinitesimal glimmer of ominous steel in the corner of my eye.

I leaped back and a streaking dazzle went past my throat. Mama's face was a replica of the mask of madness she wore the night she punched Carol's baby from her belly. Mama gripped the scissors like a dagger and glared hatred at me.

I picked up my suitcase and backed toward the hall. Then I went out the front door into the clean bright sunshine. I reached into my inside coat pocket and got Mike's sealed letter. I tore it unread into shreds and scattered the pieces in the gutter.

I didn't know where I was going or what I was going to do. But as I strode through the chaotic rubble of riot-ravaged Madison Street, I felt a peace, a surging joy I had never felt before.

I was never a religion buff, but for some mystical reason, I heard an old slave chant reverberating through my being.

Free at last! Free at last! Great God Almighty I'm free at last!

EPILOGUE

In the middle part of April in 1969, I received a telegram from a writer friend of mine in Chicago. The sad message of the telegram was to inform me that Otis Tilson had taken his own life by hanging in a skid row hotel in New York City.

I can't help but wonder what he expected to find there except the misery that is the heritage of his kind. Perhaps the final solution to the torture of spirit and body that he endured could only be death.